*Bruja*

# Bruja

## The Legend of La Llorona

Lucinda Ciddio Leyba

UNIVERSITY OF NEW MEXICO PRESS
ALBUQUERQUE

Library of Congress Cataloging-in-Publication Data
Leyba, Lucinda Ciddio, 1969–
 Bruja : the legend of La Llorona / Lucinda Ciddio Leyba.
   p. cm.
 ISBN 978-0-8263-5052-7 (pbk. : alk. paper) — ISBN 978-0-8263-5053-4
(electronic)
 1. Witches—Fiction. I. Title.
 PS3612.E99B78 2011
 813'.6—dc22

                            2010051763

Originally published as *Bruja: The Legend of La Llorona* by Lucinda Leyba
(Otsego, MI: PageFree Publishing, Inc., 2004)

# *Prologue*

The setting sun illuminated the Sangre de Cristo Mountains with a fiery orange glow. The southern edge of the Rocky Mountains was fittingly named "The Blood of Christ" by the Spanish settlers after observing the intense sunsets in the Indian-settled valley.

Estefanita sat alone on the back porch of her small adobe home as she looked out at the vast forest. The mountains were sacred and Estefanita understood the power held within their towering peaks.

A gentle breeze blew over the mountains, down into the valley, and through Santa Fe. The tall cottonwoods swayed and the leaves rustled in the wind. Estefanita's backyard was a green oasis in the dry New Mexican desert. Cedar fence posts, strung with wire, surrounded a small garden filled with tomatoes, corn, and flowering green chile. Clusters of herbs and spices lined the southern wall of the house in rock planters. At the far end of the backyard, under the shade of trees, was a small chicken coop filled with geese and chickens. The tranquil Santa Fe River could be heard past the grove of cottonwoods, and the crickets' summer mating song grew louder as the sun dipped farther behind the distant mountains.

Oblivious to the beautiful sunset, Estefanita stared intently into the distance. For her, nothing was appealing about the evening. Tonight was only a painful reminder of the suffering she'd had to endure throughout her life. She was seventy-eight and too old to make the pilgrimage into the mountains, but she'd made a pact with God, one she would never break. Vowing to make the treacherous journey into the forest each year was a pledge she'd kept for forty-five years, but her dedication had its price. With it brought a flood of painful memories that Estefanita would typically bury the rest of the year. Her difficult life could have been easier to endure with the love of her children.

Tension ominously filled the hot desert air. With her back straight, gripping a knobby wood cane between her legs, Estefanita kept a vigilant watch on the mountains. Her stout legs pushed against the weathered plank floor as she methodically rocked in the worn rocking chair. The dry wood creaked faintly under the weight of the chair with each bend.

A lone coyote howled as the sun disappeared behind the mountains. The eerie cry broke Estefanita's trance. With her head cocked, Estefanita stopped rocking and listened to the coyotes pack together for the night.

Pushing against her cane, the tired old woman stood and walked to the weathered screen door. With one last look over her shoulder, Estefanita searched the mountainside for the howling coyotes before she stepped into her dark home. The floors bowed under her weight as she walked through the small kitchen. The open-faced white cupboards were packed with jars of dried herbs, leaves, and roots. A large wood table with boxy chairs crowded the room as a cast iron woodstove radiated heat inside the already hot kitchen.

Reaching up to one of the many bundles of dried herbs hung from the low ceiling and exposed round vigas, Estefanita grabbed a handful of leaves. Relying heavily on her cane, she walked across the kitchen. Filling a kettle with water from a canning jar, she crumbled the leaves into the water. Estefanita hobbled over to the hot stove and set the kettle down with a loud clank. Water spilled from the spout and hissed as it evaporated off the hot iron stove.

Estefanita slowly made her way to the dark corner of the living room. On a table surrounded by melted candles was a hand-carved statue of the Virgin Mary. The intricately carved wood captured the beautiful essence of the saint, from her delicate praying hands to her compassionate gaze. The Blessed Mother gave Estefanita strength and hope, which she desperately needed for her last journey into the forest.

Estefanita leaned her cane against the small altar and carefully lit each candle. The dark room was illuminated by the soft glow. With a loud moan, Estefanita felt the discomfort of old age as she knelt down. Torturing her arthritic knees, Estefanita steadied herself on the hard wood floor and waited for her body to surrender to the pain. Taking the clay-beaded rosary wrapped in the praying hands of the statue, Estefanita made the sign of the cross, closed her eyes, and began to pray.

"Padre Nuestro," Estefanita began.

Outside, the pack of coyotes drew closer. Estefanita turned to stare out the window as darkness slipped through the valley. With each howl Estefanita knew the coyotes were getting closer. Clutching the rosary in her hand, she turned back to the saint and continued to pray.

"*Que estás en el cielo.*"

Searching for another bead with her fingers, Estefanita opened her eyes. Immersed in prayer, she hadn't realized she had finished the rosary and she looked around the room. The coyotes continued to howl in the darkness as they moved closer. Estefanita listened to their cries and struggled to control her mounting fear. Swallowing the lump in her throat, she took a shaky breath as her heart pounded.

Turning back to the small altar, Estefanita opened her clenched fist and studied the crucifix embedded in the palm of her hand. Tonight would be the final test of her faith. Making the sign of the cross, she kissed the crucifix and carefully returned the rosary into the statue's hands. She blew the candles out one by one and studied the transformation of the flames into twisting plumes of smoke.

The image of fire and smoke made her think of her imminent death and the uncertainty of the passage of her troubled soul into the afterlife. Estefanita slowly stood and waited for the dull ache to leave her legs. Taking a small ceramic bowl of dirt from the altar, she hobbled out of the dark living room.

After setting the bowl down on the table, Estefanita used a potholder to pick up the steaming kettle. At the sink, she poured the boiling green liquid into a glass jar.

Outside, the coyotes began to taunt the old woman with their loud cries as they circled her home. They impatiently beckoned to her, excited for the imminent battle.

Estefanita fought to ignore the wild animals and walked over to the old *trastero*. She searched the shelves lined with canning jars. Taking a jar, she unscrewed the metal lid and sniffed the dried leaves. She crinkled her nose from the pungent odor and set the jar back on the shelf. She reached into the back corner and grabbed a dusty jar.

Estefanita's breath stopped in her chest and sweat beaded over her brow as she glanced out the window. The time had drawn near and her uncertainty grew as she prayed for the courage to continue. Shutting her eyes, Estefanita shuddered and wiped the sweat from her brow. She couldn't give in to her fears, not now when the end was so close. She was in God's hands. He had taken care of her throughout her life and if it was her time to die, it was His will, not hers.

The coyotes suddenly grew quiet. Estefanita's chest tightened and her mouth went dry as she looked out the kitchen window into the darkness. The night became eerily still except for the slow creep of the full moon into the night sky. Estefanita's heart raced in her chest as she watched the moon rise over the Sangre de Cristo Mountains and cast its ominous glow over the land. The unusual silence was broken by a deep throaty howl and Estefanita looked away from the window.

Focused on the task before her, Estefanita grabbed the jar of hot liquid and poured it over the mixture of dried herbs.

"*Para los niños,*" she whispered.

Estefanita sprinkled dirt into the watery mixture and stirred the concoction. She poured the dark mixture into a bitters bottle, sealed the brew inside with a cork, and poured the remaining dirt into a small leather pouch.

With the bottle and pouch in her hands, she held them close to her chest and looked up toward heaven.

"*Ayúdame Dios,*" Estefanita whispered as she put both objects into the pocket of her long cotton dress.

"I'm getting too old for this," she mumbled as she took the wool shawl hanging next to the door and stepped out onto the porch.

From the darkness, a black wolf emerged from the shadows and walked toward her as it sniffed the air. It stopped within several feet of the porch to stare at Estefanita with its cold yellow eyes. As the wolf curled its snout over its blood-stained teeth, a growl resonated deep in its chest.

Undaunted, Estefanita walked to the edge of the porch as the pack of coyotes ran around the corner of the house.

"It's no use!" she shouted defiantly at the black wolf. "You can't stop me! La Llorona is dead!"

The chickens and geese squawked frantically, trying to escape from their cage. Feathers drifted through the air as the coyotes harassed the confined animals. Running circles around the yard, the coyotes taunted Estefanita with their cries but the black wolf remained poised, watching her every move.

The wolf didn't have to move to intimidate Estefanita. Its cold stare and watchful eyes were humanlike, both perceptive and patient, and it didn't take long for the old woman to recognize the witch. Estefanita's heart tightened in her chest and she knew tonight her fate had been determined.

With a soft thump, two coyotes leapt up onto the porch and growled as they strode toward Estefanita. With her back to the black wolf, she swung her cane at the animals as another coyote sprang from the darkness and locked its jaws into the worn stick. Trying to pull the cane from the wild dog, Estefanita didn't know what hit her until it was too late. The push from behind buckled her down to her tender knees. Pain shot through Estefanita and she felt her left knee snap from the pressure. Letting go of her wood cane, Estefanita covered her head to protect herself from the relentless assault. The wild coyotes pounced on the old woman, tearing at her clothes.

Unable to defend herself, Estefanita felt the bottle slip from the torn pocket and fall onto the porch with a thud. Estefanita searched blindly until she felt the warm glass wedged between the wood planks. Barely able to grasp the bottle with her fingers, she tugged as a coyote's jaws locked onto her forearm. Refusing to let go of the bottle, Estefanita screamed in agony as she felt the glass slip through her fingers. Estefanita watched the coyote sneer as it clenched its jaws tighter.

Feeling warm blood trickle onto her hand, Estefanita desperately tried to keep the bottle from sliding through her slippery fingers. The excruciating pain numbed her fingers as she jerked the bottle loose. Caught on a rusted nail, the cork popped from the neck of the bottle and Estefanita felt the warm water rush through her fingers.

The coyotes continued their brutal attack as Estefanita watched the liquid seep into the dry wood. Without the mixture she couldn't complete the sacred ritual. Even if she could somehow make it back inside and mix another batch, it was too late.

Losing her will, Estefanita let her body go limp. The battle was over and she lost. There was nothing left to do but pray for the hand of death to come quickly and take her.

# One

Christina held Mark Anthony on her lap and tugged the collar of her white cotton blouse. Lifting the long red hair from the back of her neck, Christina pushed the strands into her loose bun. Christina felt beads of perspiration roll down her spine and into the small curve of her back. The desert sun beat down on the half-empty Greyhound bus, and although the windows were open the breeze provided no escape from the heat.

The tall cowboy in front of Christina dried his neck with a faded blue bandana and shoved it into his back pocket as he leaned his head against the seat. The woman across the aisle fanned herself with a newspaper as she mumbled under her breath and glanced irritably at her husband, who was leaning against the open window.

With a starched handkerchief Christina patted away the moisture from her neck and dabbed her upper lip as the rambunctious three-year-old squirmed in her lap. No matter how much she'd tried to keep Mark Anthony entertained during the long trip from Chicago, he'd had his moments of boisterousness. Christina wrapped her arms tenderly but firmly around Mark Anthony as he struggled to get away. Twisting and turning his small body, Mark Anthony pushed against Christina's arms before he let out a soft whimper.

He collapsed onto his mother, let his head fall back onto her chest, and closed his eyes.

Stroking Mark Anthony's soft black hair, Christina laid her head against the seat. Tears welled up in her eyes and rolled down her cheeks. The pain of losing her mother and the uncertainty of moving to a new town had begun to take its toll. She tried to bury the sadness within her but it was no use. Sensing the rhythmic movement from the fanning newspaper next to her stop, Christina felt the woman's inquisitive eyes studying her. With her eyes closed Christina could shut out the curious glances and unwanted words of sympathy from people who pretended to know her sorrow.

Opening her eyes, Christina looked away from the woman whose curious attention had faded in the heat and resumed to restlessly fan herself. Turning to the two girls in the seat beside her, oblivious to their mother's sadness, Jessica and Marie lay sleeping. They had been quiet throughout the trip and Christina sensed it was from the pain of losing their grandmother. It had been over a month since her mother's death and it had been hard on them all, as it brought back the painful memory of losing Mark.

Christina reached over and caressed the two delicate faces. She wanted desperately to take away their sadness and longed for a time when their faces radiated with joy. She hoped in time they would forget their grandmother's slow and painful death but she knew better. Death lingered in the dark recesses of the mind.

*How do you explain death to someone whose life has just begun? How do you explain something you don't understand yourself?* After Mark died she tried to draw strength from God to help her heal, but she couldn't find comfort in the hallowed walls of church and felt abandoned.

Christina let out a long sigh and looked up at the bus driver, who was watching her through the overhead mirror. Sweat dripped down his wrinkled forehead as he stared at her with a licentious leer. His silent gaze made her uncomfortable. In her heart she was a married woman with three children. Couldn't he recognize the commitment to her family?

Rolling the gold wedding band on her finger, she felt her heart ache. She still wore the ring but she wasn't married, not according to the laws of the state and the vows she'd taken. She was a widow, and although it had been over three years since Mark's death, she still couldn't bear to face a life without him. Christina looked away from the bus driver's disgusting smile to the two sleeping girls.

Christina's sadness slowly faded at the sight of her beautiful children. Her children gave her strength and without them she knew she'd be lost in despair. As Christina gazed down at the two girls she smiled. Although there was no more than three years' age difference between Jessica and Marie, if one didn't know them, it was hard to tell they were related.

Marie was the oldest at eight years old. She resembled her father with dark hair, green eyes, and a beautiful olive complexion. Jessica looked more like her mother, with fiery red hair and a fair complexion enhanced by a splash of freckles on the bridge of her nose.

Getting another burst of energy after Christina loosened her hold around him, Mark Anthony jumped off Christina's lap and screamed excitedly as he ran down the narrow aisle, bumping the cowboy's elbow as he ran by. Instinctively, Christina reached out. Not quite out of her seat, she grabbed the tail of his white shirt and pulled him back onto her lap. Ignoring the irritable cowboy's glance over his shoulder as Mark Anthony screamed with glee, Christina tickled the child and intensified his happiness. Mark Anthony held a special place in her heart. He was her only son and, like Marie, the spitting image of his father.

The memory of her marriage to Mark flooded back with her son's laughter and took her back to when her life was filled with love, a time when life seemed perfect. She was twenty-six when she met Mark and he was four years older. He was tall and handsome beyond belief, with curly black hair and green eyes that sparkled when he smiled. They'd met in the spring of 1938 and were married a few months later that summer.

The bus turned off Old Pecos Trail onto a rutted dirt road, tearing Christina away from her memory of a life she hardly recognized. She looked out the dusty window as they bounced down the narrow road.

Christina gazed out at the small town nestled against the Sangre de Cristo Mountains. The dark green backdrop of the ponderosa- and aspen-covered mountains cradled Santa Fe. The narrow roads were lined with tall cottonwoods, dark evergreen pine trees, and yellow flowering chamisa bushes. The houses, built from stacked adobe bricks, were different from anything she had ever seen. Some of the homes were plastered with gray cement but most had a smooth mud finish, which blended beautifully with the rich brown dirt.

Nearly all the roofs were flat and covered with dirt but some were built up with sheets of metal fastened against the steep pitches. Streaks of dark rust ran down the tin folds from years of abuse under the harsh elements of the high desert and, much to Christina's surprise, weeds grew from the dirt on the flat-roofed homes. A flash of color caught her attention and Christina noticed the vibrant colors painted on the woodwork around the homes.

"Strange, isn't it?" Christina turned to the woman next to her. The woman continued to fan herself with the newspaper as she looked over at Christina. "The bright colors they use around here. You wouldn't find homes painted like that in Georgia." Christina smiled at the woman's soft Southern drawl. "The first time I came to Santa Fe I was appalled by the use of the obtrusive colors but after living here a few years I learned they had a deeper meaning." The woman leaned over into the aisle and whispered. "They paint the windows and doors to keep the evil spirits out of their homes." The woman looked over at her husband asleep against the window and straightened in her seat as she continued to move the newspaper within inches of her face. "I'm not superstitious, mind you, but it's a mighty interesting story to tell the family back home."

Christina looked out the window. The woman was right. The dark cobalt blues and deep greens were a shocking contrast against the soft earth tones. For the most part the paint around the windows and doorways was cracked and peeled from the desert heat but there was not a home that didn't incorporate the dramatic colors.

Christina woke the two girls as the bus turned into the parking lot. Lucy stood under the shade of a tall cottonwood in the back corner of the bus stop. Her long black hair was tied in a bun neatly pinned under a fashionable cream pillbox hat. A white rose sewn on the side of the hat held a wisp of cream netting that draped across

Lucy's forehead. The hat perfectly matched the stylish summer dress that delicately draped over Lucy's slender, curvaceous body. Christina smiled and waved at Lucy. She hadn't seen her in five years but recognized her immediately. She was just as beautiful as she remembered.

They had both entered nursing school at the same time but Lucy's intention of becoming a nurse had been different than her own. Christina wanted to help heal the sick, while Lucy only wanted to be a nurse until she could find herself a husband, and not just any husband. She wanted to marry a doctor. That was ten years ago and she was still a nurse.

Lucy waved back as the bus pulled into the parking lot. Taking one last puff from her cigarette, Lucy tossed it to the ground and stomped it out under her soft white pump. Dust swirled around the bus and stopped as people gathered eagerly around the door.

"Christina!" Lucy called out excitedly as Christina walked off the bus and looked uneasily at the crowd of oriental men. Christina walked through the horde unable to look at the men's faces. The despair and anger burned in the pit of her stomach with each tedious step. She didn't detest the men because of the way they looked. She despised them because a part of her blamed each of them for her husband's death.

"Christy, over here," Lucy called out again.

Holding Mark Anthony in one arm and Jessica's hand in the other, Christina walked over to Lucy. Standing timidly behind their mother, Jessica and Marie watched Christina embrace Lucy in a warm hug.

"It's so good to see you, Christy." Lucy smiled as she looked down at the two girls. "Hi there."

"This is Lucy." Christina moved aside and urged the girls out in front of her. "This is Jessica and Marie."

"Aunt Lucy," Lucy corrected with a smile. "Aren't you two the pretty ones?" She leaned over and gently stroked their hair before she turned her adoring attention to Mark Anthony. "And you're just as handsome as your father." Lucy looked uncertainly at Christina. "I'm sorry," she quickly apologized. "I didn't mean—"

"Don't apologize." Christina forced a smile as she looked over her shoulder at the men boarding the bus.

"They're sending them home," Lucy said as she motioned to the men.

"Who's sending them home?"

"The government. During the war they set up what they liked to call an internment camp at the edge of town. Now that the war is over they've started to send them back to their homes or wherever they came from."

During the war Christina heard of the atrocities inflicted on the Jewish people by Hitler and the Nazis but the image of her own country setting up concentration camps for the Japanese sent a cold chill through her.

"Come on, let's get you home." Lucy picked the heavier of the two suitcases and led Christina down the brick-lined street.

Setting Mark Anthony down, Christina grabbed the other suitcase and followed Lucy. Christina welcomed the chance to stretch her legs even if it was in the heat of the day. Looking around, she took pleasure in the splendor of her surroundings. Santa Fe was beautiful. It was peaceful, almost serene. The people were friendly, smiling at her as she walked by and her apprehension at leaving the familiarity of Chicago vanished as she walked along the Santa Fe River.

Christina was in awe of the picturesque town. Her senses were alive. Everything felt so invigorating: the gentle trickle of the river, the majestic mountains that towered into the dark blue sky, and the sound of the breeze rustling through the trees. She filled her lungs with the fresh smell of the running water and blossoming wildflowers that grew along the riverbank. Christina smiled at the children gathered around the edge of the river playing in the cool running water. *This is where I want my children to grow up*, she thought with certainty.

"This is the hospital." Lucy pointed to the four-story white building as she stopped to rest under the shade of a cottonwood.

Christina studied the out-of-place building. It was taller than the surrounding buildings and its white plastered walls stood out in sharp contrast against the others.

"You have an interview tomorrow morning with Sister Martha. The interview is really just a formality. You already have a job." Lucy spoke as she dabbed her upper lip with a white handkerchief.

"How can you be so sure?" She'd never worked in a hospital before, or anywhere else for that matter.

"Sister Martha is a good friend of mine."

Christina raised her eyebrows at Lucy. The Sisters of Charity had taught them nursing in Chicago and Lucy never considered any of them to be friends. Lucy lightheartedly claimed their vows of chastity and poverty made her uncomfortable.

"Oh, for crying out loud, quit looking at me like that," Lucy said.

"She doesn't even know me," Christina pressed.

"Would I have asked you to come out here if I wasn't sure you'd have a job?" Christina shook her head. "No," Lucy answered. "We're shorthanded at the hospital. They've tried to get nurses from other hospitals to work here but nobody wants to leave the larger cities. Working in Santa Fe may be rewarding but the pay doesn't compare to what the hospitals offer out east. Now come on, let's get you home." Christina followed Lucy over a small cement bridge down a narrow dirt road.

"*Buenos días*, Lucy." A woman stopped shelling peas to wave as Lucy and Christina walked by.

"Hello, Mrs. Romero," Lucy said. "The people around here are friendly." Lucy nodded and waved at the woman sweeping the porch across the street. "Generations of families live in these houses." She pointed to the homes built along the road. "Each compound belongs to a single family. Brothers, sisters, aunts and uncles, they all live here. As the family grew they just added on to the house."

Christina envied the strong bonds each family must have had to live together and wished she shared that kind of love with her own father.

"We're almost there." Lucy glanced at the dispirited family from the corner of her eye and felt the sadness emanate from the four deserted souls. Lucy stopped at the top of the hill. Cedar posts marked the driveway that led to a small adobe house. "This is it."

Christina admired the mud-plastered home and dark blue paint around the doors and windows. The tin roof was streaked with rust and the white porch had weathered away to a dull gray. Yellow wild rosebushes and hollyhocks bloomed along the barbed-wire fence separating the driveway from the adjoining property. Lilies and tulips grew in rock planters around the house and lush green meadow grass stretched toward the thick grove of cottonwood trees along the river's edge.

"What do you think?" Lucy asked apprehensively. She knew the homes in Santa Fe were outdated and in need of repair but once you stepped inside you couldn't help but feel the warmth of the home embrace you.

"It's beautiful." Christina smiled as she walked onto the front porch. The wood planks creaked under her feet as she opened the screen door and stepped into the kitchen. It was cool inside the house and had an earthy smell, like wet dirt after a rainstorm. Everything in the small kitchen was painted white.

"There are two rooms at the end of the hall." Lucy set down the suitcase. "The bathroom is through the first door on the left. My room is in there." She pointed to the closed door next to the refrigerator.

"You live here?" Christina asked in surprise.

"We split the rent fifty-fifty," Lucy smiled sheepishly. "We share the kitchen and bathroom. I hope you don't mind."

"Of course not." Things couldn't have been more perfect. Lucy was her only friend and having her close now when her life was so complicated was just what she needed.

"Good. Make yourself at home." Lucy looked down at her watch. "One of the nurses is getting married today and I'm the matron of honor." Lucy turned around, showing off the stylish dress. "I'll be back after the ceremony and we'll go to the reception downtown at the La Fonda."

"I don't know," Christina answered reluctantly.

"I already told the bride I was bringing you. She'd be disappointed if she didn't get a chance to meet you. It'll be fun and you'll get to sample some of the most wonderful food you've ever tasted."

"Thank you." Christina gave Lucy another hug.

"You don't have to thank me, but you're welcome." Lucy looked over at the children watching her warily and smiled before she stepped out of the house.

Through the dirty screen door Christina watched Lucy walk up the driveway. "Well?" She turned to the children. "What do you think?"

"It's nice." Marie shrugged.

"It's home now," Christina said as she looked around the kitchen.

# *Two*

Estefanita lifted her head and looked around the dark room. Her eyelids fluttered as blood rushed through her swollen brain and pressed against her skull.

Estefanita instinctively laid her head back to control the intensifying pressure but she kept her eyes open. Looking down at her battered and bruised body, Estefanita realized she was lying on a small bed. To her right she saw two silhouettes moving swiftly through the shadows. She strained to listen to their faint whispers but the blood rushing through her brain pounded in her ears.

Estefanita didn't know where she was but she knew she had to get away. She should be dead and for some reason her life had been spared. Not by God, she was certain, but by the coming evil. Struggling to sit up, Estefanita felt her chest cave. An invisible force slammed into her and roughly pushed her back onto the bed. With her arms and legs outstretched Estefanita felt an incredible heaviness move over her and pin her body down. Estefanita struggled to breathe as the weight on her chest slowly subsided.

"She's awake." Estefanita turned to the deep and raspy voice as the silhouettes walked toward her.

Estefanita struggled to sit up but her movements triggered the intense weight and pressed her body deeper into the bed. Unable to move, Estefanita watched as the hooded figures walked around her.

A cold hand grabbed Estefanita by the chin and turned her head forcefully to the side. Estefanita saw the long needle and cried out. Feeling the warm rush of poison flow into the muscles of her neck, she shut her eyes as the cold hand let go of her and quietly she began to pray. She'd hoped the poison would kill her and end her misery but Estefanita knew her torment had only just begun. She would be punished for as long as her body could endure the torture.

Distant cries for mercy caused Estefanita to open her eyes and she watched in horror as the hardened walls transformed into a cascading sea of torment. Estefanita watched the distorted images sweep across the bloody walls. A mayhem of torsos and arms surfaced as deafening screams rang in her ears. *Hell*, Estefanita thought, *I am in hell.*

Crowded on the small stage, the six-member mariachi band serenaded the couple gliding effortlessly across the floor. Circled by their family and friends, the bride dressed in beautiful white lace smiled warmly at her father. The groom watched as he stood nervously between two men who slapped him on the back in drunken merriment. The groom tugged uneasily on his collar as his father-in-law stopped and presented his daughter's hand to him. A chorus of laughter and applause filled the ballroom as the groom shyly took the bride and resumed the dance with his new wife.

In the far corner of the ballroom a group of rowdy men raised their shot glasses, toasting the newlyweds as their wives looked on with obvious displeasure.

"Didn't I tell you the food would be marvelous?" Lucy shouted over the music as she took a bite of red chile enchiladas.

Christina nodded as she reached for the glass of water and drank to soothe the fire in her mouth. The food was delicious and hot. With each bite, the sweet, roasted red chile would yield another dose of spicy fire. Christina had wanted to stop eating after the first wave of heat flooded her mouth but she couldn't resist the wonderful, sumptuous food.

The children sat quietly at the table enjoying their own tasty pleasure of sopapillas doused with honey. They had eaten two baskets of the soft, billowy fried bread and were anxiously waiting for another.

The musicians ended the romantic ballad with an energetic blaze of trumpets and couples formed a line behind the newlyweds.

"May I have this dance?"

Christina looked up at the handsome man impeccably dressed in a pressed army uniform. Christina felt her cheeks blush and didn't know if it was from the chile or the man's simple request.

"She'd love to," Lucy answered for Christina.

"No." Christina shook her head nervously at Lucy. "I can't."

"Why not?" The man asked with a gentle smile.

"I don't know how to dance," Christina stammered.

"I'll teach you," he smiled.

"The children . . ." She motioned to the children.

"I'll watch them." Lucy folded her arms and leaned back in her chair with a smile.

Not wanting to embarrass herself any further, Christina reluctantly took the man's hand and followed him to the dance floor.

"This dance is called 'La Marcha,'" he shouted over the loud music and rhythmic clapping. "It's just like follow the leader. You follow the women and I follow the men," he instructed as the line separated and he followed the long procession of men.

Christina apprehensively looked at the woman behind her. The stout Hispanic woman smiled as she danced and clapped to the music. Christina softly clapped her hands and followed the woman in front of her around the crowded ballroom. The energy from the dance was invigorating. Following the dancers around the ballroom, Christina smiled when she was reunited with the handsome man and slid her arm through his bent elbow.

"My name is Simon Garcia." He smiled as he moved behind her and gently placed his hands on her waist and led her through the long tunnel of dancers.

"Christina Digerno." She smiled when they reached the end of the tunnel. Taking Christina's hands, Simon lifted their arms to create an arch as dancers continued the procession beneath them. After the newlyweds passed, the line broke up to form a circle around the happy couple. After several minutes the circle broke as couples joined the newlyweds in the joyful dance.

Turning to Christina, Simon held her firmly by the waist and guided her around the dance floor.

"I thought you said you didn't know how to dance," Simon teased, making Christina blush. The song ended with applause and a slower ballad began.

Not loosening his hold on Christina, Simon slowed his movements to the new song.

"I really should get back to my children." Christina tried to push herself away from Simon.

"The children are fine." Simon motioned to the children eating another fresh basket of sopapillas, oblivious of their mother. "Just one more dance." He looked in her eyes. "I leave for Georgia tomorrow. Let me enjoy my last night in Santa Fe."

"How long have you been in the army?" Christina asked as they continued to dance.

"A year." Simon's smile faded. "I was drafted too late to see any action during the war."

"You should consider yourself lucky."

"Lucky?" He looked appalled. "How could you say that? I wanted to fight and be a part of the action. Now that the war's over I'm just some guy in a uniform."

Christina's stomach turned and her cheeks burned with anger. "At least you're alive. You should be grateful for that."

"I wanted to serve my country," Simon answered with a hint of anger.

"You don't have to die to serve your country."

"I wouldn't expect you to understand." Simon stiffened his back as he danced her through the crowd.

"Don't tell me I don't understand." Christina noticed the dance was turning into a struggle of wills rather than a fluidity of motion.

"I lost my husband, and my children lost their father. I understand more about that war than you'll ever know."

"I'm sorry. I didn't know." Simon stopped in the middle of the dance floor.

"Don't be sorry." Christina stepped away, looking uncomfortably at the other couples happily dancing around them. "I think I've had enough dancing for one night." She turned to walk away.

"No, wait." Simon grabbed her by the arm. "Can I call you?"

"I don't think that would be a good idea." Christina shook her head as she continued to move through the crowd.

"How about a letter? Nothing romantic," he quickly added. "I'd just like to get a letter from someone from home who isn't my mother or sister." He smiled sheepishly. "Even if it's only about the weather."

"The weather?" Christina asked.

"Have you ever been to southern Georgia?" Christina shook her head. "No mountains and no snow in the winter. Just rain."

"Don't they have hurricanes over there?"

"Do you see the suffering I have to endure?" He smiled. "So you'll write?"

"Yes, I'll write," Christina replied.

Simon led her through the crowd of drunken men gathered around the bar and quickly scribbled his address on a cocktail napkin. He handed Christina the napkin. "I hope you're not telling me you'll write just to get rid of me."

"That, Mr. Garcia, will be something you'll soon find out." Christina smiled lightheartedly as she turned and walked away.

Through the cover of darkness, the black wolf ran through the thick forest, sniffing the ground as it followed a scent. The coyotes' cry echoed as the pack kept a safe distance behind the wolf. The black wolf followed the scent to a small clearing and stopped in front of an abandoned wood shack. The wild beast sniffed crazily as it paced back and forth. Honed in on the scent, the wolf stopped and began to claw at the dirt. The coyotes slowly emerged from the forest and circled anxiously. As it continued to dig, the wolf growled and snapped angrily to keep the curious animals away. The moonlight shone through the trees, illuminating the black wolf's thick coat.

A muffled cry sounded from beneath the ground. Hearing the wail, the black wolf stopped and backed away as the coyotes grew more frantic. Watching intently, the black wolf circled as the dirt slowly began to move. A bony hand emerged and clawed at the ground. The wolf pawed at the hole.

The haunting cry grew louder as a decomposed skull, caked with black soil, emerged. White matted hair hung loosely from the skull and maggots fell from the rotted flesh. The muscles around the mouth had been eaten away to a decayed grin. Dark black eyes stared up at the moon. La Llorona forced the air out of her dry lungs. Maggots and beetles crawled out of her mouth as she let out a raspy cry.

La Llorona pulled herself out of the ground. Her torn clothes barely covered her body. She looked over to the black wolf and extended her hand to the animal. The black wolf timidly walked over and nuzzled La Llorona's hand before it moved closer and licked the oozing flesh on her face.

A coyote crept up and began to nibble the flesh on the decayed skeleton. La Llorona cried out painfully as the black wolf jumped onto the coyote and in one swift and powerful move broke the coyote's neck. The pack circled closer to La Llorona as the black wolf stood protectively by her side.

With all her strength La Llorona pulled herself from the grave and dragged her weak body toward the abandoned shack. Once safely inside, the black wolf settled in front of the door and watched the coyotes search the open grave.

Crawling across the floor through broken glass and dead leaves, she looked around at her deteriorated one-room home. Thick cobwebs blanketed the room and mice scurried away from her. Making her way to the torn and rat-infested mattress on the floor, she collapsed on the mound of loose cotton. Exhausted and unaffected by the mice, the wretched woman fell into a tormented sleep.

# *Three*

After a long and restful night, Christina leaned against the kitchen counter drinking a cup of coffee. The morning's long shadowy fingers slowly inched away from the house until the kitchen was filled with the bright morning sun. Lucy and the children were still asleep and each morning Christina started her day in peaceful solitude watching the transformation of darkness to light.

Turning to stir the sizzling bacon in the pan, Christina hummed quietly to herself. She felt incredible. The more she thought about it, the happier she was about moving to Santa Fe. It was like an incredible burden was lifted off her shoulders. Chicago held too many painful memories and the farther away she was from there, the better she felt.

Christina heard a loud knock at the door. Outside on the front porch was a woman peering through the window and Christina opened the door. The woman appeared to be in her late forties but the years of working under the desert sun had been harsh on her dark skin.

"You must be Christina." The woman smiled as she held out a plate of cookies.

"Yes?" Christina halfheartedly returned her smile, uncertain how this woman knew her name.

"Lucy told me you were moving to town and I thought your children might enjoy some homemade cookies."

"Thank you." Christina took the plate and stepped aside. "Would you like to come in, Mrs.—?"

"Dolores Sanchez. I live next door." She pointed to the gray house across the dirt road as she stepped into the kitchen.

"Is this the first time you've been to Santa Fe?" Dolores asked as she ran her hand over the kitchen counter and rubbed the dust from her fingertips.

"Yes." Christina watched the woman suspiciously.

"I won't keep you, but there are a few things you should know about the way we do things around here." Dolores moved around the kitchen inquisitively. "I said the same things to Lucy when she moved in and I'll explain them to you. People around here are generally pretty friendly but you have to be careful. There are some people who don't like outsiders. Now, everyone around here likes Lucy. She's been an absolute doll. Most people in the neighborhood will come to her instead of the doctor. They respect her," Dolores continued as she rearranged the placemats on the kitchen table. "That's not to say people won't take to you, but there are some people you will have to be careful of. I can't say who they are but I can tell you this—don't eat any food given to you by strangers."

Christina looked at the cookies on the table.

"I'm not a stranger." Dolores rolled her eyes and let out a long sigh. "Why is it so hard to explain these things to gringos?" She looked Christina in the eyes and spoke slowly as if she were addressing a child. "Many people around here believe in witches. I for one do not but then again I wouldn't eat the food given to me by a stranger and neither should you. They curse the food to make you sick and there's not a *curandera* around for miles." Taking one last look around the kitchen, Dolores walked toward the door. "Anyway, I'd better get going. If you need anything I'm right across the street." Signaling that the conversation was over, Dolores opened the door and stepped out onto the porch.

"Thank you," Christina called out as Dolores walked away.

"Just remember what I said," Dolores answered without stopping.

"Who was that, Mommy?" Jessica asked as she walked into the kitchen.

"The neighbor from across the street," Christina answered, a little confused about the eccentric woman's ramblings about witches.

"Can I have a cookie?" She reached for one of the warm oatmeal cookies.

"Why don't we wait until after breakfast?" Christina gently took the cookie from Jessica's hand and set it back on the plate. She didn't believe Dolores's outrageous warning but she wanted to talk to Lucy before she'd let the children eat any of the cookies. "Why don't you wash up and help me set the table?" Jessica walked down the hall, sleepily rubbing her eyes.

Turning to the sound of the door opening, Christina watched Lucy walk into the kitchen as she cinched the belt around her robe.

"It looks like you could use a cup of coffee." Christina smiled as she poured the black coffee.

"My head," Lucy said as she rubbed her temples. "I'm going to have to stop drinking margaritas." Taking a pack of cigarettes out of the pocket of her robe, Lucy put her feet up on a chair and lit a cigarette. Exhaling a long white plume of smoke, she set the burnt match in the ashtray next to the cookies. "I see Dolores came by this morning." She pointed to the cookies. "Did she give you her little talk about witches and not eating the food anyone gives you?"

"Yes." Christina sat across from Lucy.

"Don't pay too much attention to her." Lucy took a bite of one of the cookies. "She's the only one who ever brings food and every time she does, she gives me the same lecture. She means well but things have never been the same with her since her son was killed in the war." Lucy set the cookie down wanting desperately to take her words back.

"I can sympathize," Christina whispered as she looked down into her empty cup. "Well, she thinks the world of you."

"If she was so nice, why didn't you eat one of her cookies?" Lucy teased.

"Maybe next time," Christina laughed as she stood and poured herself more coffee. "How about some breakfast?"

"I'm too sick to eat." Lucy took another puff of her almost-finished cigarette. "How did you sleep last night?"

"Wonderful." Christina smiled at the thought of the first good sleep she'd had in what seemed like years. "The sound of the river and the peacefulness around here is incredible. Nothing like Chicago."

"Speaking of Chicago, how did dear old dad take the news you were moving here with me?"

"You know my father . . ." Christina's stomach twisted at the thought of the old man she had to call "Father." The butcher down the street took more interest in her life than he ever did. "He was angry but it wasn't because he was going to miss me or the children. He got used to having someone take care of him and now he'll have to fend for himself."

"Do you miss him?"

"Miss him?" Christina laughed. "No, I don't miss him. I do wish I could see him trying to cook himself a meal." Her smile quickly faded and her voice broke with emotion. "He never appreciated what my mother did for him. To him, she was just a financial burden. He always complained about her medical expenses and the money he wasted on nursing school for me until mom got sick. Then he claimed my education had been a good investment, one less bill he had to pay." She struggled to control her rising anger. "But he'll realize how valuable and special Mom really was." Christina tried to shake the image of her heartless father. "Enough about him. How about you? What have you been up to? In your last letter you didn't mention anything about the doctor you were dating."

"That's because there was nothing to tell. Turned out he was married. It came as a big surprise to everyone when his wife showed up one day. She was an actress working on Broadway while her husband was acting out his own play with me. When the sisters found out he was married, I nearly lost my job."

"What did you do?" Christina's heart went out to Lucy. Lucy didn't go out looking for married men but no matter how hard she tried it seemed like the lying bastards always found her.

"I gave Sister Martha a piece of my mind. He was the one who was married and *lied* about it to everyone." Lucy stubbed her cigarette out in the ashtray.

"You didn't!"

"You're damn right I did. I figured, what could it hurt? They were going to fire me anyway."

"And what did they do?"

"You know the sisters, they didn't want to cause any problems but he was committing adultery, so they encouraged him to find a job somewhere else."

"What did they do to you?" Christina smiled at her friend's courage.

"They all prayed for my condemned soul." Lucy rolled her eyes toward heaven.

"I don't believe you—you're actually braver now than you were in nursing school."

"Are you ready for your interview?" Lucy asked.

"I think so." The thought sent butterflies dancing in Christina's stomach.

"Well, don't worry about it too much. Sister Martha will take care of you." Lucy stifled a yawn. "I'll watch the kids."

"No, you get some rest. I'll take them with me. They can wait for me in the hall."

"It's really not a problem for me to watch them."

"I know, but I want to take a walk into town after the interview and pick up a few things."

"Your interview is at nine thirty." Lucy yawned again. "I'm sorry I'm not better company but my head is pounding."

"Don't apologize. Now go get some rest."

"I missed you." Lucy smiled. "I'm glad you're here."

"I missed you too."

Lucy closed the door behind her as Christina walked down the hall into her bedroom. The room was small but the brightly painted walls made the room feel bigger. The bed's iron headboard was pushed against the wall next to a large window overlooking the lush green backyard. A single rug woven from strips of cloth lay in front of the bed and partially covered the wood plank floor. The floor creaked under her weight as she walked over to the three-drawer dresser and picked up a double-picture frame. She held the metal frame gently in her hands as she looked down at the two pictures. Her wedding picture and Mark in his military uniform. Christina traced her fingers over Mark's face and smiled. "I think we finally found a place to call home," she whispered.

# *Four*

The midmorning sun shone through a tall stained-glass window, brightly reflecting the color onto the perfectly waxed floors.

As Christina had expected, the hospital was built in the shape of a cross. Past the front entrance, midway down the hall, the corridor branched out into four directions. She'd recognized the layout from the hospitals in Chicago run by the Sisters of Charity and knew everything the nuns did was carefully designed with their faith in God etched into every detail of their lives.

Christina and the children waited outside Sister Martha's office on the first floor at the far end of the long hall. Christina fidgeted as she tried to hide her growing anxiety.

She'd arrived at the hospital twenty minutes early for her interview. When she walked through the hospital's front entrance, she felt a sense of calm. The familiar smell of antiseptic eased her insecurity and renewed her sense of confidence. For the first time since she'd gotten Lucy's letter inviting her to Santa Fe her uncertainty over being able to take care of her family vanished. But now as she waited, her confidence slipped away with each passing minute.

Irritated for being so nervous and tired of watching doctors and nurses walking in and out of patients' rooms, Christina sprang out of her chair and paced in front of the children. Smoothing the sleeves of her blouse, Christina brushed invisible lint from her gray skirt.

"What's the matter, Mom?" Jessica asked.

"Nothing, sweetie. I'm just a little nervous, that's all."

"Why?"

"I don't know. I just am," she lied. Lucy said the job was hers but how could it be that easy? She married Mark shortly before she graduated from nursing school, and shortly thereafter she was pregnant. Mark refused to let her work while she was pregnant and that was the end of her career in nursing until she cared for her sick mother.

Turning to the sound of the door opening, Christina saw a petite woman in her fifties dressed in a white uniform and habit step out into the hall.

"Christina?" Sister Martha looked over her wire-rimmed glasses at the application in her hand.

"Yes," Christina managed to mutter through her dry throat.

"Why don't you step into my office?" Sister Martha stepped aside to let Christina by as she studied the three children sitting next to the office door. "Your mom will be right back." She gently reassured them before she closed the door.

"Have a seat." Sister Martha motioned to the empty chair in front of the desk. Christina glanced around the office and sat down. Filing cabinets filled the small room. Drawers left half open were jammed with folders and loose papers. Stacks of binders were piled high on Sister Martha's desk and Christina quickly realized this nun was not like any other she'd met. Although Sister Martha was probably a good nurse, her organizational skills needed refining. This, Christina guessed, was why Lucy liked her.

Sister Martha walked around the desk, sat in her chair, and looked over at Christina. Unable to see Christina through the mounds of paperwork, Sister Martha mumbled under her breath and moved a stack of folders onto the floor.

"Lucy tells me you went to nursing school together." Sister Martha didn't look up as she read through the application.

"Yes." Christina pulled her skirt over her knees as she sat at the edge of the hard wood chair.

"Do you have any work experience?"

"No. I took care of my mother before she died but I've never worked in a hospital," Christina answered, drying her palms on her skirt.

Sister Martha set the application down in front of her and took off her reading glasses to get a better look at Christina. "Well, we prefer to hire nurses with experience, but you did learn from our sisters in Chicago, which means you're familiar with how we operate and if you're anything like Lucy, you'll make a fine nurse. When can you start?"

"Start?" Christina said in astonishment. That was it? Could it actually be as easy as Lucy promised?

"Don't sound so surprised. I told Lucy we'd hire you if you moved to town," Sister Martha laughed. "It's no secret we need nurses around here. We've got several openings." She picked up a sheet of paper and put her glasses back on. "We've got an opening in the emergency room—no, wait, you need experience for that one." She read farther down the paper. "There's an opening in surgery from seven until four p.m., there's another in pediatrics from four until eleven p.m., and we have an opening on the fourth floor for the night shift, eleven to seven a.m." She read the paper again to make sure she didn't miss anything before she looked up at Christina.

"I'll take the night shift, eleven to seven."

"Are you sure? That's a hard shift to get used to."

"Yes." Christina nodded.

"You'll need to fill out a few more forms. Can you start tonight?"

"Yes," Christina answered eagerly. The sooner the better.

"Okay." Sister Martha stood and walked around her desk as Christina followed her to the door. "Go down the hall to the personnel office. Tell them I sent you. They have the payroll forms you need to fill out."

"Thank you." Christina smiled as she shook Sister Martha's hand and walked out into the hall.

⁓

A steady stream of people walked into the hospital carrying bundles of flowers and bags of goodies. The friendly nods and smiles couldn't hide their uneasiness of calling on a loved one who had the misfortune of being sick.

Christina closed her eyes and smiled. She couldn't believe how everything had begun to fall into place for her. A warm feeling of comfort washed over her and for the first time since her mother's death Christina felt her mother's loving presence. She couldn't see her but when she looked up at the gently rustling leaves in the cottonwood trees, she felt serene. She could have dismissed the sensation as elation from getting her first job but she knew better. It was as if her mother were letting her know she wasn't alone.

Taking a small envelope from her purse, Christina tapped the letter on her hand as she stood in front of the mailbox outside the hospital.

"What's that, Mom?" Marie asked.

"It's a letter." She hadn't planned on writing Simon but when she woke up this morning she wanted to know more about him, and letters were simple. Carefully chosen conversations could easily be ended if they became too complicated.

"Is it to Grandpa?" Jessica tried to read the address.

"No." Christina shoved the envelope back into her purse.

"I bet it's to the man you danced with last night," Marie teased.

"Come on, let's get to town." Christina felt the warmth in her cheeks as she took Mark Anthony's hand.

Hand in hand the young family walked around the front of the hospital onto the cracked cement streets of Palace Avenue. Christina looked up at the four-story building. Studying each detail of the white hospital, she immediately recognized the adjacent compound. The words *Marion Hall* were etched in the stone over the main entrance to the sisters' dormitory. It was a home for the sisters who dedicated their life to helping the sick.

Walking farther down the street toward the center of town, Christina looked across a small green park to an incredible stone cathedral. The construction was unlike anything she'd ever seen. Massive stone bricks formed the high walls that encompassed the tall, arched stained-glass windows. The front of the church featured two towering bell towers and enormous double doors. The hand-carved doors were supported with immense iron hinges. With the doors wide open, the bells resonated loudly, beckoning patrons to the daily Mass.

Christina and the children continued past the church and stopped when they reached the plaza. It was more beautiful than Lucy had described in her letters. Rustic adobe buildings with covered portals surrounded a circular park dotted with tall cottonwood trees. A brick-paved street separated the businesses from the plaza. This was the center of town. Women dressed in skirts and matching hats gathered outside Woolworth's, while the men preferred to meet in the center of the plaza around the fountain.

Crossing Palace Avenue, Christina wanted to explore the majestic town and started toward the oldest building on the street. The Palace of the Governors faced the plaza to the south. American Indians sat under the shade of the portal with ceramic pottery and turquoise and silver jewelry laid out before them on woven wool blankets. Tourists strolled past the open market display of jewelry and Christina slipped between several couples to admire the artistic exhibit.

"Who are they, Momma?" Jessica asked as she walked timidly behind her mother.

"They're Indians selling their jewelry."

"Will they hurt us?" Jessica stepped behind her mother in fear.

"Of course not. How could you even ask such a question?" Christina looked uncomfortably at the old Indian woman sitting on the hard brick floor.

Ignoring Jessica's remark, the woman leaned over and picked up a silver bracelet. Her long braided gray hair was entwined with beaded leather and she wore a red velvet dress with an intricately decorated turquoise belt and matching necklace. Silver bracelets wrapped around each of her wrists and each ring finger was adorned with a large turquoise ring.

"Because of the movies, the Indians are always bad and trying to kill the good guys."

"Honey, that was only a movie. It wasn't real." Christina looked uneasily at the woman. When she'd taken them to the movies, she'd never realized how negatively the Indians had been portrayed until now.

"Do they live in teepees?" Jessica continued.

Christina didn't know how to answer. She didn't know anything about American Indians other than what she'd seen in the movies. She didn't know where or how they lived and now her daughter wanted a history lesson.

"I live in a house like you." The old woman looked up at Jessica as she polished the silver bracelet with a red bandana and set it back on the blanket. The sun reflected brightly off its smooth finish. "When I was a child I was told to stay away from the white man because my people believed they wanted to hurt us." The woman spoke slowly so Jessica would understand her through her strong Tewa accent. "Do you want to hurt me?" Jessica slowly shook her head. "Do you think I want to hurt you?" Again she shook her head. "Good." The woman smiled. "The next time you see a movie with Indians, you won't think we're all savages and the next time I see the white man I won't think you all want to hurt us." Jessica nodded again.

"Thank you." Christina smiled at the woman.

The woman nodded as the next wave of tourists streamed by her wares, moving Christina and the children to the next display. Christina glanced at the woman polishing her jewelry, wishing she could hear more about her incredible life.

Christina sat on the grassy embankment along the Santa Fe River as the children laughed and played in the water. She'd brought the kids to the river after they came back from town. Lucy was still asleep when they'd gotten home and Christina didn't want to wake her. So she packed a small lunch and headed for the river. The river was only about a hundred yards from the house but it seemed much farther when they walked through the thick grove of cottonwood and elm trees that grew along the embankment.

They'd found a small grassy clearing yesterday, and Christina wanted to spend time with her children there before she went to work. She knew she should be resting for her new job but it had been such a long time since the children played with such uninhibited joy that she didn't want it to end. Here, in Santa Fe, they all felt at ease as a family, and it was as if the pain of their lives had been forgotten. Leaning back on her elbows, Christina closed her eyes and listened to her children's laughter mingle with the rippling water.

"I thought I'd find you here." Lucy walked up behind Christina and sat beside her on the wool blanket.

"Hi. Would you like a sandwich?" She reached into the brown paper sack and took out a sandwich wrapped in waxed paper.

"Thanks." Lucy took the sandwich. "How'd the interview go with Sister Martha?"

"Great. I start tonight."

"Tonight?" Lucy nearly choked on her food.

"Are you okay?" Christina asked as she poured Lucy a glass of lemonade.

"What's the matter with that crazy old lady? Why would she make you work the night shift? I specifically asked her to give you a decent schedule." Lucy took a drink from the glass.

"It wasn't her fault. I asked for the night shift," Christina tried to explain.

"What?" Lucy turned to Christina. "Why would you want to work the night shift?"

"So I can spend time with the kids during the day," Christina answered innocently.

"I don't know if that was such a good idea. Working at the hospital is tough enough but the night shift can be brutal. I ought to know—I worked that shift for two years. What floor will you be working on?"

"The fourth floor."

"You've got to be kidding." Lucy shook her head as she set the sandwich down on the waxed paper.

"What?" Christina looked at her best friend in bewilderment.

"Not only is the night supervisor a bitch, but strange things go on up there. Martha should have known better than to let you work under Jenny. But don't worry. I'll talk to her this afternoon and see if you can transfer to another ward."

"How can you say that about a nun?" Christina was mortified Lucy had used such a harsh word to describe a woman who dedicated her life to God.

"Jenny's not a nun." Lucy laughed. "And she *is* a bitch. Look, the patients on the fourth floor are long-term patients and require a tremendous amount of care and attention, but there's something else about that place. It's almost like it's haunted or something. None of the other nurses will go up there after dark."

"Lucy, I appreciate your wanting to help but the fourth floor was the only place with an opening for the night shift."

"It's a rough shift, Christy, and Jenny is tough." Lucy hoped Christina would change her mind.

"You've said that already but I can take care of myself." Christina said.

"Okay, but—"

"No buts," Christina cut in. "I can do this. I have to do this for me and the children."

"It's good to see you again." Changing the subject, Lucy put her arm around Christina and squeezed.

"It has been a long time," Christina said as she leaned her head on Lucy's shoulder.

"The kids seem to be having fun."

"They love it here and so do I."

"This is a good town to raise a family."

"I know." Christina smiled as she watched Jessica and Marie splash water at each other and Mark Anthony dig holes in the sandy embankment. "I know," she whispered.

# *Five*

Christina looked at her reflection in the small bathroom mirror as she pinned on the nurse's cap and turned her head from side to side to check her hair. Stepping away from the mirror to get a better look, Christina ran her hands over the pressed white uniform Lucy lent her until she could save enough money to buy her own. She and Lucy both wore a size six but her body definitely didn't fill out the simple uniform like Lucy's curvaceous body could. Christina checked her hair one last time before she stepped out of the bathroom.

Walking down the dark hall, Christina quietly opened the door and tiptoed across the squeaky wood floor. All three children slept comfortably in the same bed, with Mark Anthony nestled protectively between his two older sisters. Christina sat on the edge of the bed and gently stroked Jessica's soft red hair. She used the soft moonlight to check her watch and stood. It was ten thirty. She knew the short walk to the hospital would only take fifteen minutes but she didn't want to be late. Leaning over, Christina gently kissed each of her children on the cheek and walked out of the room.

Stepping out onto the front porch, Christina searched the darkness at the sound of a coyote howling in the distance. She rubbed the chill from her arms and stepped off the porch. With no street-lights to guide her except for the occasional porch light, Christina walked under the glow of the full moon.

Christina slowly walked down the middle of the road, her eyes darting to every shadow as the bushes rustled around her. Christina was startled as a gray squirrel scampered down from a tree and crossed the road in front of her. With a nervous laugh she quick-ened her pace, ignoring the night's frightening sounds. In Chicago, Christina had become accustomed to the mercury lamps that illu-minated the neighborhood streets and walking down a desolate road at night was something she'd never done.

Christina walked around the corner off Canyon Road and breathed a sigh of relief. In the distance she could see the brightly lit hospital. She hurried across the empty parking lot, through the front entrance, and into the quiet building.

The nun behind the front desk smiled kindly at Christina as she walked toward the elevator. Christina watched several doctors and nurses walk through the large metal doors into the emergency room, which was busy with activity unlike the rest of the first floor. In the elevator, Christina fidgeted with her uniform while she was carried to the fourth floor. The door slid open and she hesitated. Taking a deep breath, she straightened her shoulders and stepped out of the elevator. As she walked slowly down the long hall, the stillness was unsettling. Focusing at the light at the far end of the hall, she saw three women working quietly behind the nurses' sta-tion. Drying her damp hands on her uniform, Christina timidly walked up to the women.

"Hello," Christina whispered through her tight throat.

The women looked up in surprise. "You must be Christina." The oldest of the three smiled warmly. "I'm Michelle," she said as she extended her hand. "This is Monica and Amanda."

Christina relaxed. "It's nice to—"

"What's going on?" A gravelly voice growled as Michelle quickly pulled her hand away and Christina turned to the woman stepping out of the shadows. Offering her hand and forcing a smile, Chris-tina tensed at the sight of the large woman walking toward her.

"I'm Christina. I was hired to fill the opening," she began.

"I wasn't talking to you." Jenny snapped as she looked over at Michelle. "Why wasn't I notified about this?"

"We just got the paperwork." Michelle held out a sheet of paper and quickly stepped away as Jenny snatched the form out of her hand.

"Get to work," Jenny ordered as the three nurses quickly retreated down the hall. She waited for them to disappear into the patients' rooms before she turned to her attention back to Christina. Christina watched Jenny as she slowly walked around her. Straightening her shoulders, Christina stood still for Jenny's thorough inspection.

Jenny was in her late fifties but was taller than Christina and solid. Her body was built from years of lifting and moving patients. Her gray hair was tied neatly in a bun and Christina guessed no matter how hot or how hectic it got around the hospital, she never looked haggard in her crisp white uniform. Jenny stopped in front of Christina and looked contemptuously down at her.

"You don't have any experience," Jenny began.

"I—"

"I'm not finished," she growled. "I don't have the time or the patience to train inexperienced nurses. How you got this job is beyond me but it seems like you've got a friend downstairs so let's get something straight. You will do what I say when I say. I don't want to hear any excuses. If you can't do the job, I'll find someone else with more experience who can. Am I making myself clear?" Too intimidated to answer, Christina nodded instead. "Good. As far as I'm concerned you are not worthy of calling yourself a nurse. So from now on, your nights will consist of cleaning. There are sixty rooms on this floor, all of them occupied. Every night you will start by clearing the dinner trays, then emptying and cleaning the bedpans. After you're finished with that, mop and disinfect the rooms." She didn't give Christina a chance to answer as she turned and walked away.

Although Lucy warned Christina about Jenny, there was nothing that could have prepared her for what she'd just experienced.

She stood alone in the empty hall, her head throbbing and wishing she could go back home. Regaining her composure, Christina slowly walked down the hall. *I can do this,* she thought, *and I will prove it to anyone who doubts me, including myself.*

Christina walked into the last room down the hall. Michelle was inside checking the young man's blood pressure and smiled at Christina. Christina glanced down at the man as she walked over to pick up the dinner tray. From the outline of the thin sheet she could see both of his legs ended just above the knees. His arms were scarred from second-degree burns but it was his face that held Christina's eyes. He couldn't have been older than thirty but his face was aged beyond his years and his pale gray skin withered over his frail bones. Blood stained the bandage wrapped around his head and Christina wondered how someone so young could have ended up here.

After Monica finished her brief examination, she folded the arm cuff and put it back into a small black handbag.

"How are you doing?" Michelle asked kindly.

"I'm fine." Christina forced a smiled as she turned toward the door.

"Jenny is tough on all of us. Don't let it get to you." Christina nodded. She could only imagine how she treated the other nurses. "Do what you're told and she'll eventually leave you alone." Michelle walked in front of Christina and stopped before she opened the door. "Jenny blends into the walls around here. Just remember, she's always watching." With that, Michelle opened the door and let Christina by. Lucy's warnings echoed in her ears but it didn't matter; she was here to do a job and that was what she was going to do.

Michelle stopped. "That patient"—she pointed—"is the only one allowed to receive visitors after hours. His fiancée works as a nurse downstairs and usually comes in after her shift."

Christina walked quickly down the hall carrying a tray of small paper cups filled with medications. It was two thirty in the morning and the hospital was still muggy from the hot summer day. Christina was exhausted. She'd worked hard to please Jenny, but she soon realized it was close to impossible to please that woman. Her hair hung limp around her face and fell out of her cap. She tried to blow the stray strands out of her eyes as she walked around the corner and ran into Jenny.

"Where are you going with those medications?" Her voiced echoed loudly through the empty hall.

"I was taking them to the front desk," Christina answered timidly.

"You're not authorized to handle the medications. I thought I made it perfectly clear what your responsibilities were around here," Jenny snapped as she grabbed the tray from Christina. "If you can't follow my simple instructions I'll find someone else who can."

Christina wanted to snap back at the bitter old woman but bit her tongue instead. She needed this job and Jenny knew it. Jenny had made it tough on her all night but if she lost this job, she'd be forced to go back to her father in Chicago and she'd do anything to make sure that didn't happen, even if it meant losing a bit of dignity.

Jenny looked narrowly at Christina and waited for her to respond. "I didn't think so," she snickered. "Clean the bedpan in room 431."

"Yes, ma'am." Christina turned and walked away, refusing to be beat by the woman. She lifted her head, pushed her shoulders back, and walked squarely down the hall.

# *Six*

Estefanita slowly opened her eyes and looked around the dark room. The glow from the moon reflected off the sterile walls, giving just enough light for her to make out where she was. Pain shot through Estefanita's body as she tried to move. Her heart raced and her head spun from the rush of blood and she started to lose consciousness. Laying her head back on the stiff pillow, Estefanita stared at the white ceiling tiles and tried to remember. Her whole body ached with even the slightest movement. She gradually remembered the black wolf, the coyotes, and the attack. Looking over at the white walls, her heart began to pound as the bloody visions of hell raced through her. The cries of grief rang in her ears as she tried to forget their torment. She was still groggy and weak from the shot, but as she looked around the room, Estefanita knew now was her only chance to get away.

Estefanita's mind was jumbled with questions as she looked out the window into the dark night and wondered how long she'd been unconscious. Other than the brief encounter with her captors and the vague memory of the poisoned shot, she couldn't remember anything after the attack. The fear of her failed mission sank into the pit of her stomach. *Was I too late?* Not once in fifty years had she fallen victim to the powerful witch and she couldn't fail now.

Swinging her legs off the bed, the old woman sat up. Expecting the hidden power to force her back onto the bed, Estefanita cautiously looked around the room and breathed a sigh of relief. She was alone. The evil presence she'd felt earlier was gone. As she touched the cool tile floor with one foot, the room began to spin. She tried to swallow the nausea rising in her throat and fought the overwhelming urge to lie down. Stepping off the bed, Estefanita buckled from the pain shooting through her tender knee. Cradling her bandaged forearm, she remembered the coyote's bloodthirsty glare as his teeth tore into her.

Estefanita braced herself against the bed. Each step brought a flood of razor-sharp pain. Her bruised ribs cracked with each breath and she felt as if her leg would snap at the knee. Forcing herself to continue, she hobbled across the room. Slowly opening the door, Estefanita peeked out into the dark hall. Satisfied no one was around, she stepped into the hall, knowing this was her only chance to escape. The injured old woman struggled to walk toward the elevator, using the metal handrail bolted to the wall to steady herself.

Focusing all her energy on her escape, Estefanita didn't see Jenny step out from the shadows.

"I don't think you're going to make it." Jenny stepped in front of Estefanita and sneered at her. "Not in your condition."

"You . . ." Estefanita let go of the handrail and fell to her knees.

Christina stood in the doorway of room 431 and sighed. In the moonlight she could see the silhouette of the large man fast asleep. The rise and fall of the sheet draped over his body synchronized with the loud snores. When she entered nursing school she had the romantic idea she'd be helping people. She never imagined all of her training would be spent cleaning and changing bedpans.

With her hand on the mattress, Christina crouched down and saw the pan on the floor. She watched the rise and fall of the sheet and, satisfied the man was sleeping, she slid the metal pan from under the bed. The pan was full and heavy and Christina cautiously balanced the weight as she tried to keep it from spilling onto the floor. Steadying the pan in one hand, she tried to get a better grip with the other when a loud scream broke the tranquility and silence of the ward.

Looking over her shoulder, Christina forgot about the bedpan until it was too late. The man grumbled in his sleep, disturbed by the frantic screaming, and knocked the pan out of her hands with his knee. The force from the kick sent the pan into her chest. Turning her head, Christina barely avoided being splashed in the face but felt the wetness soak through her uniform. Letting the metal pan slip from her fingers, she dropped it onto the floor with a loud clang. Staring at the urine dripping off her uniform, Christina felt the first wave of nausea rise and gagged.

"Christina! Get over here and help with this patient!" Jenny's voice echoed over the hysterical screams.

Christina looked over at the man in shock. *How could this have happened? And how could he still be asleep?* She dried her arms and patted her uniform with the man's robe on the chair next to the bed.

"Christina, get over here now!" Jenny yelled again as the screams grew louder.

Christina dropped the robe onto the chair and ran out of the room down the hall. Around the corner, Jenny stood over the three nurses and watched them struggle to keep Estefanita on the floor. Estefanita's arms and legs flung wildly.

Jenny looked up at Christina and for a second was shocked to see her soiled uniform. "Don't just stand there, grab her legs!" she ordered.

Christina leaned over and grabbed a leg. She struggled to hold on but with one leg free, Estefanita kicked with all her might. Kicked in the face, Christina fell onto her back. Dazed by the powerful blow, Christina sat and watched the old woman continue to fight.

"Grab both legs!" Jenny's yell snapped Christina out of her shock.

Nodding, she jumped on both flinging legs and held on tight. Christina barely hung onto the moving legs while Michelle and the other two nurses pinned Estefanita down long enough for Jenny to shove a needle into the old woman's arm.

The fear in Estefanita's eyes was undeniable as she watched the needle pierce her skin and after several seconds she felt the numbing effect of the drug pulsating through her blood. Estefanita's eyelids fluttered and her body went limp.

"You can let her go now," Jenny scoffed as Christina opened her eyes and looked up at the four women watching her. "What's the matter with you? Didn't you learn anything in nursing school?" Jenny snapped as she smoothed her hands over her uniform. "Next time we have a disorderly patient, grab both legs. One of us could have gotten hurt."

"Yes, ma'am." Christina slumped her shoulders and looked down at the floor as she gently touched her tender cheek.

"It disgusts me to know there are women out there like you who think they can call themselves a nurse. Now get back to work," Jenny barked.

Sickened by the stench of her uniform, Christina looked up pleadingly at Jenny and the other nurses. "May I clean up first?"

"No, clean the mess first," Jenny scoffed. "Maybe the next time you're doing something as simple as cleaning a bedpan you'll be more careful." Jenny turned her back to Christina. "What are you doing just standing there? Get her back into her room." She pointed to Estefanita lying semiconscious on the floor. "And restrain her to the bed. I don't want her getting loose again."

Christina watched the three women drag Estefanita out of the hall into the room and slowly walked away.

# Seven

Lucy jumped when she heard the kitchen door swing open and hit the water heater in the corner of the kitchen. "What in the hell happened to you?" Lucy asked as she stubbed her cigarette out in the ashtray.

Christina knew she looked ridiculous in the large green surgeon's gown. The pant legs were folded around her ankles and she had to cinch the suit around her waist but she didn't care. It was clean and that was all that mattered. Exhausted, Christina set the brown paper bag with her dirty uniform on the floor and sat in the chair across from Lucy. Tears burned her tired eyes and she dropped her face into her hands.

"I'm sorry, honey, I didn't mean to make you cry." Lucy stood and poured a cup of coffee.

"It's not your fault," Christina muttered between sobs.

"What happened to your cheek?" Lucy asked as she handed her the coffee and gently brushed the hair from Christina's face to examine the bruise.

"I don't know if I can take it," Christina managed to say as she dried her eyes with her sleeve. "I loved nursing school and the thought of helping people but I don't know if I can do this."

"What did Jenny do to you?" Lucy spoke through clenched teeth.

"Nothing." Jenny hadn't actually done anything to her. "Everything that went wrong last night was because of my own stupidity."

"Stop talking like that," Lucy said.

"I was hopeless. I couldn't do anything right."

"None of this would have happened if Jenny was any kind of supervisor. I'm getting you transferred to another ward."

"Please don't," Christina sobbed.

"Why not?" Lucy sat back down in her chair and lit another cigarette.

"Because I can't afford to lose this job."

"You're not going to lose your job. You're just going to work on another floor."

"What about the kids?"

"What about them?"

"Who's going to take care of them while I'm at work?"

"Me."

"I couldn't ask you to do that. You have your own life."

"You're not asking, I'm offering."

"That's not the point. I want to spend as much time with them as I can. They need me."

"If you won't take my help, then don't let Jenny push you around. She's only making it hard on you because she knows she can. You've got to put your foot down and stand up to her."

Christina stared into the steaming cup of coffee in her hands. "I just don't understand how my life got so screwed up. Why did Mark have to leave me?"

"This isn't about Mark. This is about you. You have to stand up to that bitch."

"And if I get fired?"

"So what? At least you won't be miserable." Lucy inhaled a breath of smoke. "Everyone knows she's a bitch, all the way up to Mother Superior. I doubt you'll get fired for standing up for yourself. Besides, it can't be any worse than the way things are now."

"Maybe you're right," Christina reluctantly admitted as she rubbed her tired eyes and leaned back in the chair.

"Why don't you get some rest? I'll take care of the kids this morning."

"You watched them all night."

"They slept all night. Believe me, it wasn't that hard. Besides, I don't have kids and it'll give me a chance to see what I'm missing out on."

"I can't." Christina stifled a yawn.

"You can't do it all by yourself. You work the night shift so you can be with the kids during the day but you've got to take some time to rest."

"I don't want to be a burden."

"How are you a burden? I don't have to go to work until four. I'll have the kids back by two. Plenty of time for me to get ready for work."

Christina looked over at her friend. She was exhausted and as much as she hated to admit it, she desperately wanted to crawl into bed and sleep. "Thank you."

"You don't have to thank me. Now get to bed before the kids hear you and wake up."

Christina picked up the sack by her feet and stood. She walked down the hall into the bedroom. The heavy curtains were pulled over the window, darkening the cool room. She dropped the bag down by the door and collapsed on the bed. Not bothering to get under the covers, Christina closed her eyes and drifted off to sleep.

Christina reached over for the windup clock on the nightstand. It was one thirty. She had been asleep for almost six hours. Rolling over on her back, Christina stretched out under the soft cotton bedspread and closed her eyes. Even though she worked all night, she felt a little guilty for sleeping through the morning. Listening in the empty house for the children, Christina wished she'd awakened them before she fell asleep.

It was hard for her to remember a time when she had been without her children and not once since Jessica was born had she been alone. Staying in bed until the late afternoon was an indulgence she'd only shared with Mark.

Christina reluctantly got up. Putting on her robe, she walked down the narrow hall into the kitchen. Christina filled a glass with water and sat at the table. With her back to the sink she sipped the water and waited. She felt strangely alone without her children. They were like an extension of her soul. She knew Lucy would take care of them but she still fidgeted nervously until she saw them walk into the driveway.

Christina opened the door and stepped out onto the porch. The hot July afternoon hit her like an oven and she ran out to meet them halfway up the drive.

"Mommy! Mommy!" Mark Anthony called and ran to her.

"I missed you so much!" Christina scooped the small boy into her arms as she reached out for Jessica and Marie. "Where were you?"

"Aunt Lucy took us to town," Jessica answered excitedly.

"To buy candy!" Mark Anthony held up a small white bag filled with butterscotch candy and stuck out his tongue to show her the one in his mouth.

"You're all sticky." Christina noticed his dirty face and looked over at Lucy who smiled sheepishly as she sucked on a lollipop. Mark Anthony wiped his sticky hand on his shirt. "Don't get your clothes dirty. Come on, we'll clean you up inside." She put Mark Anthony down and took his sticky hand in hers.

"How did it go?" Christina asked Lucy.

"Fine, but why don't we can talk about it in the house? I need to get you inside before the neighbors see you parading around in your nightgown." Lucy smiled as Christina cinched the robe's belt tighter around her waist.

# Eight

Stepping out onto the front porch, Christina watched the moon rise into the clear night sky. In the warm night the stars twinkled brighter than she'd ever seen. She felt good. She was rested and ready to work. Last night she had felt uneasy walking to work but tonight she welcomed the darkness and quiet peacefulness. The moon illuminated the road and she even recognized the barks of the neighborhood dogs, from the deep throaty howl of the neighbor's German shepherd to the high-pitched yap of the pug at the end of the road.

Christina opened the stairwell door and trotted up the metal staircase. Turning the corner onto the second floor, Christina jumped away from the door as it swung open and almost hit her. Lucy laughed as she seductively led a handsome young doctor into the stairwell. She pulled him close as she backed into Christina.

"Christy." Lucy quickly turned as she let go of the doctor. "What are you doing here?"

Christina didn't answer as she looked between Lucy and the doctor.

"I'd better get back to my patients." The blushing doctor excused himself and backed out of the stairwell.

"I'm sorry," Christina apologized. "I didn't mean to interrupt."

"Don't be." Lucy looked over her shoulder as the door clicked shut. "What are you doing taking the stairs? Is the elevator broken again?"

"No, I just needed a little time to think before my shift starts," Christina answered uneasily, knowing Lucy could sense her apprehension.

"The sooner you stand up to Jenny, the better. Don't take any shit from her."

"I know." Christina agreed but had trouble believing her own words.

"How do you feel?" Lucy reached into her pocket and took out a worn pack of cigarettes.

"Good. Thanks again for taking care of the kids."

Lucy lit the cigarette and took in a deep breath. "It was nothing. You've got good kids. Did you lock the door before you left the house?"

"Yes, and I called Dolores. Are you sure it's okay to leave the kids alone?"

"They're not alone. Dolores will check in on them and I'll be home as soon as I get off work."

"I just I hate to leave them, that's all."

"Don't worry, this is a nice town. I've lived here five years and nothing has ever happened. This isn't Chicago."

"I know," Christina admitted as a metal door opened above them and footsteps echoed down the stairwell.

"I'd better get going. I don't want to be late." Christina checked her watch.

"I'll see you in the morning." Lucy took another puff from her cigarette.

Christina climbed the stairs. As she rounded the corner, she bumped into Lucy's young doctor. He smiled sheepishly and without saying anything stepped out of her way to let her by. Christina quickly stepped by and continued to climb as Lucy's playful laugh echoed throughout the stairwell.

Christina reached the top of the stairs and stepped out into the dark hall. Knowing she couldn't avoid the inevitable she slowly made her way toward the nurses' station. Jenny sat behind the desk sorting stacks of papers and files.

"You're late," Jenny snapped when Christina reached the station. Christina checked her watch. She was ten minutes early. "I don't care what time you have on your watch. You're still late."

Christina didn't answer as she set her purse behind the desk. Realizing it was going to be another rough night, Christina refused to start it with an argument and walked away. At the end of the hall she slipped into the last room.

The room was hot and stuffy. In the dark room Christina saw Estefanita tied to the bed and her heart went out to the old woman. Even though she'd kicked Christina in the face, Christina couldn't help but feel sorry for her.

With her arms and legs tied to the corners of the bed, Estefanita lay motionless as she stared up at the white ceiling. The cuts on her arms and legs had been bandaged but the harsh method of control was shocking. To Christina there was no reason a patient should be tied up like an animal. Striding across the floor, Christina cranked open the metal window to let the summer's evening breeze into the sweltering room.

Hearing Estefanita's throaty moan, Christina quickly turned to the old woman. With her back arched off the bed, Estefanita's dark and terrified eyes looked past Christina into the darkness, and she began to thrash violently on the bed as she tugged on her restraints.

Sensing Estefanita's fear, Christina quickly closed the window. She saw the fear slowly disappear from the old woman's face as her body eased back onto the bed. Christina locked the window and walked toward the bed. Watching Estefanita's eyelids grow heavy over her eyes, Christina could see the torment in the woman's face as she turned her head toward the ceiling.

"Are you hungry?" Christina asked as she walked around the bed to the untouched bowl of oatmeal. Estefanita began to mumble softly to herself. "Is there anything I can get for you?" she asked again, feeling foolish for talking to the delusional old woman. Taking the food tray from the end table, Christina left Estefanita alone in the dark.

Estefanita waited for the door to close before she began to pull on the restraints. She struggled with all her might to loosen the straps but her efforts only caused the cloth to cut painfully into her wrists and reluctantly she gave up. Her heart pounded in her chest and her breathing was short and labored. Sweat poured from her skin, drenching her thin nightgown and for the first time in her life not even prayer could calm her.

Focusing her eyes toward heaven, she prayed for guidance. She didn't know how much longer she could defend herself from the bruja guarding the halls. She hadn't eaten since the night of the attack, and her body was growing weaker with each passing day. Without food or water she would slowly die but she knew better than to eat the food brought to her.

The redheaded nurse had been the only person who had been in her room since last night. Her eyes were kind and gentle but Estefanita didn't know if she could trust her. The brujas were waiting for her to lose her faith and take the poison, but how long would they wait? If they couldn't control her spirit, Estefanita knew they would soon grow impatient and come for her. The time was nearing and she had to be ready.

# Nine

Stirring restlessly on the mattress, La Llorona's body trembled and twitched uncontrollably. The moonlight shone through the trees and illuminated her grotesquely thin figure. La Llorona painfully sat up as mice scurried around her to feed on the fallen maggots left on the mattress where she laid.

She searched around the room until her gaze fixed on the dusty shelf against the back wall. She squinted at the accumulated dust and cobwebs covering the glass jars. A cool wind blew through the broken window, scattering dirt and leaves across the room. The wind swirled around her as she reached out for the chair on the floor next to her. With all her strength, she pulled herself off the mattress. She stood still for a moment, unable to move. Fighting through the pain, she moved the chair out in front of her, dragging her feet across the splintered wood floor and ripping the soft flesh from her feet.

Pushing through broken glass and thick cobwebs, La Llorona stopped when she reached the wood shelf. Cobwebs hung from her hair as she studied the dusty jars filled with powders, dried leaves, and roots. She reached up and knocked jars off the shelf as she searched through the dirt and cobwebs. Her search became frenzied as she ran her hands over the shelf. Feeling the soft leather pouch, she gripped it in her hand. The rotted muscle snapped and popped as it pulled away from her blackened teeth into a hideous grin. She carefully took the dusty pouch from the shelf and held it against her chest.

Forcing herself to walk to the pile of blankets on the floor in the corner, La Llorona picked up a sheet and wrapped it around her head, leaving an opening for her dark eyes. She shook the mice from the blanket and draped it over her shoulders.

Still clutching the pouch, La Llorona sat on the floor. The rage grew inside her as she looked around the shack. *How long had she been held captive by Estefanita's spell?* She studied her decayed hand. Tendons popped and rotted skin peeled away from the decaying muscle as she made a fist. How could her clan have forgotten about her for so long? How could they have left her to rot in her grave?

No longer able control her fury, La Llorona threw her head back and screamed. Outside the shack the black wolf sat up and howled in unison with her cries, breaking the silence of the forest.

# Ten

Stepping into Estefanita's dark room, Christina hesitated when she realized the woman's condition hadn't changed since she'd last been there. Estefanita continued to stare blankly at the ceiling, softly muttering her prayers. Christina reached under the bed and looked up at the catatonic woman. Christina caught a glimpse of Estefanita's purple hand, which was dangling off the bed. Slowly Christina stood and gently inspected the swollen hand. The restraints had been wrapped too tightly, digging into the old woman's skin and cutting off the circulation. Leaning over Estefanita, Christina lifted the other tender hand. Christina pulled the blanket away from Estefanita's legs. "Oh, my God," she whispered when she saw the bruised and inflamed feet.

Christina could see Estefanita's body tremble from the pain and tenderly tugged the restraint on Estefanita's wrist. Christina looked into the woman's dark brown eyes staring blankly past her.

Christina heard Jenny's stern voice at the far end of the hall giving orders and turned back to Estefanita. Christina knew she should mind her business, but she couldn't let the old woman continue to suffer. Not forgetting the woman's strength from last night, she gently lifted Estefanita's frail hand and dropped it onto the bed.

Estefanita was as weak as she looked. Certain the old woman didn't have the strength to escape, Christina slowly began loosen the restraints. She began to work faster. Listening carefully to make sure Jenny was still at the nurses' station, Christina unfastened the bandage and let the blood flow back into Estefanita's hand.

With quick and strong reflexes, Estefanita grabbed Christina's wrist. Shocked by the woman's sudden strength, Christina looked into Estefanita's eyes. No longer dulled with confusion, the woman's eyes were surprisingly alert. They held a hint of kindness but Christina was captivated by the intensity of the woman's stare as Estefanita searched the depths of her soul. Christina struggled to break free from the firm grip and pulled at the bony fingers digging into her arm.

Christina heard Jenny's quick footsteps coming down the hall. Ignoring Estefanita's penetrating stare, Christina frantically twisted and yanked her arm trying to pry herself free as Jenny's footsteps got closer.

"She's alive," Estefanita whispered, her voice dry and raspy. Her words startled Christina and for a moment she stopped her struggle and looked at the old woman. "She's alive," Estefanita whispered again, making sure Christina understood before she let go of her wrist.

The footsteps stopped outside the door and Christina spun as the door swung open.

"What are you doing?" Jenny snapped.

"I was—" Christina stammered as she looked over her shoulder at Estefanita who had resumed her blank stare toward the ceiling. "I was changing the bedpan."

From the doorway Jenny looked over at Estefanita. "Well, hurry up. You've got other rooms to clean, and try not to make a mess tonight," she smirked before she let the door close.

Christina turned to Estefanita as she rubbed her hand. Estefanita's powerful grip left red marks around her wrist. Although the incident left Christina a little shaky, she knew Estefanita hadn't meant to hurt her. There was a gentleness about the woman; she saw it in her eyes. Leaving the bedpan, Christina quickly loosened the other bandages on Estefanita's arm and legs before she turned to leave. As she walked toward the door she saw writing scrawled over the doorway. After studying the Spanish words written in black Christina turned to Estefanita.

"Do you want me to wash it off?" She asked and Estefanita shook her head. "I'll leave it as long as no one else sees it," she said as she walked out of the room. If it made her feel more comfortable, Christina didn't see the harm.

Christina glanced over to the nurses' station. Jenny was sifting through paperwork, but when Christina stepped into the hall she stopped and looked up. Christina held Jenny's cold stare for several seconds before she turned and stepped into the young man's room.

Christina had begun to name the patients in her care. She thought each name suited the patients' dispositions. There was the Fat Man, who knocked the bedpan out of her hands. There was Grandma, a woman in her nineties, with Coke-bottle glasses perched crookedly on her face. Christina never knew her own grandma but imagined she would have been much like this woman. No matter how quiet Christina was during the night, Grandma would always wake up, put on her glasses, and smile. She spoke with a soft gentle voice, and although she only spoke Spanish, Christina would smile and nod at her kind words. She didn't have a name for all sixty patients and she didn't have a name for Estefanita, but she did name the man with the amputated legs: Young Man. She'd read Young Man's medical chart and knew the name suited him when she discovered he was only twenty-seven.

Tonight when she stepped into Young Man's room, there was a young nurse sitting vigilantly next to the bed holding his limp hand in hers. When she heard Christina come into the room she quickly sat up and smiled as she wiped away her tears.

"Would you like for me to come back later?" Christina whispered as she looked into the woman's red eyes.

"No," the nurse answered as she let out a long sigh. "You must be Lucy's friend." She forced a smile.

"Christina." Christina walked over and extended her hand.

"Sarah." She smiled and shook Christina's warm hand.

"How long have you been working here?" Christina asked as she walked over to the untouched dinner tray. She knew Sarah was fighting an emotional battle and didn't want to add to her grief with questions about her relationship with Young Man.

"I've been a nurse for almost three years. What about you?" Sarah blew her nose into her handkerchief.

"This is my second night." Christina smiled warily.

"This is your first job?" Sarah asked in bewilderment. Christina nodded as she picked up the tray. "What in the world would make you work the nightshift with—" Sarah looked over her shoulder and whispered. "Jenny? Didn't Lucy warn you about her?"

"Yes, Lucy warned me." Christina laughed, finding it amusing everyone knew what a tyrant Jenny was. "I need the job and the night shift gives me time to spend with my children."

"You have children?" Christina recognized the yearning in Sarah's voice.

"Three," Christina said.

"Where does your husband work?"

"I lost my husband three years ago." Christina's voice softened with emotion.

"I'm sorry." Sarah sank back in her chair. "How?"

"The war." Christina's heart tightened in her chest.

"I should have known. That damn war left this whole country in turmoil. Some of us lost our whole lives."

"Is he your husband?" Christina asked as she motioned to Young Man, who was lying unconscious on the bed.

"No." Sarah shook her head slowly and her voice trembled. "We were supposed to get married when the war was over but Roman got hurt and he broke off our engagement." Sarah wiped the tears rolling down her cheeks. "He said he didn't love me anymore but I know he does. I can see it in his eyes. He thinks I only want to marry him because I feel sorry for him. He can't understand I love him for what's in his heart, with or without his legs. I've tried so hard to make him understand how I feel about him but he just keeps pushing me away." Sarah dropped her head and twisted the wet handkerchief in her hands. "His mother blames me for what he did."

Christina set the tray down on the floor and knelt beside Sarah. "And a part of me does, too. If I'd just left him alone maybe he wouldn't be here." Sarah leaned back in her chair and let out a long sigh. "He tried to kill himself with his father's gun."

"That is not your fault." Christina took Sarah's hand and held it firmly. "Roman made the choice to pull the trigger, not you."

"I know, but maybe if I left him alone . . ." Sarah began.

"What do you want to do?" Christina gently turned Sarah's face to her.

"I love him. I don't want to let him go."

"He needs time to heal. Not just from his wounds, but to cope with what's in his mind. You and I will never know the violence he had to face. Give him time to deal with the pain and when he's done he'll realize he needs you just as much as you need him."

"Thank you," Sarah whispered.

"You're welcome." Christina smiled as she picked up the tray and walked out the door.

# Eleven

The night air hung with humidity from the evening rain. Christina stepped off the porch as her eyes darted around nervously. Something was strangely different tonight. She sensed it in the air. The night was remarkably quiet; not even the neighborhood dogs ventured out to bark as she passed their homes. Christina heard a flutter over her head as she turned off Canyon Road and walked toward the hospital. Searching the dark starry sky, Christina couldn't see anything as a strange sensation of being stalked swept through her. Christina walked faster as the sound grew louder.

Out of the darkness an owl swooped down with its sharp claws outstretched and dug into her head, pulling on her nurse's cap. Screaming out, Christina fell to her knees with her arms protecting her head as the owl beat it wings against her. Her long red hair came loose from its bun and fell around her face as the owl continued its attack. Still screaming, Christina swung her purse, blindly struggling to protect herself from the powerful animal. Disoriented by the deafening sound of the owl's wings slamming against her head, Christina managed to strike the bird's soft body. Unyielding, the owl grabbed the purse as Christina beat the owl with her other hand. Knocked off balance, the bird released the purse as Christina cowered on the ground. Christina listened to the sound of the owl's wings as it flew away. Straining to hear through the ringing in her ears, Christina listened until everything went still.

Slowly rising, Christina looked toward the hospital and stared in disbelief. She watched a flock of owls circling the building. The birds swooped and soared in an aerobatic display.

Christina timidly watched the birds. Glancing uncertainly over her shoulder, Christina searched the darkness. She looked toward the hospital. She couldn't stay outside, as she'd already been attacked by one owl, and she didn't want to see what the large flock could do. Poised for another attack, Christina walked closer to the hospital. She stepped out of the darkness and into the light surrounding the hospital. Sensing her vulnerability in the open, she made a dash for the door.

Covering her head with her arms, Christina ran as the owls swooped down on her with their sharp claws and beating wings. Christina reached the glass doors and ran inside. She slammed the door and caught one of the owls by the wing. The owl screeched as it frantically beat itself against the glass door.

"Doesn't feel so good, does it?" Christina pulled the door harder as the owl thrashed wildly. Christina held the door shut for several seconds before she shoved it open and knocked the owl to the ground. The large bird slammed into the sidewalk and quickly hopped to its feet. Staring at Christina with its haunting eyes, the owl hopped toward Christina. Christina quickly stepped back from the door and watched the owl beat its wings violently before it flew away.

Christina watched the birds disappear into the night sky and slowly backed away from the door. Christina swallowed the lump in her throat as she scanned the deserted hall. The chair where the nurse usually sat behind the front desk was empty, and the halls were silent. Still shaking, Christina quickly walked to the elevator. Her whole body trembled as she struggled to regain her composure. She waited as the elevator door slid open and immediately stepped inside. She pushed the fourth-floor button as the elevator door closed and stared at her reflection in the steel door. Her usually light complexion was pasty and her eyes were wide from shock. Her hands trembled as she fumbled with her hair. Closing her eyes, Christina took a deep breath. The dull onset of a headache throbbed as the elevator reached the fourth floor. Christina slowly walked toward the nurses' station.

"She's not here yet," Amanda whispered when she saw the worry on Christina's face.

"She probably got trapped outside with the owls," Christina answered as she pinned her cap back onto her head.

"What owls?" Monica asked.

"You didn't see all the owls flying around the hospital?" The three nurses looked at each other baffled and shook their heads. "There were at least fifteen flying around under the lights." Christina studied them intently. "I even trapped one in the door."

"I got here just before you and I didn't see any owls." Amanda looked at the two women next to her. "What about you?"

"I didn't see anything," Monica agreed.

"Neither did I," Michelle added. "But whatever the reason Jenny's late, we'll have hell to pay if she found us standing here talking." Without saying another word she walked from behind the desk and disappeared into a patient's room down the hall.

Christina readily took Michelle's advice and stepped into Estefanita's room.

The hall light shone through the small window in the door and cast a dull glow in the otherwise dark room. Still tied to the bed, Estefanita stared blankly at the ceiling. Somehow she'd managed to kick the thin blanket off the bed and the light blue hospital gown stuck to her sweaty body. Breathing rapidly, Estefanita turned to Christina, locking her dark eyes on her. Unable to look away from the old woman's stare, Christina stood still until Estefanita looked away and stared back toward the ceiling.

Christina walked through the stuffy room and cranked open the window. Pulled from her trance, Estefanita turned to the window and her whole body trembled with fear.

"Don't worry," Christina softly reassured. "I'm right here. I won't let anything happen to you."

Estefanita looked nervously between Christina and the open window. Although the night was muggy from the evening rain, the fresh air was a welcome change in the sweltering room. Estefanita watched Christina as she walked around the bed and picked up the water pitcher.

"I'm going to get you some water," Christina said as she walked into the bathroom to fill the pitcher. Gently lifting Estefanita's head off the pillow, Christina put the glass to her lips.

"Slow down," Christina cautioned as Estefanita choked and spilled water down her chin. "When was the last time you had anything to drink?" Christina filled the empty glass again and lifted Estefanita's head but this time the woman took her time to savor each drink.

Christina took a washcloth from a drawer and poured the remaining water into a small washbowl. Christina wiped Estefanita's face and arms with the wet cloth as the woman looked up gratefully at her.

"You haven't eaten." Christina motioned to the bowl of cold oatmeal on the table. "The kitchen is closed, but I brought an extra sandwich for dinner."

Before Estefanita could respond, the door swung open and Jenny's dark shadow cast across the floor as she stood in the doorway. "What are you doing?" She moved to step inside but stopped.

"I was giving the patient water and wiping her down. She's—" Christina looked over at Estefanita, who had resumed staring at the ceiling.

"Leave this patient alone. There's nothing wrong with her," Jenny ordered sharply.

"But her arms and legs are tied. She can't move." Christina couldn't believe what Jenny had asked her to do. This woman was being neglected and it seemed as if Jenny wanted her to die.

Estefanita turned her head and Jenny quickly stepped back into the hall to avoid the old woman's piercing stare. "I said leave her alone," Jenny growled as the door closed.

"I'm sorry," Christina whispered as she put down the washcloth and walked around the bed to the window. Estefanita watched

Christina close the window and take the dinner tray from the nightstand.

"I'll be back as soon as I can," Christina reassured quietly before she left the room.

Waiting in the hall, Jenny watched as Christina fumbled with the dinner tray. Not knowing Jenny was behind her, Christina turned and ran into her.

"I'm sorry," Christina quickly apologized as she struggled to balance the tray. Jenny stepped away from Christina and rubbed her arm. "Are you all right? Did I hurt you?" Christina took a step toward Jenny.

"Of course I'm all right." Jenny raised her chin and smoothed her uniform. "Now get back to work." Straightening her shoulders, Jenny pivoted on her heel and walked away.

Christina watched Jenny walk away as she set the tray on the metal cart. She stopped outside Roman's room. Expecting to find Sarah with Roman, Christina knocked softly before she walked inside. Roman lay sleeping on the bed and for a moment Christina wished Sarah had been there. She hated when people meddled in her personal life and last night she'd taken the liberty of giving Sarah advice about a situation she'd known nothing about. She'd loved Mark with all her soul and naïvely believed everyone she met shared that same kind of love. After their conversation last night, Christina thought she'd been wrong about Sarah and Roman. Maybe they didn't belong together and it was better for them to be apart.

Christina took the tray off the end table. She thought she saw Roman blink. Christina stepped closer to the bed as she stared at Roman's cold, gray face. His eyelids were hidden in dark, sunken circles and Christina doubted he would ever wake up. According to his chart, the self-inflicted wound occurred nearly ten days ago and each day the doctor's comments were the same: "No voluntary movement, not responding to external stimuli." Maybe Roman had finally gotten his wish. His body was still alive but maybe the bullet lodged in his brain had ended his misery.

A sudden uneasiness swept through Christina as she studied Roman. Her hands got cold and clammy and the hairs on the back of her neck stood on end. Christina grabbed the empty dinner tray and quietly slipped out of the room.

# Twelve

Praying silently in the dark room, Estefanita stared at the closed window. The scratching outside had grown steadily louder. She was trapped and all she could do was pray for deliverance from the evil that haunted her. She looked away from the window and dug her thumbnail into the palm of her hand. Without her beaded rosary, she used the pain to help track the mysteries. The Our Fathers and Hail Marys easily rolled off her lips with a gentle, pleasant hum. Concentrating on each whispered word of faith, Estefanita ignored the coming evil outside her window.

A steaming kettle sat on a bed of smoldering coals. A plume of smoke drifted from the fire, lifted by a gentle breeze, and carried through the forest into the dark sky. Draped in the red and black wool blanket, La Llorona walked slowly over to the fire and looked down into the bubbling water. Studying her every move, the black wolf remained by her side as the pack of coyotes emerged from the forest. The coyotes rambled in and out of the darkness yelping and howling.

Reaching into the leather pouch, La Llorona took out a handful of dried leaves and crumbled them into the boiling water. A thick yellow plume of smoke spilled from the kettle and blanketed the ground.

With all her strength La Llorona lifted the kettle off the smoking embers. Using a gnarled stick, she carried the steaming cauldron to the shack, leaving a trail of yellow smoke behind her. The black wolf obediently followed the decrepit woman up onto the eroded porch and stopped at the door. With the door closed the black wolf lay down and watched the yelping coyotes.

La Llorona set the iron kettle on the table and searched the floor around her. She picked up a piece of broken glass and held it up to the moonlight to examine the sharp edge. Mesmerized, La Llorona slowly twisted the glass and distorted the haunting image of the moon.

Turning away from the window back to the kettle, La Llorona put her hand over the boiling liquid. Running the sharp glass over her palm, she sliced open her rotted flesh. Black blood oozed from the cut and dripped into the mixture, burning and sizzling like acid. She squeezed her decomposed hand to expel as much blood as she could and let the last few drops fall into the kettle.

She stirred the bubbling brew with a metal cup, filled the cup, and raised it over her head. Her eyes rolled back and her body shook. Deep in her chest she groaned a chant. Her eyes opened wide as she held the cup to her lips and swallowed the hot mixture.

Screaming out in pain, La Llorona dropped the cup to the floor and gagged as the hot brew burned her throat. Holding her hand firmly over her mouth, she resisted the urge to spit out the bitter drink. The blackened brew seeped from the corners of her mouth and dripped down her chin. Waiting several minutes for the pain and nausea to pass, she collapsed wearily into the chair. She leaned over and picked up the cup off the floor. She filled the cup again, held the steaming liquid to her lips, closed her eyes, and drank.

Estefanita turned toward the door as Christina slipped into the room. Relieved, the old woman laid her head back on the pillow. Christina tiptoed across the room as she unwrapped a sandwich and held it to Estefanita's mouth. Estefanita's eyes were wide as she looked at the sandwich. Her stomach grumbled because she hadn't eaten in days, but she wouldn't be deceived by the bruja.

"It's okay," Christina reassured as she took a bite. "It's tuna, see?"

Estefanita's mouth watered as Christina put the food to her mouth again and this time she ate.

"Slow down. You're going to choke," Christina whispered as Estefanita quickly chewed the food and took another bite. Christina put the half-eaten sandwich down on the nightstand and poured a glass of water.

Estefanita leaned her head back on the pillow and chewed the last mouthful of food.

"You were hungry," Christina remarked and much to her surprise Estefanita nodded. "I can bring you another sandwich tomorrow night if you'd like." Again she nodded.

"*Cuidado con la bruja,*" Estefanita whispered.

"What?" Christina asked as she leaned closer.

"*Cuidado con la bruja,*" she stressed.

Hearing the quick, sharp sound of Jenny's footsteps in the hall, Christina turned to the door. "I'm sorry, but I've got to get back to work. I'll be back as soon as I can," she whispered and quickly walked out of the room.

Estefanita stared at the door for a moment before she looked back up at the ceiling. She couldn't remember where she stopped her prayers. Digging her thumbnail into the tender blister on her hand, she started from the beginning.

Staring up at the white ceiling tiles, Estefanita prayed for God's help. She was frightened and the only thing she knew to help was prayer. She couldn't remember how she'd gotten to the hospital and she was thankful to be alive but now she wondered if death would have been easier than the torture she would endure at the hands of La Llorona and her clan of witches.

She tried to leave the night she was brought in before anyone could recognize her, but it was too late. They had been waiting for her. She had been bound to the bed for three days now, unable to do anything but pray. She entrusted her life to God and knew he would send someone to help her. Tonight her prayers had been answered with the redheaded nurse.

She didn't know the nurse's name but she was kind and willing to help, no matter the consequence. Estefanita trusted the young nurse and soon it would be time to give her the gift.

Estefanita heard the latch on the window click. She turned and watched in fear as the window unlocked and slowly opened.

When Christina heard the ear-piercing scream echo through the hall she knew immediately it was Estefanita. Knocking her chair back onto the floor, Christina jumped up and ran down the hall into the dark room. Estefanita thrashed violently on the bed as she stared out the window. Christina ran to the window and tried to pull it shut. The metal frame was jammed and wouldn't budge. Leaving the window, Christina turned to comfort Estefanita as an owl landed on the windowsill. Startled, Christina stumbled back as Estefanita screamed hysterically. Christina looked around the bare room. Leaning over Estefanita, she grabbed the reading lamp off the end table and yanked the cord out of the socket. Christina turned to the owl as Monica and Michelle ran into the room and tried to subdue Estefanita. Holding the lamp out in front of her like a sword, Christina walked toward the window.

The owl beat its wings threateningly. Christina turned her head to protect herself from the owl's beating wings and charged. Ramming the lamp into the owl's soft body, she shoved the bird off the ledge. Still holding the lamp, she reached out into the darkness and pulled on the window. Concentrating on closing the window, Christina didn't see the owl attack and screamed as the bird grabbed her wrist.

The owl dug its sharp claws into Christina's soft flesh as it screeched wildly. Unable to pull her arm from the powerful claws, Christina beat the owl with the lamp. Stunned, the owl flopped out of the window, ripping Christina's flesh as it fell.

Christina shut the window and turned to help Michelle restrain Estefanita. Estefanita continued to thrash violently until the she saw the window was closed and her body went limp. Christina watched the quick rise and fall of the old woman's chest. Estefanita breaths came in quick gasps as she continued to stare out the window. Christina closed the drapes and rushed to Estefanita's side as Monica ran into the room with a hypodermic needle.

"What's that for?" Christina asked as Monica grabbed Estefanita's arm to search for a vein.

"Jenny's orders. Anytime she has an outburst she has to be sedated." Monica touched the needle to Estefanita's arm and pierced the soft skin.

Christina watched Estefanita stare fearfully at the needle. "Wait!" Christina shouted and reached out to stop Monica.

"What's wrong?" Monica looked up but kept the needle in Estefanita's arm.

"She doesn't need to be sedated. Look at her—she's fine."

"You saw her. She was crazy, and any one of us could have gotten hurt."

"Could you blame her? What would you have done if that damn bird flew through your window while you were asleep?"

"Jenny's orders were specific when it came to this patient." Monica shook her head.

"I'll take full responsibility if Jenny finds out, but she's not even here," Christina pleaded.

Monica looked over at Michelle who shrugged, leaving the decision to her.

"If Jenny finds out—" Monica began.

"She won't. I'm not going to say anything and I know she's not going to say anything." Christina pointed to Estefanita. "Michelle?"

"No."

"Monica?" Christina asked hopefully.

"Okay." Monica reluctantly pulled the needle out of Estefanita's arm. "But it'll be your head if Jenny finds out."

"Thank you." Christina sighed as Estefanita closed her eyes and let her head fall back on the pillow.

"We'd better help Amanda with the other patients," Monica said to Michelle as they walked to the door.

Walking around the bed, Christina looked into Estefanita's pleading eyes. "Would you mind if I stayed here for a while?" she asked Monica.

"You're on break," she reminded.

"I know." Last night she took a nice walk along the river but knowing the owls were still around she wouldn't be going out tonight. "I'll take my break here."

"Suit yourself," Monica said as she and Michelle walked out of the room.

Christina walked over to the window and peeked through the heavy curtains into the darkness. She couldn't see anything but knew the owl was still out there, watching and waiting. Letting the curtain fall, she stepped away from the window and looked down at her arm. Her hand throbbed painfully and for the first time she noticed the deep cuts on her wrist and hand. Christina took down a bottle of peroxide from the metal cabinet against the wall and carefully poured the medicine over the deep scratches.

Wrapping her hand and wrist in gauze, Christina slid the chair from the wall and set it next to the hospital bed. Christina watched the old woman's lips move as she whispered her prayers. Christina leaned her head against the chair, closed her eyes, and listened to the rhythmic whispers.

Perched on the window ledge, the owl looked through the small crease in the curtain and watched Estefanita and Christina intently before it flew away into the night.

# *Thirteen*

A cool breeze drifted from the Sangre de Cristo Mountains and filled Santa Fe with the fresh sweet smell of summer. It was a beautiful bright morning. Birds sang and the aroma of coffee and bacon drifted from the neighborhood homes. The dogs, out from hiding, barked as Christina walked down the narrow dirt road. She was tired. Her hand ached but the cool morning air helped clear her head as she walked. Smiling halfheartedly at the neighbors preparing for another day in the fields, Christina lowered her head as she walked faster down the busy side street.

Christina turned down the drive and stopped when she saw the new black Oldsmobile two-door coup parked in front of the house. She ran her hand over the smooth metal already warm from the sun. Stepping up onto the front porch, Christina unlocked the door and walked into the kitchen.

Inside, Lucy was cooking breakfast as the young doctor held her from behind kissing her neck and caressing her thigh. Startled by the door, the doctor let go of Lucy and leaned sheepishly against the sink.

Christina didn't see them at first as she fumbled with her key in the lock. Closing the door, Christina turned as the young doctor smiled guiltily and Lucy continued to stir the bacon.

"Christy, we're just getting ready to have breakfast. Can I fix you something?" Lucy smiled over her shoulder.

"No, thank you." Christina glanced anxiously down the hall, wanting to make a hasty retreat to the children's room.

"You haven't met John, have you?" Lucy asked without turning around.

"No. Just in the stairs." Christina smiled uneasily.

"Hi." John smiled as he reached out his hand.

Christina took John's hand and let out a small gasp as he gently squeezed hers.

"What happened?" John asked as he looked down at her hand.

"I was—" Christina's eyes darted between John and Lucy. She didn't want to tell them about the owls and pulled her hand away.

"Are you okay, Christy?" Lucy stopped stirring the bacon to look at her.

"It's nothing, really. We had an incident with an owl trying to get into one of the patient's rooms and I got scratched pushing it out the window."

Lucy walked away from the stove toward Christina. "You mean it just attacked you?"

"You could say that." Christina shrugged.

"You should let me take a look," John said.

"It's okay. I cleaned it with some peroxide." Christina held her arm firmly to her side.

"The scratches are deep and could get infected," John pointed out.

"John's right, Christy," Lucy started.

"I'm fine," Christina said. "Besides, I'm sure people get scratched by owls around here all the time."

"Why would you think something like that?" Lucy asked as she walked back to the stove.

"There are so many around here."

"I've lived here five years and I've never seen one before." Lucy looked over at John. "What about you?"

"Can't say that I have." John folded his arms as he leaned against the sink.

Christina watched them in disbelief. What was the matter with people around here? If Monica and Michelle hadn't seen the owl last night they wouldn't have believed her either.

"You didn't see any owls when you got off work?" Christina asked as Lucy looked over at John curiously. "You can't be serious." Christina started to laugh but realized they weren't joking.

"Christy, I think you're working too hard. Maybe you should take some time off." Lucy said.

"I've only been working three days. I don't think Jenny would appreciate me asking for time off."

"The night shift isn't for everyone. Maybe you should reconsider transferring to one of the day shifts."

"I don't need to take any time off and I don't need to change my shift," Christina defended.

"Maybe you're right," John interrupted. "I was a little preoccupied when I got off work last night and didn't notice the owls." He smiled mischievously at Lucy before he turned back to Christina. "But do me a favor and let me take a look."

Christina looked over at Lucy. Knowing it would be useless to argue, she held out her hand. "All right, but you're wasting your time. I already disinfected the scratches."

John took Christina's hand gently and pulled her close to him. After getting a better look at her wrist, he let out a short sigh. "These are pretty deep. You could use a few stitches."

Christina had had enough. There was no way she was going to get stitches for a few scratches and she pulled her hand away.

"I'm fine, really. Now if you'll excuse me I want to wake the children before it gets much later." Christina excused herself as she hurried out of the kitchen and practically ran down the hall.

Christina heard Lucy giggle as she closed the door behind her and walked over to the bed. Smiling at her beautiful children sleeping soundly, she slid under the covers and closed her eyes.

Christina thought back to the last time she'd been with a man: the night before Mark left for the war, the night Mark Anthony was conceived.

Christina often thought of her last night with Mark, replaying each precious moment over and over in her mind. They stayed up all night talking. It was as if they both knew it would be the last time they'd be together and didn't want it to end. But it did. It ended with the most incredible sunrise.

They watched it together as they held each other. Neither spoke as they waited with anticipation for the sun to start the day. In the days that passed after Mark left, Christina couldn't bring herself to watch the sunrise. After a few weeks she received a letter from Mark and in it he wrote about watching the sunrise every morning. Closing his eyes, he'd imagine holding her and together they'd watch the magical transformation together. After Mark's letter she never missed the morning sun until the day she received a telegram informing her she was a widow.

After Mark had been killed, Christina shut out the world and hid in her dark apartment. Her only visitor was her mother. Her mother helped care for Jessica and Marie while Mark Anthony grew inside her. It was her mother who comforted her through her hopeless misery and it was her mother who pulled her out of her depression.

Sleeping through her grief, Christina had become weaker and was slowly losing her desire to live. One month before she was due to deliver Mark Anthony she woke up to find her mother standing over her holding Jessica in one arm and Marie's hand in the other. Setting Jessica down on the bed, Christina's mother walked over to the heavy drapes covering the windows and pulled them open with one quick tug. The bright afternoon sun poured into the room and Christina instinctively covered her eyes.

"Get up and take care of your family." Her mother's words were firm but gentle and without another word she left Christina alone to pick up the pieces of her broken life. It wasn't easy for her mother to leave but Christina knew it was the only way she could save her and it worked.

Christina stared up at the wood ceiling as Mark Anthony crawled over Jessica and snuggled against her.

"Good morning," she whispered and kissed his thick curly hair.

Hearing her voice, Jessica and Marie woke up and moved closer.

"How was work, Mommy?" Marie asked as she rubbed her tired eyes.

"Work was fine, sweetie," she answered as she brushed the hair out of Marie's eyes. "How did everyone sleep?"

"I didn't sleep good," Jessica answered without opening her eyes.

"How come?"

"Aunt Lucy was making too much noise. I think she had a stomachache or something. She was up all night moaning and groaning. It sounded like it hurt."

Christina closed her eyes and smiled.

"What's the matter, Mommy?" Marie asked.

"Nothing, but let's not say anything to Aunt Lucy, okay?" Christina sat up when she heard the front door close and watched from the window as John got into his car and drove away. "Wash up while I fix us some breakfast."

The kids jumped off the bed and raced each other down the hall into the bathroom. Christina walked into the kitchen. Lucy was sitting at the table drinking coffee and smoking a cigarette. The bacon she'd been cooking sat on the kitchen table drying on a greased-soaked napkin.

"What happened to breakfast?" Christina smiled as she took a strip of bacon and chewed on it.

"What usually happens—the sun comes up and my usefulness is over." Lucy let out a long puff of smoke.

"Why do you do that? Why do you always put yourself down?" Christina was upset. "You are more than just a beautiful woman. You have a lot to offer any man."

"If I'm such a great catch, why haven't I been caught yet?" Lucy put out her cigarette in the full ashtray.

"Because you haven't found the right man yet, that's why."

"Not everyone can be like you and find true love the first time around," Lucy answered sarcastically.

"Yes, I married the man of my dreams, but look at me. I'm a thirty-six-year-old widow with three children. Life doesn't always turn out the way you plan. But you've got to make the most of it."

"I'm sorry, Christy. I didn't mean to throw that at you."

"Don't be sorry." Christina smiled. "There isn't a thing I would change about my life."

Lucy smiled at Christina. She was her best friend, the only one who looked beyond her physical beauty and knew her for who she was.

"Look what came in the mail yesterday." Lucy took a white envelope sitting on the table and held it up to the light.

"Who is it from?" Christina reached over for the letter.

"The postmark is from Santa Fe." Lucy moved the letter out of Christina's reach. "I think someone's taken a liking to my best friend." Lucy smiled mischievously.

"Give me that." Christina reached over and grabbed the letter out of Lucy's hand.

"He must have sent it before he left." Lucy looked over her coffee cup. "Aren't you going to open it?"

"I don't understand." Christina studied the return address in Georgia neatly written on the envelope. "I didn't give him my address." Christina looked up at Lucy who suddenly became immersed in reading the daily newspaper. "So I wonder how he got my address."

"Hmm?" Lucy looked up with a guilty smile. "I wonder."

"How could you?" Christina laughed.

"He was afraid you wouldn't write so he asked me for your address. Was he right? Were you going to break the poor boy's heart?" Lucy raised her eyebrows.

"I wrote him," Christina whispered.

"What?" Lucy sat up in excitement. "When?"

"A couple of days ago, but I haven't mailed the letter yet."

"A couple of days ago?" Lucy chuckled. "You only met him a couple of days ago. So what are you waiting for? Why don't you send him your letter?"

"I don't know." Christina tapped the envelope nervously on the table. "I don't know if I'm ready yet."

"Ready for what?" Lucy sipped her coffee. "It's only a letter."

"I know it's only a letter, but I don't think it would be fair to him. He might get the wrong idea."

"And what might that be?"

"Lucy, I have three children. They're all I have time for in my life." Christina set the letter on the table, stood up, and poured a glass of milk.

"Gee, thanks."

"That's not what I meant."

"I know what you meant." Lucy reached over and took the letter. "You have to move on, Christy."

"I can't." Christina shook her head. "Mark was everything to me. How could I possibly give that same commitment to someone else?"

"Don't you think you're jumping to conclusions? Nobody said you had to marry Simon," Lucy said, reading the name on the envelope.

"I know, but . . ." Christina reluctantly admitted.

"But nothing. Quit making excuses. Nobody can blame you for wanting to move on with your life. You're young and beautiful."

"And still in love with my husband," Christina interrupted, not liking the way her stomach was beginning to tie up in knots.

"Who's been dead for more than three years," Lucy sighed. "You don't have to justify your love for Mark. I was with you the day you met and the day you got married. I know the commitment and love you both shared but it's time to move on. Christy, I'm not pushing you to go out and get married. I'm just saying if this Simon fellow interests you, then give him a chance and see where it goes. Read the letter." Lucy pushed the letter across the table and Christina slowly picked it up. She opened the envelope and took out the neatly written letter.

"Well?" Lucy pried when Christina set down the letter with a smile.

"He's a nice man."

"And?" Lucy reached for the letter.

"And he just wants to know about the weather." Christina grabbed the letter out of Lucy's fingers and folded it neatly back into the envelope.

"No chance of him wanting to get married if all he wants is a weather report," Lucy mused. "That's all he wants?"

"That's it." Christina smiled and tucked the letter into her uniform.

# Fourteen

Slumped over on the wood table, La Llorona rested her head on her arm. The kettle, tipped on its side, spilled black brew on the table and soaked into her long white hair. With the metal cup clutched in her hand, her body began to convulse. Gagging and no longer able to control the sickening feeling in the pit of her stomach, she threw up. Maggots and beetles poured from her mouth mixed in the foamy black liquid. Heaving again, La Llorona spit out the last of the brew and groggily raised her head off the table.

She studied the cut on her palm and smiled. The spell was beginning to work and her body had begun to heal. She peeled away the loose dead skin down to the soft pink muscle.

Opening and closing her hand, she enjoyed her newfound strength. She slowly pushed against the table and stood up. The pain was gone but she was still weak. Seeing her reflection in the broken window, La Llorona turned her head from side to side. She ran her fingers over her grotesque face and dead skin flaked off as the anger in her raged and she tore furiously at her withered skin. She studied the scarred flesh around her blackened teeth. Disgusted by her hideous reflection, she turned away from the window.

Taking the stained sheet from the chair, La Llorona carefully wrapped it around her head and draped her naked body with the wool blanket. Walking to the door, she stepped out into the warm summer night.

The black wolf anxiously awaited its master at the door. Smiling down at the animal, La Llorona extended her hand as the wolf hunched down and nuzzled her hand. The wolf was gentle and showed no sign of its wild instincts as it stepped closer to allow La Llorona to stroke its fur.

Stepping off the porch with her wood cane, La Llorona followed the wolf. She ventured out into the forest. Driven by a hatred that festered deep in her soul, she made her way to the peaceful town she'd once called home.

The sound of Christina's footsteps echoed softly as she stopped at Estefanita's door and looked around. She arrived fifteen minutes before her shift and to her surprise the fourth floor was deserted. The soft twang of country music echoed from a room down the hall but there was no one around. Christina quietly slipped into Estefanita's dark room.

Estefanita struggled against her restraints. Visions of the dark forest and the black wolf flashed through her. She tossed and turned, trying to block the images.

Christina walked over to the restless woman and gently stroked the matted gray hair from her sweat-covered forehead.

Estefanita trembled under Christina's touch. Her eyes were open, but they looked beyond the white ceiling.

"Estefanita?" Christina whispered softly.

Estefanita didn't respond as she continued to struggle. Taking a wet washcloth, Christina wiped the perspiration from Estefenita's face. Feeling the cool cloth against her skin, Estefanita looked away from the ceiling at Christina.

"She's coming," Estefanita whispered, her eyes filled with desperation.

"Who's coming?"

"*Alistense.*"

"I'm sorry. I don't understand." Christina shook her head.

"Things are not what they seem. Do not be controlled by la bruja."

"What is a bruja?" Christina repeated the word but without Estefanita's Spanish accent.

"The witch. You must be careful." Estefanita looked past Christina to the door as it swung open. Jenny's large silhouette cast a dark shadow in the room.

"I want to talk to you," Jenny snapped. "In the hall."

Christina put down the washcloth and stepped into the hall.

"I want you to administer the patient her medication." Jenny held a hypodermic needle in front of Christina's face.

"What is it?" Christina asked as she took the syringe and studied the clear liquid.

"It's her medication, what does it look like?" Jenny answered sharply.

"What kind of medication is it?" Christina pressed.

"A sedative."

"Why does she need a—"

"That is none of your business. You only need to know how to administer the shot. You do know how to do that, don't you?" Jenny's words stung with criticism.

"Of course." Christina tried to hide her apprehension.

"Well, what are you waiting for?" Jenny glared at Christina. "The doctor ordered the medication. You either give her the shot or you're fired for insubordination."

Christina looked at Jenny and knew she was about to lose her patience but she pressed further. Christina wanted Jenny to know she wasn't intimidated anymore. "It's just that I don't think she needs a sedative. There's nothing wrong with her."

"You don't think? Who are you to question a doctor's orders, and how dare you disobey me?" Jenny snarled and suddenly Christina wished she hadn't pushed the point. "I know what happened last night and if you ever disobey one of my orders again, I'll have you fired. I don't care who you know downstairs. Am I making myself clear?"

Christina couldn't hide her shock. How could Jenny have known about last night? Who told her? Monica? Michelle? They agreed last night not to say anything, so how could she have known?

"Now go give the patient her shot."

Christina turned and walked into the dark room. She hadn't given a shot since she was in nursing school and she was nervous. She walked over to the lamp on the end table and turned it on. With the syringe in her hand, she searched Estefanita's arm for a suitable vein. Christina trembled as her fingers ran over Estefanita's wrinkled skin. *It's no good*, Christina thought. Her veins were too thin. Walking around the bed to check the other arm, Christina purposefully avoided Estefanita's gaze until she found a suitable vein. Putting the needle to Estefanita's arm, she looked into the old woman's pleading eyes.

"I'm sorry, but I have to," Christina tried to explain.

"You must do what's best for you," Estefanita answered sympathetically.

Christina pushed the needle into Estefanita's arm. Estefanita turned and began to pray as tears rolled down her cheeks. Christina slowly emptied the syringe and watched Estefanita's eyes flutter as she slipped into unconsciousness.

"I'm sorry," Christina whispered softly before she left the room.

Jenny held out her hand as Christina walked out the door. Christina fought the urge to drive the needle into Jenny's hand. Sensing Christina's anger, Jenny narrowed her eyes, refusing to be intimidated and Christina placed the needle in her hand.

"If you can get her to start eating, she wouldn't have to be sedated."

"She's too drugged to eat." Christina couldn't believe Jenny's rationalization.

"If she wants to stop the medication, she has to start eating her meals." Jenny turned around and took a few steps before she stopped and looked over her shoulder at Christina. "Oh, and you might want to have a doctor look at those scratches. They look infected." Jenny smiled and walked away.

Christina looked down at her bandaged hand and for the first time that night the scratches burned painfully. After waiting for Jenny to walk around the corner, Christina slipped back into Estefanita's room.

Even under heavy sedation, Estefanita still had the discipline to pray. Christina felt horrible for giving her the shot. Everything in her knew it was wrong but she couldn't go against Jenny, not now anyway. Christina knew she needed to find a way to help Estefanita. She wasn't as dangerous as Jenny made her out to be, so why was Jenny so afraid of Estefanita?

Christina didn't have the answers but she knew Estefanita did. The old woman trusted her and that was to her advantage. Now she had to keep her off the medication.

# Fifteen

The wolf led La Llorona through the forest and waited patiently as she struggled through the thick underbrush. La Llorona stopped and leaned against a tree for support. Behind her the pack of coyotes circled. Their cries echoed through the forest.

La Llorona pushed herself off the tree and followed the black wolf to the edge of the forest. She looked down into the moonlit valley and was filled with awe. Santa Fe was different from what she had remembered. There were houses built on the land once used for farming and the cattle that grazed freely in the open meadows were no more. She wondered how long she had been held captive by Estefanita's spell, but it didn't matter. She had been reborn, just as she'd promised, and now she'd unleash her fury on those who cast her away. One by one she'd find redemption through the lives of the innocent.

The moonlight illuminated the adobe houses clustered along the green valley. A gentle wind blew through the tall alfalfa and flapped the clothes that were hung out to dry.

Transfixed by the trickle of the river running through the valley, La Llorona raised her hand to quiet the coyotes and she squinted her black eyes to search for the source of the sound. The moon reflected off the Santa Fe River as it wound through the valley. Emerging from the cover of the forest, La Llorona slowly made her way toward the sleeping town. With the wolf walking at her side, the domesticated dogs sensed her evil presence and began to bark. Stopping at the first house, La Llorona walked through the wood gate and followed the walkway to the clothesline.

At the sound of the gate opening, a large German shepherd ran from behind the house and barked at the intruders. La Llorona motioned to the wolf. The wolf growled as it strode across the yard. With ferocity and cunning intuition, it quickly overpowered the German shepherd. With its powerful jaws and killer instinct, the wolf swiftly ripped the German shepherd's throat open. With one last shake of its jaws, the wolf released the lifeless dog and walked back to its master. Pleased, La Llorona reached out and tenderly stroked the wolf's thick fur.

Awakened by the commotion outside, José Mercedes walked through the house, turning on lights as he made his way to the front door. La Llorona quickly grabbed a cotton dress from the clothesline and hid in the darkness next to the house as the old man stepped out onto the front porch. In his bare feet the plump man pulled his suspenders over his shoulders. Running his hands over his rumpled white hair and unshaven face, José looked out into the darkness and whistled.

"Gordo!" José called out as he cautiously walked along the porch listening to the coyotes bark in the distance.

Pressing against the wall, La Llorona held back the growling wolf as the old man got closer to the edge of the porch.

"Gordo!" José searched the darkness and called out again as the coyotes got closer. Hearing their cries, he backed away.

Letting go of the wolf, La Llorona watched the powerful animal leap onto the porch. Startled, the old man stumbled and fell. Scooting on his butt using his arms and legs, José tried to get away from the vicious animal.

The wolf growled at José as the old man continued to back away. Too afraid to take his eyes off the beast, José reached for a shovel next to the front door. Stepping onto the porch behind the black wolf, La Llorona motioned the pack of coyotes over the wood fence to feed on the dead dog.

"W—who's there?" José Mercedes strained to see the woman walking toward him. "What do you want?"

La Llorona smiled. She'd forgotten the fear she evoked in people. "You know who I am." Her voice was raspy and deep. "I haven't been dead long enough for you to forget," she said and stepped into the light.

The old man watched the woman coming toward him. Looking away from the face hidden behind the gray sheet down the wool blanket, he caught a glimpse of her bare legs. Seeing the scarred and rotted flesh, José screamed in fear.

La Llorona took another step toward José and stopped when the front door swung open. Mana Mercedes stood in the doorway pointing a large double-barrel shotgun out the door. Mana Mercedes aimed the gun and shot into the pack of coyotes feasting on the dead dog. All the coyotes scattered at the sound of the blast, except one. Unable to run with its injured leg, it yelped as it struggled to crawl away. Stepping farther out onto the porch, Mana Mercedes pointed the long barrel at the woman and for an instant she was overcome with fear as she stared into La Llorona's evil eyes.

"Shoot her!" José yelled, still on his back.

Mana Mercedes closed her eyes and pulled the trigger. Jumping to his feet, José grabbed the gun and walked cautiously through the smoky haze as he searched for La Llorona.

"She's gone." José looked around in disbelief. "How could you have missed? She was right in front of you."

Mana Mercedes didn't answer.

"Next time, give me the gun," he ordered.

Close by, the wolf let out a haunting howl to remind the couple he and La Llorona were still there.

"Come on, let's get inside." José grabbed Mana Mercedes by the arm. Unable to move, Mana Mercedes stood still as she stared out into the darkness. The coyotes began to circle the house but the wolf's distinctive howl remained in the distance. José forced Mana Mercedes into the house and quickly locked the door.

"You remember, Mana," La Llorona whispered, watching Mana Mercedes from the shadows. "And I remember you."

La Llorona turned and walked through the grassy meadow. The coyotes circled as she made her way to the river. Falling to her knees, La Llorona let the cool river run through her fingers.

Filled with a deep sadness, La Llorona rocked back and forth as she wept softly until she could no longer bear the pain and cried out.

"*Ay, mis hijos.* Don't leave me," she cried as the black wolf joined her eerie cry.

Hearing the haunting cry, Mana Mercedes looked out from her bedroom window.

"Come to bed," José mumbled as he climbed under the covers.

Mana Mercedes stepped away from the window. Taking the rosary from the dresser, she made the sign of the cross and began to pray quietly as she climbed into bed.

# Sixteen

Christina stood at the end of the long hall and watched the beautiful sunrise over the Sangre de Cristo Mountains. She held her sore hand against her body. The infection had begun to spread. Her hand had swollen to twice the normal size and the scratches stung.

The dark orange glow gradually softened as the sun rose over the Sangre de Cristo Mountains. Turning away from the window, Christina walked down the hallway to the nurses' station. Walking around the corner, she watched Jenny working diligently behind the desk. Jenny's energy was incredible. After working all night she showed no signs of fatigue.

"Take the old woman her breakfast." Jenny pointed to the tray sitting on the corner of the desk.

"Estefanita?" Christina knew the question would piss off Jenny but annoying Jenny this morning didn't bother her. She was exhausted. Her hand hurt and she was fed up with Jenny's condescending demeanor.

"Yes, her." Jenny stopped writing and glared at Christina.

With a nod, Christina smiled and took the tray from the desk.

"If she eats, she can stop being sedated," Jenny reminded as Christina turned the corner.

Estefanita lay motionless on the bed but turned her head and watched Christina set the tray down next to her and gently loosen her restraints.

"If you eat, the doctor will take you off the medication." Christina spoke gently, hoping she understood. Taking the glass of orange juice, Christina lifted Estefanita's head and put the drink to her lips. With her mouth clamped shut, Estefanita shook her head and spit the juice down her chin onto her hospital gown.

"You have to eat," Christina pleaded as she cleaned Estefanita with a towel. Christina took a spoonful of the warm cereal to Estefanita's mouth. Again Estefanita shut her mouth and refused to eat.

"The only way they're going to stop sedating you is if you eat. Please, just one bite." Estefanita shook her head again. "Why not? I know you're hungry," she urged. "It's good." Turning the spoon of food, Christina opened her mouth.

Estefanita watched as Christina put the spoon to her mouth. Lifting her arm, Estefanita hit Christina's tender hand and sent the spoon flying to the floor. Estefanita swung her arm again and knocked the bowl out of her hand.

"Why did you do that?" Holding her throbbing hand, Christina's voice trembled from the pain as she went down to her knees to pick up the spilled oatmeal. Hoping Jenny hadn't heard the commotion, Christina quickly scooped the oatmeal into the bowl. Christina smelled the oatmeal. Repulsed by the foul stench, Christina set the bowl on the tray.

"I will not be tricked." Estefanita was angry.

"Tricked?" Christina was surprised.

"She is using you to trick me but I know the food is poisoned." Estefanita pointed to the bowl of oatmeal.

"The food isn't poisoned," Christina reassured.

"I will not eat her food. I don't care what she does to me. I will not eat." Estefanita looked down at Christina's swollen hand. "She has cursed you."

"What?"

"Your hand. It's the work of the bruja."

"It's only an infection."

"Go to Mana Mercedes. She can break the spell. She lives on Palace Avenue at the end of the road in the gray house." Christina smiled. Half of the houses in Santa Fe were gray. "Take some tobacco with you. She likes the kind in the red can. Show her your hand. She'll know how to cure the spell."

Christina didn't believe in witchcraft but she politely agreed to please the old woman. Christina walked into the bathroom and flushed the juice and oatmeal down the toilet.

"I'll bring you a sandwich tonight and I'll log it on your chart that you ate so you don't have to get anymore shots." Christina walked out of the bathroom.

"Thank you," Estefanita muttered quietly.

"You're welcome." Christina took the tray from the table. "My shift is almost over. I'll see you tonight."

"Go to Mana Mercedes. She will help you," Estefanita advised as Christina left the room.

"Well?" Jenny waited in the hall to inspect the tray. "Did she eat?"

"Yes," Christina held out the tray for Jenny.

"Good." Jenny smiled as she took the tray. "Bandage your hand before you come into work tonight. I don't want you spreading germs to our patients."

Christina's hand burned as the words left Jenny's lips. Looking down at her swollen hand, she noticed one of the scratches was bleeding from where Estefanita hit her. Christina took a handkerchief from her pocket and held it against the cut as she watched Jenny walk down the hall. There was something different about Jenny this morning. Christina had never seen her carry a food tray before. Jenny usually left the menial work for Christina.

## *Seventeen*

Christina stopped to rest under the shade of a large cotton-wood next to an irrigation ditch. Holding a small brown paper bag in her bandaged hand, she looked up at the long road ahead of her and wiped perspiration from her forehead. Behind her, the three children walked along the ditch picking flowers.

"Where are we going, Mom?" Jessica asked as she plucked the white petals off a wild daisy.

"I don't know." Christina didn't know exactly where she was going. She hadn't planned on looking for Mana Mercedes but she hadn't been able to sleep with the pain, so she decided to try to find the woman Estefanita told her about.

"What's in the bag?" Marie asked.

"A gift."

"For who?"

Another question she didn't know how to answer. Christina looked around at the houses and felt the anxiety rising in her chest. They were all gray. Hell, she didn't even know if she was on the right road.

After walking for more than thirty minutes, Christina wondered why she was out looking for a woman who might only exist in Estefanita's irrational mind. But Estefanita intrigued her and if this Mana Mercedes could tell her more about the old woman then it might be worth the while. Christina wanted to give up and turn around. She was tired and hot and the pain in her hand was almost unbearable, but she knew going home to get some rest was out of the question.

"Mom?" Marie nearly yelled to get Christina's attention. "Are you okay?"

"I'm fine." Christina forced a smile. "Come on, let's keep going. We're almost there."

Continuing to walk along the dirt road, Christina looked down at the alfalfa fields and the curving Santa Fe River. The road wound around the desert mountain filled with pine trees, yuccas, and flowering cacti. Christina walked for another ten minutes before she stopped and looked up at the gray house on the green plateau abutting the forest.

Mana Mercedes sat under the shade of the front porch shelling peas as she rocked in a weathered chair. When she saw Christina and the children, she set down the bowl of peas and smiled as if she'd been expecting them.

Christina stood outside the front gate as José pushed a wheelbarrow containing two dead dogs. Flies swarmed around the animals. Christina shielded Jessica and Marie's curious eyes and waited for José to walk by before she looked over at the petite woman.

"I've been expecting you." Mana Mercedes smiled as she opened the wood gate to let Christina and the children into her yard.

"How could you know I was coming?" Christina asked as she followed the woman onto the porch.

"Estefanita told me." Mana Mercedes smiled knowingly.

"You visited Estefanita at the hospital?" Christina was shocked. She'd checked the visitors' log this morning and no one had been to see her.

"No," Mana Mercedes answered as she stared eagerly at the brown paper bag.

Christina held out the bag to Mana Mercedes. "This is for you."

Mana Mercedes opened the bag and took out the red tin of tobacco. "My favorite."

"Estefanita told me," Christina answered shyly.

Mana Mercedes sat in the rocking chair and sprinkled a rolling paper with the fresh tobacco. Wetting the edge of the paper, Mana Mercedes rolled a nearly perfect cigarette and held it between her lips as she searched the pocket of her apron.

"There's a box in the bag." Christina pointed.

Taking out a match, Mana Mercedes stuck the white tip with her thumbnail. Easing back in her chair, Mana Mercedes lit her cigarette and deeply inhaled the smoke. A look of contentment washed over her face. She took another puff before she turned her attention back to her guests.

Christina watched Mana Mercedes from the edge of the porch as she held Mark Anthony in her arms and Jessica and Marie hid behind her.

"You have a beautiful family." Mana Mercedes smiled at the children, causing them to cringe.

"Thank you." Christina smiled politely.

"Perhaps the children would like to play with my kittens." Mana Mercedes motioned with her hand as three small kittens ran from around the corner of the house toward the children. Jessica and Marie let go of their mother and Mark Anthony pushed himself out of her arms to play with the animals. "Now you and I can go inside and talk about your hand." Mana Mercedes stood up and motioned Christina into the house.

With one last look at the children, Christina followed Mana Mercedes into the small house.

"Have a seat." Mana Mercedes walked around the wood table to a white hutch in the corner of the kitchen. Christina sat down and watched Mana Mercedes take several glass jars filled with dried leaves from the cupboard. She filled a small ceramic bowl with boiling water and placed some dried leaves in the bowl to soak. Next she poured some oil onto a shallow grinding stone. The dark stone was coarse on the exterior edges but the inside was smooth from years of use.

Christina had never seen anything like it before but she knew it was old and could have been used by the ancient Indians to grind their foods. Mana Mercedes removed the leaves from the hot water and placed them into the stone with the oil. From a black ceramic jar she took a pinch of gray powder and sprinkled it into the oily mixture. With a cylindrical black stone Mana Mercedes ground the ingredients into a green paste. Christina watched intently as Mana Mercedes sat next to her.

"Show me your hand." Mana Mercedes motioned to Christina's hand.

Christina unwrapped the bandages. Her hand was pale in comparison to the deep scratches oozing yellow pus. Her fingers were swollen and she could no longer close her hand. Mana Mercedes scooped the green paste with her fingers and rubbed it gently on the cuts.

"You can put the bandages back on your hand," Mana Mercedes said as she rubbed the last of the paste on the scratches. As Christina wrapped her hand with the soft gauze, Mana Mercedes rolled another cigarette.

"I don't understand how Estefanita told you I was coming. She has been in and out of consciousness since she was brought into the hospital four days ago and I've checked the visitors' log. No one has been in to see her."

"Estefanita is a very special woman." Mana Mercedes smiled. "I've known her for many years. She is a good judge of character and she has taken a great liking to you. She trusts you even though you are ignorant of our customs." She took another puff from her cigarette. "She can teach you but you must be willing to learn."

"Learn what?"

"The ways of the curandera."

"What is a curan—?" Christina struggled to pronounce the word.

"This town was founded by the Spaniards many years ago. They brought religion to this area and forced the native Indians to give up their religious customs. The Indians knew many things about the native plants and their uses for medicinal cures. Several were intrigued by their knowledge and learned from those who were willing to teach. Some used this knowledge to help others while others used it to inflict pain and suffering. A curandera uses this knowledge to help others."

"Estefanita is a curandera?"

"Yes."

"And you are a curandera."

"Yes."

Christina leaned back in her chair. The green mixture felt warm and the pain in her hand was going away.

"Estefanita is at the end of her life and she has chosen you to pass her knowledge to."

"Me? Doesn't she have any family?"

Mana Mercedes wet her thumb and forefinger and pinched the cigarette out between her fingers. Rolling another cigarette, she leaned back in her chair. "No, Estefanita does not have any family." She lit the match as she chose her words carefully. "She lost her family many years ago."

"What happened?" Christina knew it wasn't any of her business but she wanted to know as much about Estefanita as Mana Mercedes was willing to share.

Mana Mercedes stared at her for a moment, forgetting about the burning match until she felt the heat on her fingers and lit her cigarette. "Her family was taken away from her by a witch." Mana Mercedes blew out the match with a puff of smoke and picked several pieces of tobacco from her lips. "Estefanita nearly went crazy with grief."

Christina's heart went out to Estefanita but she wanted to know more. "If Estefanita wants you to know about her life, she'll tell you, but beware of what you ask for. The evil she once destroyed has been reborn."

"What?" Christina asked as a chill raced down her spine. Christina's image of witches flying across the sky on brooms and gathering around large caldrons of brew vanished, replaced by another image more terrifying. She'd never believed in witches but because of the way Mana Mercedes talked about the Indians and curanderas with such conviction, their existence suddenly became a shocking reality.

Mana Mercedes stood up from the table to indicate the conversation was over and Christina reluctantly followed. Christina wanted to know more about Estefanita but knew Mana Mercedes was right. If she wanted to know about Estefanita, she needed to ask Estefanita, not try to pry the information out of Mana Mercedes. The children happily played with the kittens on the porch.

"It's time to go," Christina said as she stepped out onto the porch.

"Can we take them home with us?" Marie pleaded as she held the purring kitten close.

"No." Christina shook her head. "They don't belong to us."

"Please, Mom," Jessica added as if her pleas would change her mother's mind.

"Take them." Mana Mercedes smiled. "They need a good home and they've taken well to your children."

Christina looked at the children and couldn't find it in her heart to tell them no. "Okay," she agreed reluctantly.

"Thanks, Mom!" Jessica hugged Christina's leg.

"Don't thank me. Thank Mana Mercedes."

"Thank you." Jessica smiled warmly at the old woman.

"You're welcome."

Mana Mercedes looked thoughtfully at Christina. "The evil I told you about lurks in the darkness. She is weak but will soon grow stronger. Her thirst for vengeance can never be quenched and she will once again prey on the innocent. Take care of your family and trust your instincts with those around you." Sitting back in her rocking chair, Mana Mercedes picked up the bowl of peas and continued where she'd left off.

Mana Mercedes's words sent a shiver through Christina. Trying to forget the old woman's warning, Christina watched the three kittens follow her children down the dirt road.

# *Eighteen*

Christina opened the door to check on the children and smiled. At the foot of the bed the three small kittens curled together and purred quietly as they slept.

When Mana Mercedes told her the kittens had taken a liking to the children, she had dismissed the woman's words as flattery, a way to get rid of the unwanted pets. But as she'd watched Jessica cuddle and play with the runt, and now, as they slept, she was glad she'd relented. The kittens were good for the children. They needed something to love and take care of, something to call their own.

Christina walked out into the cool summer night. A storm had been brewing all evening and it seemed as if it was going to rain. She hurried down the dirt road. The wind swirled dust around her as bolts of lightning flashed across the dark clouds. Feeling the first few drops of rain, Christina began to walk faster. Rain poured out of the dark clouds. Holding her purse over her head and clutching her sweater around her neck, Christina ran around the corner of Canyon Road.

Soaked from the sudden downpour, Christina shivered as she waited for the elevator. She patted her face and neck with her handkerchief and stepped off the elevator. Walking down the hall to the nurses' station she felt herself tense when she saw Jenny behind the desk. Jenny looked up from her paperwork as Christina walked up to the desk.

"Hello." Christina half smiled as she walked around the desk to set her purse on the floor.

"What's that on your hand?" Jenny asked as she sniffed the air.

"I covered my hand like you asked." Christina ran her hand over the clean gauze bandages.

"Well, it smells like shit. Take it off." Jenny crinkled her nose, repulsed by the odor.

"What?"

"You heard me, I said take it off." Jenny glared at her.

"No," Christina answered defiantly.

"What did you say?" Jenny lowered her voice to a growl.

"I'm not taking it off. My hand is infected and I'm treating the infection."

Jenny stood from the chair and moved closer to Christina. Christina straightened her shoulders. This was one argument she wasn't going to back away from. Whatever Mana Mercedes had put on her hand had worked. The swelling was down and the pain was gone. As the two women glared at each other, Michelle and Monica walked around the corner.

"Get to work," Jenny growled before the two women walked up to the nurses' station.

Christina quickly turned and walked away to start her nightly routine. She started in Estefanita's room as she normally did. She slipped quietly into the room. She was surprised when the old woman turned and smiled at her.

"Hi," Christina whispered as she took out a sandwich from the pocket of her dress and unwrapped it from the waxed paper.

Estefanita took several bites and savored the taste of the sandwich. Christina placed the half-eaten sandwich on the nightstand, poured a glass of water, and lifted Estefanita's head off the pillow to help her drink. Christina struggled to keep the water from spilling as the old woman shook her head.

"What's the matter?" Christina asked.

Estefanita didn't answer as she continued to chew her food. Christina knew she was thirsty and she couldn't understand why she wouldn't drink. She lifted the glass and looked at the cloudy water. Putting the glass to her nose Christina recognized the foul odor from the morning oatmeal. Christina walked into the bathroom, poured the rancid water down the drain, and filled the pitcher with fresh water. She poured a glass of water and this time Estefanita lifted her head to drink.

"I went to Mana Mercedes's today," Christina said as she fed the rest of the sandwich to Estefanita. "She fixed my hand. Thank you." Estefanita smiled as she chewed the last of the sandwich and drank more water. "I've got to get back to work but I'll be back later to check on you." Christina turned and walked out of the room.

Jenny waited for Christina outside Estefanita's room. Christina was startled when she saw Jenny and tried to walk by but Jenny stepped in front of her.

"You need to administer the patient another sedative." Jenny held out the syringe.

"I thought you said she wasn't going to get anymore shots."

"She never ate her food," Jenny answered sharply.

"Yes she—" Christina began.

"Don't lie to me," Jenny barked. "I know she didn't eat."

"How do you know?" Christina challenged.

"Don't fuck with me, you little bitch." Jenny took a step toward Christina. "I won't be made a fool of, do you understand?" It took everything in Christina not to step away from Jenny but she didn't move. "Now get in there and give the patient her shot." Jenny held the syringe in front of Christina's face.

Christina stared at the syringe for a moment before she took it and turned around. She walked back into the room but Estefanita didn't smile at her this time as she watched her walk over to the bed with the syringe in her hand. Christina avoided Estefanita's pleading eyes as she took her frail arm in her hand and searched for a vein. She put the needle to her skin, looked up at Estefanita, and knew she couldn't give her another shot.

"If I don't give you the shot, you've got to promise me you won't cause any problems, okay?" Christina whispered as Estefanita nodded eagerly.

Christina moved the needle from Estefanita's arm and stuck it into the mattress. She pushed the liquid into the cotton mattress as Estefanita let out a sigh of relief, looked up at the ceiling, and began to pray. Christina let go of Estefanita's arm and walked out of the room.

# Nineteen

L a Llorona walked aimlessly along the riverbank. The white
cotton gown she'd taken from Mana Mercedes's clothesline hung loosely on her thin frame. Staggering on the slippery rocks, La Llorona splashed black mud and water onto the
clean gown. The flesh around her mouth had begun to heal but
the damage had been done and her face was grossly deformed.
La Llorona's long white hair blew in the wind.

Beside her, the black wolf remained close as the coyotes circled
in search of food. Still weak, La Llorona stumbled to her knees and
fell into the river. Feeling the cool water run over her hands, she
began to sob.

La Llorona shut her eyes as a vision of two small children
flashed through her. "No!" She whimpered softly. The children
were neatly dressed, the boy in blue trousers and a white shirt and
the little girl in a yellow cotton dress with matching bows tied in her
long black hair. Their laughter filled the air as they ran and played
in the lush meadow filled with wildflowers and dancing butterflies.
She watched the children dance with joy around her as she sat on
the red and black Indian blanket. Looking down at the swaddled
infant nursing at her breast, she was overcome with joy. The lover

beside her leaned over and lovingly kissed the baby on the head. He gazed into her eyes and tenderly caressed her face before he went to the children.

The ache in her soul festered and she slammed her fists into the water. "No!" La Llorona screamed as muddy water splashed onto her face. Hearing her wretched cry, the coyotes stopped their hunt to watch the delusional woman. Captivated by La Llorona's eerie moan, the wolf threw his head back and unleashed a reverberating howl.

"*¿Mis hijos, donde esta?*" La Llorona crawled out of the water. "Children, where have you gone?" Slowly getting to her feet she followed the river into town. "*Mis hijos vente con to momma.*" She stumbled along the river and sobbed. "Come to your momma."

Estefanita's body was covered with sweat. Her heart pounded in her chest and she felt as though the air was being squeezed out of her. Her stomach burned as the taste of bitter bile rose in her throat. Flinging her head from side to side, she struggled to suppress her haunting vision. Blurred images of the forest and river flashed through her like a silent movie. She tried to suppress the haunting visions but she was too weak.

Unable to fight any longer, her soul was pulled from the safety of her body and hurled through the darkness. Standing at the edge of the river Estefanita watched La Llorona lying in the sand. The river splashed over La Llorona's curled body. La Llorona pulled her knees to her chest while the wolf sat by her side. Sensing Estefanita's presence, the wolf jumped to its feet and growled.

Estefanita watched from the shadows as La Llorona stood. Searching the darkness with her black eyes, La Llorona slowly walked toward Estefanita. The wolf sat obediently and growled. Limping across the rocky embankment, La Llorona stopped within inches of Estefanita.

Christina tried to comfort Estefanita by wiping her face with a wet washcloth but the cool water wasn't having an effect on the woman's condition as she continued to fight. Christina looked down at Estefanita's bruised and raw wrists. Christina wondered if not giving

Estefanita the sedative had been the right decision. Maybe Jenny was right; maybe Estefanita needed the sedatives. Estefanita's condition had worsened, there was no doubt about it, and it was her fault. She felt sorry for the woman. She'd only wanted to help but she couldn't let Estefanita suffer, even if it meant telling Jenny what she'd done.

"Calm down. I'm right here," Christina whispered gently as she continued to wipe Estefanita's face and neck with the washcloth. Christina looked into Estefanita's distant stare.

Christina wondered if any of the other nurses would find out about Estefanita. Telling Jenny what she'd done would only get her fired and she couldn't have that happen. Her children needed her and her life was going so well. She looked down at the helpless woman, and Estefanita needed her too. She had to keep Estefanita as comfortable as possible and pray she didn't have another crazed outburst. Not wanting Jenny to find her in Estefanita's room again and knowing there was nothing more she could do for the woman, Christina quietly slipped out of the room.

Estefanita smelled the decay on La Llorona as they stood face to face. Both women stared into each other's eyes and searched the other's soul. Nothing could have prepared Estefanita for the evil she saw within La Llorona, an evil she knew existed but never had seen. La Llorona sensed her fear and began to laugh.

"It has been a long time, Estefanita." Estefanita could feel La Llorona's breath on her face. "Don't you have anything to say to your old friend?" La Llorona's smile faded as she grabbed Estefanita's throat with her bony hand. "For years you kept me buried but nothing you do now can stop me. I am getting stronger while you are slowly dying." Estefanita didn't struggle as La Llorona squeezed harder. "You're not afraid of me," she snickered. "But then again, why should you be afraid of what you created? We share a special bond, Estefanita, one that can never be broken. Our lives are entwined in life and death. We need each other. One cannot exist without the other, like good and evil." Estefanita closed her eyes and began to pray. "Always the devoted Catholic. Your useless

prayers won't be answered because your God can't help you now."
La Llorona put her free hand over Estefanita's eyes. "I want you to
see what you created."

Estefanita's body stiffened. She felt the darkness well up inside
her. Hatred and anger seethed through her soul. She struggled to
control the hate but it consumed her.

"Yes," La Llorona whispered. "Feel the hatred."

As soon as Christina walked out of Estefanita's room, she heard
the old woman scream. Christina turned and ran back into the
room and saw Estefanita sitting up in bed. Somehow Estefanita
had untied one of the restraints and was using her hand to free the
other. Estefanita's short gray hair stood up wildly. Her eyes were
filled with rage, and she looked at Christina with utter contempt.

Christina quickly ran across the room, grabbed Estefanita's
hand, and pushed her back onto the bed. Estefanita screamed as
Christina struggled to keep her pinned to the bed. Christina frantically covered Estefanita's mouth with her bandaged hand to muffle
her screams but it was no use.

Estefanita continued to fight and it took all of Christina's
strength to hold her down. Christina began to tire against the old
woman's relentless struggle as Estefanita bit the bandages on her
hand like a wild animal. Not knowing what else to do, Christina
struck Estefanita across the face. Stunned, Estefanita stopped
and looked into Christina's eyes. Christina could see the hatred in
Estefanita eyes and fearfully eased off the old woman. Estefanita
swiftly grabbed Christina's wrist with her cold hand.

Christina panicked as she tried to pull away, but it was useless;
the old woman's grip was too powerful. In her desperate attempt to
free herself, Christina didn't notice Estefanita's face soften and the
hatred vanish.

"I'm sorry," Estefanita whispered. Christina stopped and looked
up at her. "I don't know what else to do," she muttered softly. "You
are my last hope."

Estefanita closed her eyes as Christina felt the energy pulsate
through her from the old woman's hand. Initially the sensation was

warm and pleasant but then her body began to twitch from the powerful force generating through her and the pleasure quickly turned to pain. Christina fell to her knees as Estefanita continued to hold her wrist and drive the pulsating energy through her. Christina's heart pounded in her chest, her veins throbbed against her skin with each heartbeat, and the pressure in her built until it felt like she would explode. Unable to take the pain, Christina collapsed onto the floor. With one last burst of energy Estefanita let go of Christina's hand before she collapsed onto the bed.

Christina struggled to regain her strength as she crawled away from the bed. Using the chair against the wall, Christina pulled herself up off the floor. Blood rushed to her head, causing the room to spin, and she collapsed back into the chair. Rubbing her temples, Christina waited for the wave of nausea to subside before she looked over at Estefanita.

Christina stood and walked over to the bed. Both of Estefanita's wrists were tied in the restraints. Dumbfounded, Christina rubbed her arm, the painful reminder of what had just happened.

Estefanita's eyes were closed but her lips moved quickly with whispered prayers. Christina watched the woman in disbelief. Did she imagine what just happened? She turned and walked out of the room.

"What's the matter with you?" Jenny snapped.

"Nothing," Christina managed to answer through her surprise.

"I thought I heard screaming. What were you doing in there?"

"I was, uh, changing the bedpan," Christina muttered.

Jenny glanced at the closed door before she looked down at Christina's wrinkled uniform in disgust. "Get back to work."

Taking every ounce of energy she had, Christina walked around Jenny and staggered into Roman's room. Christina collapsed against the door.

"You don't look so good." Roman's words startled Christina and she forced herself to stand up straight.

"You—you're?" Christina stammered. Roman's room had been a place of refuge for her, a place where she wasn't expected to listen to drug-induced ramblings, and now he was awake.

"Yes, I'm awake," he grunted irritably.

"When? Does Sarah know? Is there anything I can get you?" Christina managed to ask as Estefanita's electrical charge still pulsated through her body.

"I need to get out of here." Roman tried to sit up and collapsed back onto the bed.

"You're not going anywhere." Christina raced across the room, forgetting the dull ache in her head, and poured a glass of water. Holding the glass to Roman's dry lips, she eased his head off the pillow as he sipped the water. "I'm going to get you a doctor."

"Don't bother," he answered as he let his head fall back onto the pillow. "The doctors have been here all day sticking needles in me, trying to figure out why I'm still alive."

"What about your family and Sarah?" Christina asked as she set down the glass.

"The doctors ordered my family to leave after I woke up. They don't want me getting all excited and falling back into a coma." Roman closed his eyes and tenderly touched the bandage around his head. "And I don't want Sarah anywhere around me, is that understood?" he ordered sharply.

"Yes, but don't you think she has a right to know you're going to be all right?" Christina asked, wishing she'd kept her promise to mind her own business.

"Sarah needs to get on with her life, just like I've gotten on with mine," he mumbled.

"Putting a gun to your head is getting on with your life?" Christina bit her lower lip.

"What are you, some kind of shrink?" Roman snapped. "I don't have to explain myself to you."

"You're right and I am sorry. I had no right to intrude." Christina looked out the open window as mariachi music drifted into the room from the plaza. Christina listened to the energetic beat and smiled as the trumpets and violins carried the melody.

"Close the window, please," Roman asked.

"Don't you like the music?" Christina asked as she walked over and felt the cool breeze blow over her.

"The music is fine," he mumbled. "I just don't feel like celebrating fiestas this year, although I wouldn't mind seeing my troubles going up in flames with Zozobra."

"Zozobra?" Christina asked as she closed the window, leaving the room filled with a somber silence.

"You're not from around here, are you?" Roman smiled. "During Fiestas de Santa Fe they burn a twenty-foot paper puppet named Zozobra—or Old Man Gloom for you gringos. It's believed if you tell Zozobra your troubles, they will burn in the fire and disappear in the smoke." Roman's eyes stared blankly at the image of his problems being carried away and sighed. "If only it were that easy. Each year there's a weeklong celebration to mark the Spaniards' triumphant return to Santa Fe. During the Pueblo Revolt, the Indians drove the Spaniards out of Santa Fe, but only for a while. Several years later Spain sent back another army of conquistadors to reclaim the small village."

"You don't sound pleased with Santa Fe's history." Christina walked around the bed to take the tray.

"I'm not pleased that hundreds of Indians were killed by men who forced their religious beliefs and themselves on the Indians."

"Aren't you Spanish?"

"Yes, a part of me is Spanish but my grandmother was Indian and her way of life was stripped away from her. This so-called celebration is a ploy to bury what really happened. The people around here try to claim this is a celebration of the unity between the Spanish and the Indians but it was nothing more than a slaughter of innocent women and children and like every other war was justified by those doing the killing."

"You don't like war," Christina mumbled absently.

"War?" Roman hissed. "No, I don't like war. I didn't like being shot at, I didn't like to hear friends plead for their lives after they'd been shot, and I certainly didn't like losing my legs." He pulled back the sheets to show Christina the blunt nubs where his knees used to be. "I wish I were dead!" He slammed his fists into his legs.

Christina stood beside the bed and watched tears stream down Roman's face. Christina reached down and stroked his dark brown hair.

"I'm sorry," she whispered. "But killing yourself isn't the answer."

"What could you possibly know?" Roman glared at Christina with his red eyes.

"I know that I'd give anything to have my husband home with me and my children. I wouldn't give a damn if he'd lost his legs and his arms!" Hot tears stung Christina's cheeks. "I just want him home!" Wiping away her tears, Christina shook her head and nearly sprinted out of the room.

# *Twenty*

C hristina stared out the window at the far end of the corridor and watched a small crowd of people walk along the dark street off the plaza. The mariachi music had ended several hours ago but the vendors slowly made their way home. Michelle explained the celebration would commence at dawn with morning Mass at the cathedral and end with its usual nightly revelry.

Christina sighed as she pressed her forehead against the window and thought about what Roman had told her about Zozobra. She wished there were a ritual where you could burn your troubles away. Her shoulders slouched under the burden she'd carried since Mark's death and she knew there wasn't a fire big enough to burn away her sorrow.

La Llorona stepped out of the dark forest, using a thick branch as a cane. In one arm she carried kindling for the fire. She was stronger but she still tired easily. Walking over to the fire burning outside the wood shack, she threw the logs into the flames, sending sparks up into the darkness. The fire raged and the orange flames stretched over La Llorona's head.

The black wolf lay on the front porch and watched as La Llorona walked into the shack. She took down a jar from the shelf and walked back to the fire. La Llorona took out a handful of dried leaves covered with white powder and threw them into the burning flames. The fire burned the leaves and blue smoke rose from the embers. The smoke swirled around La Llorona and covered the ground.

La Llorona danced around the fire. Her body was stiff and rigid as pain shot though her with every move. She closed her eyes as she swung her head around. Her long white hair fell around her face. Her movements become more dramatic as she forgot the pain and immersed herself in her dance. Dancing wildly, La Llorona stepped closer to the fire and the flames rose. She extended her arms and the flames reached out and surrounded her hands but there was no pain. La Llorona stepped into the hot embers. She continued her ritual dance. A ball of fire rose from the flames and floated a few feet off the ground. The black wolf watched intently as the ball slowly lifted higher into the night sky and bounced along the tops of the trees.

Mana Mercedes stood on her front porch and watched as the fireball soared at the edge of the forest. Another ball of fire shot across the dark sky. The two danced around each other for several minutes and the sky was filled with blazing flashes of light. Although the fireballs looked almost the same she recognized the distinction in each of them. She watched the fiery display for several minutes before she went inside.

Christina leaned against the wall at the end of the hall. She was exhausted. The open windows let a cool breeze blow down the hall, a sharp contrast from the patients' rooms where the windows were rarely opened. Drying her brow with a handkerchief, she closed her eyes and enjoyed the breeze blowing over her body.

Christina turned her head to the open window and quickly stepped away from the wall when she saw Jenny's dark silhouette. With her back to Christina, Jenny stared out the window.

Christina watched Jenny and knew she should walk away but instead she walked quietly toward Jenny. Stopping a few feet behind

Jenny, Christina stood on her toes to look out the window. Beyond the lights from town she saw the majestic balls of fire dance at the edge of the forest. Transfixed by the incredible display, she stepped closer to the window for a better look. It was unlike anything she'd ever seen. The graceful ballet of fire captivated her, and she yearned to be a part of it.

"What is it?" Christina whispered softly.

Jenny had been so engrossed watching the balls of fire she hadn't realized Christina was next to her. Straightening her shoulders, Jenny stepped in front of Christina. "Get to work," she snapped.

"What is it?" Christina asked again as she tried to look around Jenny.

"There's nothing for you to see." Jenny stepped toward Christina, blocking her view.

"But—"

"I said get back to work." Jenny took another step toward Christina. With one last look, Christina reluctantly turned and walked away.

# Twenty-One

Sitting on the swing on the back porch, Christina watched the children run around the backyard as they played with the three kittens. She hadn't been able to sleep after she'd gotten off work that morning. She was exhausted, but every time she closed her eyes her encounter with Estefanita replayed in her mind.

She fell under the rhythmic spell of the swing's gentle rocking and closed her eyes. Listening to the children's sweet laughter, she slowly drifted off to sleep.

The sun warmed her face. Christina found herself in a beautiful green meadow filled with wildflowers and butterflies. Two children, a boy and girl, ran through the meadow laughing as they blew dandelion seeds into the air. They weren't her children but she felt a strong affection toward them. Looking down at the black and red wool blanket spread out on the ground under her, she saw the infant dressed in a beautiful white gown. Gently she reached down and stroked its soft cheek.

Next to her was a handsome man, not Mark but equally attractive. His eyes were filled with love as he leaned over and kissed her tenderly. Her stomach fluttered from the gentleness of his kiss and she yearned for another.

When Christina opened her eyes from the kiss she found herself alone in the meadow. The wind howled and the bright day quickly changed into darkness as rain clouds raced across the sky. Lightning struck around her and the love and tenderness she'd just felt seethed into an uncontrollable rage. Christina looked around and frantically searched the meadow with each flash of lightning. She saw something move at the edge of the meadow and in another flash she saw the two children run into the forest. The frightened young boy carried the infant in one arm and he held his sister's hand in the other. Christina chased them through the thick forest unable to see where they'd run. She stopped and waited for another flash of lightning. Deafening thunder rumbled through the clouds and the rain poured down. Christina ran through the rain as she screamed out for the children.

The young boy stopped behind a fallen tree and cradled the crying baby against his small body as he protectively held his little sister. Trying to muffle the baby's cries, he held the infant closer to his chest but it was no use. She heard the crying. Stepping around the fallen tree, Christina looked down at the three rain-soaked children. The young boy looked up at her. The fear in his eyes was undeniable as she reached down and grabbed their arms, dragging them behind her through the darkness.

The sound of the rushing water muffled the children's pleas for mercy. She looked down at their tear-stained faces and her heart hardened as she stepped into the river, dragging them behind her.

"Christy." Lucy gently nudged her shoulder. Christina woke up. The anger in her still raged and she glared at Lucy. "You were having a nightmare." Lucy stepped away.

Christina searched the backyard for the children.

"They're inside having lunch," Lucy reassured.

"How long was I asleep?"

"About an hour. I would have let you sleep longer but you started yelling and I wanted to wake you before the children heard you."

"Yelling? What was I saying?"

"I'm not sure, but it sounded like you were pretty upset with the children."

"It was a strange dream." Christina shook her head.

"You look exhausted." Lucy sat next to her on the swing.

"I'm all right." Christina smiled but knew she couldn't hide the dark circles under her eyes.

"You're not all right. I want you to quit working the night shift."

"I can't." Christina rubbed her forehead.

"Yes, you can." Lucy's voice was firm.

"What about the children?"

"Hire a sitter."

"I can't afford to pay a babysitter."

"You can't afford not to. Look, if it's about the money, I'll help you."

"I couldn't ask you for money."

"You're not asking. I'm offering." Christina shook her head and Lucy knew she wasn't going to change her mind. "Why are you so stubborn?"

"Lucy, I appreciate everything you've done for me but I've got to do what's right for me and the children."

"You can't do it all by yourself."

"I've depended on someone to take care of me my whole life. My mother and Mark and now they're gone." Christina's voice broke. "I don't want to depend on anyone anymore."

"I just want to help you." Lucy held Christina as she cried.

"I know, but this is something I've got to do on my own. I have to know I can take care of myself and my family." Christina wiped tears from her eyes. "Everyone I've ever loved is gone. You're the only friend I've got, and I don't want to lose you."

"You're not going to lose me. Friends help each other," Christina started to protest. "But I'll leave you alone about the night shift. Now, why don't you go inside and get some rest?" Lucy helped her up from the swing.

"What about the kids?"

"I'll watch them until I leave for work."

Christina wanted to protest but she was exhausted. The children were sitting at the kitchen table eating peanut butter and jelly sandwiches when Christina and Lucy walked into the room.

"Tired, Mommy?" Mark Anthony asked, his face smeared with a mixture of peanut butter and strawberry jam.

"Yes, Mommy's tired. Aunt Lucy is going to watch you while I take a little nap."

The three nodded as they watched their tired mom walk down the hall.

"Your mom's going to need her rest so we need to be extra quiet, okay?" Lucy whispered.

"How come Mommy's so tired?" Mark Anthony asked.

"Your mom works hard all night while you're sleeping so she can be with you when you're awake. Now, why don't we put on our swimsuits and go the river?"

"We don't have any swimsuits," Jessica answered sadly.

"You have an old pair of shorts, don't you?" They nodded. "Well, put them on and tomorrow we'll go to town and buy you some suits."

# Twenty-Two

The howling coyotes woke La Llorona from an uneasy sleep. She stood up from the dirty mattress and looked out the broken window to watch the sun set in the orange sky. The coyotes circled the shack barking and howling as they anxiously waited for her. She stepped out onto the porch and the black wolf immediately moved to her side. She smiled at her companion and gently ran her hand over its fur. The coyotes yelped excitedly as she followed the wolf into the forest. La Llorona followed the setting sun as she walked through the thick maze of trees and listened to the coyotes' howl echo through the still forest.

It was nearly dark when La Llorona reached the edge of the forest. With a wave of her hand she silenced the coyotes as she stood on a high ridge overlooking Santa Fe and listened to laughter drift on the warm breeze. As dusk settled, people moved inside for the evening.

La Llorona emerged from the cover of the forest. Drawn to the sound of the river, she made her way down into the green valley. Triggered by the sound of the trickling waters, the memory of her dark past rushed through her. La Llorona covered her ears to stop the powerful sensation and she fell to her knees. The tormented pleas of her children echoed in her ears as their innocent faces haunted her. She remembered the painful memory of her rage and collapsed to the ground.

"Mis hijos, what have I done?" she cried as she slammed her fists into the river. The wolf gently nuzzled her. Comforted by its presence, La Llorona stood and looked around. She searched the river for her children as the wolf nuzzled her again and urged her to continue. La Llorona took great care to conceal herself in the thick grove of cottonwoods as she stumbled through the muddy river. The wolf walked at her side as the coyotes hunted for food.

La Llorona heard laughter and stopped. She raised her hand to silence the coyotes and listened. The wolf watched as she walked away from the river through the thick cottonwoods and quietly made her way to the sound of children's laughter.

La Llorona hid in the shadows and watched three young children playing on the grass. The small yard was lit by a single light bulb on the back porch. Two young girls in plain cotton dresses played with their rag dolls as a young boy watched. He sat alone on the steps of the porch. He threw a worn baseball into his glove as he watched the two girls play.

"C'mon, you guys," he whined.

"Johnny, you're a boy, and boys don't play with dolls," the older of the two girls informed him as she combed her doll's yellow yarn hair.

"I don't want to play with your stupid dolls," Johnny pouted. "I want to play catch."

"Well, girls don't play catch." The other girl looked over her shoulder. "So you'll just have to play by yourself."

"I wish I had a brother," Johnny grumbled as he threw the ball harder into his glove.

La Llorona watched the young boy with his dark hair and round face, which reminded her of her own son and she yearned to hold him. She blew into the air and her breath transformed into a cluster of fireflies. With a wave of her hand she sent them out to the young boy. The fireflies danced around Johnny's head and landed on the brim of his hat. He stopped playing with his baseball. He looked up and smiled at the insects dancing around him. He set down his glove and reached out to catch one of the fireflies.

La Llorona moved her hand and silently beckoned the fireflies back to her. The insects slowly began to fly through the backyard toward the cottonwoods. Intrigued, Johnny stepped off the porch and walked past the two girls to the edge of the yard. The fireflies continued to dance around him and lured him farther into the woods. Johnny stopped and looked behind him at the two girls as they played with their dolls. Johnny turned back to the fireflies and followed them into the darkness. No longer afraid, Johnny chased after the insects trying to catch them in his baseball hat.

Stepping out from behind a tall cottonwood, La Llorona drew the fireflies into her mouth in a long breath. Startled, Johnny looked up at the old woman. His smile faded and fear took its place as La Llorona reached out to him.

A scream echoed throughout the forest and the birds roosting in the trees flew out into the darkness. La Llorona watched the birds fly noisily into the air. Johnny turned when the wolf emerged from the darkness. He screamed when he felt La Llorona's bony hand on his shoulder and ran. Weak and unable to run, La Llorona motioned to the wolf. The beast sprinted, following Johnny's scent through the thick underbrush. Seeing the flash of white T-shirt, the wolf leapt through the air. Johnny could feel the animal's hot breath on his neck. Too scared to move, the young boy screamed as the wolf pinned him to the ground. La Llorona limped out of the darkness and motioned the wolf back to her side.

La Llorona extended her hand to the crying boy. "Don't be afraid, mi hijo. I won't hurt you." Johnny looked into her disfigured face and screamed. He tried to get to his feet as La Llorona gripped his small arm. Angered by his reaction, she grabbed his shirt and pulled him to his feet. She put her hand over his mouth to muffle his screams, lifted him off the ground, and carried him away.

Christina screamed as she lifted her head off the kitchen table. Looking around the room, she rubbed her eyes. It was nine thirty. She'd put the children to bed an hour ago, and she'd fallen asleep at the table. She tried to forget her nightmare but the fear in the young boy's eyes haunted her. Never had she had a dream so terrifying and so real. She pushed herself up from the table and walked down the hall to check on the children. Relieved they were still asleep, she closed the door and walked into the bathroom. She splashed cold water on her face, looked up at the mirror, and opened the medicine cabinet. Running her fingers over the bottles on the shelf, Christina stopped at the only prescription bottle in the cabinet and stared at it for a moment before she took down the bottle of aspirin. She didn't have a headache but the thought of taking one seemed to calm her. She set the aspirin back on the shelf and took another look at the prescription bottle before she closed the cabinet.

Sarah ran into Christina as she walked around the corner. Tears streamed down Sarah's cheeks and her face grimaced in agony.

"What's the matter?" Christina grabbed Sarah by the shoulders.

"Roman," Sarah sobbed. "His family won't let me see him anymore."

"What?"

"They found out I was seeing him after hours and now they won't let me see him." Sarah dried her eyes with a damp handkerchief. "Someone's always with him now and they won't let me in. Why are they doing this to me?"

"I'm sorry," Christina managed to mutter. Because Sarah wasn't married to Roman, his family could refuse to let her see him. "Did you try talking to them?"

"Yes," Sarah nodded, "but his sister won't let me into his room. What if he wakes up and I'm not there? He'll think I don't care. What am I going to do?"

"Go home and get some rest. I'll watch him and if anything should change, I'll let you know," Christina urged.

"You'd do that for me?" Sarah asked in disbelief.

"Yes." Christina smiled.

"Thank you." Sarah let out a sigh of relief.

Christina watched Sarah step into the elevator before she walked down the hall into Roman's room. She didn't try to act surprised when Roman's sister tried to stop her from coming into the room, thinking she was Sarah.

Christina looked down at the short Hispanic woman. Her petite features resembled her brother's and the anger in her dark brown eyes quickly faded when she looked at Christina's uniform.

"If you don't mind, I need to clean the room." Christina waited for the woman to step aside and let her into the room.

"I'm sorry," the young woman answered as she sat on the chair next to the bed. "I thought you were somebody else."

"You thought I was Sarah," Christina answered as she slid her hand under the bed and removed the bedpan.

"Yes," the young woman answered. "I suppose you're a friend of hers."

"No," Christina answered as she walked into the bathroom. "I've seen her almost every night with your brother, though."

"She had no business being here," the young woman answered harshly.

"She loves him." Christina motioned to Roman.

"Well, he doesn't love her," she snapped.

"He loved her before he left to fight in the war, right?" Christina stopped and looked down at the woman. "Her love probably was the single most important thing to him while he was away. When do you suppose he changed his mind?"

"That's none of your business."

"I'll tell you when he changed his mind. It was when he lost his legs."

"Shut up," the young woman hissed.

"He's hiding behind his injuries and you're letting him."

"You don't know what you're talking about." The young woman stood as Christina looked into her eyes.

"I know what it's like to lose someone, but you didn't lose your brother."

"We may as well have. Look at him! He can't walk and he can't work!"

"He's alive. He doesn't need his legs to be useful." Christina was shocked by the young woman's indifference toward her brother.

"Work is all our family has," the young woman snapped. "How could anyone love him? He can't work, so how will he support a family?"

"It bothers you that Sarah could still love him even when you don't," Christina replied. The young woman's back stiffened as she sat down. "Don't you think your brother deserves a chance to be happy?" Christina whispered before she turned and walked out of the room.

La Llorona cradled Johnny in her arms. She ran her hand over his cheek and softly combed his hair out of his eyes.

"Mi hijo, I thought I'd lost you," she mumbled, sitting at the edge of the river and rocking Johnny gently in her arms. She filled her cupped hand with water from the river and poured it over Johnny's face to wake him.

Disoriented, Johnny struggled to focus and looked up at the moon. He turned to the sound of the river and watched the water crashing over the rocks. Feeling La Llorona's grip tightening around his waist, he turned to her and screamed. He struggled to break free from the wretched old woman and thrashed wildly. He cried out as she grabbed his face with her bony hands and forced him to look into her eyes. Looking into the depths of his soul, she realized he was not her son and screamed out in frustration.

Christina stood in the middle of the empty hall. The tray she'd been carrying lay scattered across the floor. Her heart raced in her chest, a cold sweat chilled her body, and her vision blurred.

In a flash Christina found herself alone at the edge of the river. The moon reflected off the water and for a moment she felt the river's tranquility. Hearing a cry for help, she turned. Beside her she saw the young boy from her nightmare struggle to get away from the old woman pulling him into the river.

Monica ran around the corner. "Are you okay?" she asked as she looked down at the food scattered across the floor.

Christina couldn't hear her. In her mind she was no longer at the hospital. She could only focus on the woman before her. She watched in horror as La Llorona dragged the boy into the river and pushed him into the rushing current. Christina watched the boy gasp for air as he tried to keep his head above water. Behind her, she heard a deep throaty growl and turned as the black wolf sniffed the ground around her. Unable to see Christina but sensing her presence, the wolf growled. Christina backed away from the vicious animal coming toward her and stumbled into the rushing water. Christina was pulled into the strong current and thrashed against the rocks as she quickly drifted away from the black wolf.

"What's the matter?" Michelle asked as she walked up behind Monica.

Christina struggled to breathe and collapsed onto the floor. Her whole body trembled and convulsed.

"Grab her legs!" Michelle ordered as she held Christina down.

Christina thrashed on the floor. Her eyes fluttered to the back of her head and she began to choke.

"What's the matter with her?" Jenny snapped as she stepped out of the stairwell.

"I don't know. She just started screaming." Michelle struggled to hold her when Christina suddenly stopped breathing. "Oh my God, she stopped breathing!" Michelle laid Christina down and checked for a pulse on her neck. "Help me!" Michelle pleaded for Jenny's help but she didn't move.

Monica let go of Christina's limp legs and began compressions on her chest. "One and two and three and four and ..." Jenny smirked as she watched Christina. "Thirteen, fourteen, fifteen, and now!" Monica ordered as Michelle pinched Christina's nose and breathed into her mouth. Coughing out a mouthful of water, Christina gasped as she grabbed Michelle's arm and fearfully held onto her.

"Are you okay?" Michelle asked as she looked into Christina's eyes.

"What happened?" Disoriented, Christina struggled to sit up.

"I knew there wasn't anything wrong with her," Jenny snickered.

Michelle ignored Jenny. "Can you sit up?"

"How did I get here?" Puzzled, Christina looked around.

"You fainted."

"I did?"

"Don't you remember anything?" Monica asked in disbelief.

"I was clearing the dinner trays and—" Christina stopped as the vision of the scared young boy raced through her.

"And?" Monica urged.

"I don't know. I can't remember." Christina rubbed her temples and couldn't believe she'd had another nightmare.

"It's obvious there's nothing wrong with her." Jenny continued to glare at Christina. "Now that the drama is over, get back to work." Monica and Michelle looked worriedly at Christina as they stood. "Go on." Jenny motioned to the two nurses and waited for them to leave before she turned to Christina. "If you're done taking your break, the old woman is ready for her shot." Jenny reached into her uniform pocket and took out a syringe.

Christina slowly stood. Her legs were still weak, and she took the needle from Jenny. With Jenny one step behind her, Christina walked down the hall into Estefanita's room, closed the door behind her, and collapsed against the door.

Christina began to tremble. She held her hand over her mouth and ran into the bathroom where she gagged into the toilet. She spit the bitter bile out of her mouth and stood. Leaning against the sink, she splashed water on her face and looked at her reflection in the mirror. She tried to forget the terrible dream and remembered Jenny was still outside. She picked up the syringe from the floor and squirted the liquid into the sink.

"She heard you."

Christina ignored Estefanita as she stepped out of the room.

# Twenty-Three

Christina tried to forget the image of the boy and the old woman as she stirred dried oatmeal into a pan of boiling water. The mere thought of the young boy's gruesome death made her heart ache and she had to keep reminding herself it had only been a dream. Christina poured a cup of raisins into the bubbling oatmeal when Lucy walked out of her room with John behind her.

"Morning," Lucy sang as she took the coffeepot off the stove and poured two cups.

"Morning," Christina answered as she lowered her head, devoting more attention than necessary to stirring the oatmeal.

"How's the hand?" John asked as he took the cup of coffee from Lucy and sat down comfortably at the table.

"What?" Christina turned to John.

"Your hand." He pointed with his cup.

Christina looked at her hand. She hadn't thought much about it since she'd visited Mana Mercedes. "It's fine," she answered as she stretched out her fingers.

"You look tired, Christy." Lucy stood next to her and watched her stir the oatmeal.

"I'm fine." Christina deliberately let her long red hair fall around face. She didn't want Lucy to see how tired she really was.

"Why don't I take the kids with me so you can rest?" Lucy moved the hair from Christina's face to look at her.

"You don't have to—" Christina began.

"I know I don't have to. I want to," Lucy interrupted. "John and I are going to take a hike into the forest for an afternoon picnic."

Christina turned to John, certain Lucy hadn't told him about her plans but was surprised when he nodded.

"I was kind of hoping to spend a little time with them."

"You can spend this afternoon with them, after you've rested."

"Okay," Christina reluctantly agreed.

"I'll wake up the kids and get lunch ready." Lucy set down her coffee and walked out of the kitchen.

"She's a wonderful woman." John smiled as he watched Lucy leave the room.

"Yes, she is," Christina agreed. "Are you sure you don't mind taking the kids with you?"

"Of course not. I love kids. I want to have as many as my wife will give me."

"Wife?"

"Oh, I'm not married yet, but I plan to be as soon as I finish my internship at the end of the summer."

Christina smiled and knew Lucy had finally found her doctor. The love in John's eyes was unmistakable when Lucy walked back in the room.

"The kids are up and getting ready," Lucy let her arm glide lovingly over John's shoulder as she walked over to the breadbox.

"I'll help them get ready." Christina left the kitchen. Mark Anthony sat on the rug in the middle of the room as Jessica slipped a T-shirt over his head. Seeing her walk into the room, he stood and ran to her with the shirt only half on.

"Mommy!" He jumped into her arms and laid his tired head on her shoulder.

"Good morning, my angels." Christina kissed him on the neck and hugged Jessica and Marie.

"We're going on a picnic with Aunt Lucy!" Jessica was excited. "Are you coming with us?"

"I can't today," she apologized.

"Why not?" Marie asked as she slipped on a pair of socks.

"I need to get some rest, but tomorrow is my day off and I promise we'll all do something together, okay?"

"I hate your job," Marie pouted.

"Why?" Christina asked as she sat on the bed still holding Mark Anthony.

"Because you're always tired. I wish you could just stay home with us all the time." Marie laid her head on Christina's lap.

"I wish I could stay home with you all the time too, but I can't. Now come on and finish getting ready so you can go on your picnic."

"I bought these for the kids yesterday on my lunch break." Lucy walked into the room and handed Lucy a brown paper bag.

"What is it?" Jessica asked excitedly as Christina opened the bag.

"Swimsuits. I hope they fit." Lucy smiled as the kids excitedly held up their suits.

"Thank you!" Jessica ran up to her and hugged her leg.

"You're welcome." Lucy hugged her back as Mark Anthony and Marie grabbed her other leg. "Now hurry up and get ready, and bring your suits. We'll stop at the river on the way home."

Christina waved good-bye from the front porch. Watching her children leave with Lucy and John stirred a deep sadness within her. After she changed into her nightgown she lay down on the bed and closed her eyes. Images of the terrified little boy flashed though her. She rolled onto her side and tried to erase the chilling image of the boy being swept away in the river. Unable to sleep, Christina got out of bed and walked to the bathroom. The light bulb over the medicine cabinet cast a soft glow against the walls. She looked at her reflection in the mirror. The dark circles under her eyes stood out in contrast against her fair complexion and her hair, once full and shiny, was now dull and listless. Christina splashed cold water on her face but nothing she did could change the stark image of her reflection.

Opening the medicine cabinet, she reached for the aspirin. She took two tablets, turned on the water, and drank from her cupped hand. As she set the bottle back on the shelf, she took the brown prescription bottle. "Lucy Chainza," she read. "Morphine. Take one tablet as directed for recurring back pain."

Christina opened the bottle and poured the white pills into the palm of her hand. She held up one of the pills and studied it before she put it in her mouth. With the water still running, she drank from her hand and tilted her head back to help ease the pill down her throat. She wiped the water from her chin. Ashamed of what she'd done, Christina turned off the light and quickly walked out of the bathroom.

She slid back under the covers, closed her eyes, and waited for the drug to take effect.

# Twenty-Four

Christina pushed the leftover meatloaf around her plate as she listened to the children talking excitedly about their day with Aunt Lucy and Uncle John. She nodded and pretended to listen but her head ached. She was exhausted, and although she'd slept most of the morning, her dreams were plagued with visions of the boy, the wicked woman, and the wolf. She woke up exhausted. Every inch of her body ached, and she couldn't put the images out of her mind even when she was awake.

Walking in a haze through the dark hall, Christina still felt the effects of the morphine and collapsed onto the chair behind the nurses' desk. She sighed as she checked her watch. It was one thirty. Leaning her head back, she closed her eyes. Everyone was on break. Monica, Michelle, and Amanda were probably down in the cafeteria, and Jenny was gone. She had no idea where Jenny disappeared to every night and really didn't care. Christina welcomed the chance to relax.

Not long after Christina closed her eyes, her heart began to race in her chest. The pulsating beat throbbed in her ears and her breathing became labored. The room spun and the floor warped under her feet. She opened her eyes and found herself in the dark forest surrounded by a pack of howling coyotes. Turning around frantically, she watched the wild animals circle.

She saw a young girl in a cotton nightgown crying as she clutched a rag doll. The girl tried to get away from the coyotes and scooted across the ground until she backed into a cottonwood. With her back to the tree, she held onto her doll and watched the coyotes barking menacingly. Christina stood protectively in front of the girl. Without taking her eyes away from the wild coyotes, she reached down and grabbed a stick.

The girl screamed. Christina didn't have a good grip on the stick and it slipped out of her hand as she turned to the girl. Following the girl's stare, Christina searched the darkness until she saw the silhouette of La Llorona and the black wolf. La Llorona's long white hair blew in the cool wind and although her face was masked in darkness, Christina didn't have to see her face to recognize her. La Llorona held up her hand and silenced the coyotes as she stepped out into moonlight.

The visions from last night raced through her when Christina saw La Llorona's hideous face and evil eyes. Christina tried to scream but no sound came from her tight throat. Seeing La Llorona, the girl cried for help as she stood and ran into the darkness. Laughing wickedly, La Llorona watched the girl trip and fall, and with the wave of her hand she commanded the coyotes to chase her. The girl got to her feet and ran farther into the forest as La Llorona slowly limped after her.

"Leave her alone!" Christina stepped in front of La Llorona but it was if she wasn't there. The wretched old woman walked by with the wolf at her side.

Christina followed La Llorona through the dark forest, keeping her distance until she saw the girl lying on the ground. The coyotes circled around the girl, nipping at her as she struggled to untangle her foot from a strand of barbed wire.

Christina ran toward the girl and yelled. An eerie cry echoed loudly through the forest.

The coyotes howled as La Llorona searched the darkness with her black eyes. Christina stepped back into the shadows to hide from La Llorona's piercing eyes.

Taking advantage of the distraction, the girl unraveled the wire from around her foot and ran. She dropped her doll and stopped to pick it up but when she saw La Llorona turn to her, she continued to run. La Llorona picked up the doll. Squeezing the toy tightly in her hands, she ripped the soft fabric as she fell to her knees and cried out as the cotton stuffing drifted around her.

Christina backed away from the crazed old woman and tripped over a tree stump. The wolf turned and growled. Christina grabbed her knee as the wolf crept toward her. She tried to stand up but the pain was too great and she fell back to the ground. The wolf crept closer. Unable to move, Christina huddled on the ground as she held her knee and closed her eyes. The cool wind swirled around her. She could hear the wolf's throaty growl get closer with each step.

Suddenly everything went silent. Christina opened her eyes and found herself on the cool tile floor next to the nurses' desk. Confused, Christina looked around for the woman and quickly got to her feet. Her left knee still hurt and blood trickled from the scrape. Christina searched the dark halls as she wiped the perspiration from her forehead. Her whole body trembled. Realizing she'd had another dream, Christina checked her watch and breathed a sigh of relief. It was one thirty-seven. She'd fallen asleep but only for a few minutes. With trembling hands she rummaged through the files on the desk in a futile attempt to calm herself. She shoved her hands into the pockets of her uniform and looked around as she slid open the top drawer in the nurses' desk. She took a single key from the drawer and quickly walked down the hall to a white door. She fumbled with the lock as she anxiously watched the elevator, and quickly slipped into the room. She walked through the dark room to the large cabinet against the wall and slid the glass door open. Studying the shelves lined with medication, she grabbed a bottle. Barely able to unscrew the lid with her trembling hands, she took two pills and shoved them into her pocket. She set the bottle back on the shelf, closed the cabinet, and stepped into the hall just as the elevator rang. Christina ran the short distance to the elevator and stopped when the door slid open and the three nurses stepped out into the hall.

"Are you ready for your break?" Michelle asked Christina.

"Yes," Christina stammered as she glanced nervously over her shoulder when the door to the medication room clicked shut. "I just need to get my purse from the desk." She walked ahead of the nurses to the desk and quickly put the key back in the drawer.

"What are you doing?" Jenny snapped as she stepped out of the shadows.

Christina turned to Jenny as she closed the drawer with her leg. "I'm getting my purse."

Jenny looked down at the drawer and the purse clutched in Christina's hand. "Get to work," she ordered the three nurses over her shoulder. "What were you doing in the top drawer?" Jenny walked up to Christina and stopped within inches of her face.

"I was getting my purse," Christina stammered.

Without taking her eyes off Christina, Jenny opened the drawer and took out the key. "Be back in ten minutes."

"Break is fifteen minutes."

"I said be back in ten."

Christina turned around, slid her hand into her pocket, and felt the comfort of the pills as she walked toward the elevator.

Christina stepped out of the hospital into the cool night. Looking around, she cautiously popped one of the pills into her mouth. She walked around the front of the building along the road and stopped on the bridge to look at the water rushing below. The river usually calmed her but tonight was different. Tonight the river made her uneasy as she searched for the young boy in her dreams. Her imagination transformed every submerged rock and fallen log into the boy's bloated and lifeless body. Forcing herself to look away from the river, she stared up at the moon.

Behind her, Christina heard a pack of howling coyotes. She turned around and searched the darkness around her. Images from her nightmares plagued her as she listened to the haunting howls moving up the river, making their way into the mountains. Christina ran to the hospital, desperate to get away from the ghostly memories triggered by their cries.

La Llorona stood up, bundles of cotton stuffing swirling around her feet as she searched the darkness. "Estefanita," she whispered, her voice deep and raspy, "it is time." She motioned to the black wolf and followed him through the thick forest to the wood shack.

Once inside, she gathered several jars from the shelf and set them on the table. She took out several dried leaves and a handful of powder and walked to the smoldering fire. A large owl swooped down over the fire and landed on the roof of the shack.

She sprinkled the leaves and powder over the fire. The leaves smoldered on the hot coals creating a thick blanket of smoke around her. Taking a deep breath she pulled the smoke over her face. She slowly exhaled and took another deep breath, filling her lungs with the thick smoke. Her whole body was engulfed in smoke. She fell to her knees as she coughed and gasped for air. With one last breath she collapsed and lay motionless.

Curious, the owl watched. La Llorona's sinister black spirit emerged from her body and mingled with the smoke. The owl flew down from the roof and landed next to the lifeless body. La Llorona's spirit waited for the owl to get closer before it invaded the unsuspecting animal. The owl flapped its wings, wildly struggling against the powerful force. No longer able to fight, the bird collapsed helplessly to the ground. The owl lay paralyzed for several seconds, its body twitched, and then it hopped to its feet. With its wings outstretched the owl flew out of the smoke.

Leaving her body behind, La Llorona's spirit soared through the air. The freedom was exhilarating. Flying high over a green meadow, La Llorona searched the pasture with her keen eyes and swooped down. With her claws extended she grabbed a field mouse and lifted the squirming animal off the ground. Flying up into the sky, she took great pleasure in the freedom the majestic bird provided her.

La Llorona flew toward the bright lights of the hospital and perched on a windowsill. Peering through a crease in the closed curtain, she watched Estefanita struggle against her restraints.

Christina carried a stack of files to the nurses' station. The pill had taken effect; she was calm and felt completely in control. Maybe this was how Jenny kept herself motivated through the long night. She laughed silently and wished she'd taken more than two pills. Next time she'd need to take a few more.

Christina's stomach fluttered and her breath stopped in her throat. She smiled at the exhilarating sensation but the elation turned to fear as she began having visions of flying through the darkness. Rubbing her eyes, she tried to stop the image. Her stomached flipped and turned with every swoop. Her heart raced as she leaned against the desk for support. Fighting the rising nausea, she closed her eyes until the sensation passed.

Christina opened her eyes and looked around. Making sure no one had seen her, she quickly walked down the hall to the bathroom. The color slowly came back into her cheeks as she regained her composure.

"Christina!" Jenny yelled from outside the locked door.

Christina stepped into the hall where Jenny waited impatiently.

"What's the matter with you?" Jenny looked down at her in disgust.

"My stomach was a little upset."

"The old lady needs her shot." Jenny held out the needle.

Taking the syringe, Christina walked down the hall as Jenny followed. Christina stood in the dark room as she had another vision. In flashes she saw a stark white room. A bed stood in the middle of the room with blankets pulled over a body. Christina recognized the room from the hospital and tried to focus on the person in the bed but the image faded. Confused, she waited for the vision to return. The vision had been different from the others. This one didn't bring with it the fear and anxiety she'd felt with the others.

She walked over to Estefanita's motionless body as the vision replayed in her mind. She felt uneasy as she looked around the room and recognized every detail from her vision. Panic rose in her throat as another image flashed and she saw herself in the room next to the bed. She watched in horror as she backed away from the bed. The realization that she was seeing herself from behind the closed curtain sent a cold chill through her spine and her mouth went dry.

Slowly she walked around the bed and crept toward the drapes. Trying to reassure herself the vision was a hallucination from the pill, she reached out with her trembling hand, pulled back the heavy curtain, and saw the owl perched on the windowsill.

Christina's eyes locked with the owl's. She couldn't move and she couldn't look away from the animal's gripping stare. The only sound she heard was her heart beating as the owl continued to stare into her soul. La Llorona looked over Christina's shoulder at Estefanita before she beat her wings against the window and disappeared into the darkness.

Christina let the curtain fall as she backed away from the window.

"She knows who you are," Estefanita whispered. Christina didn't answer as she turned to walk out of the room. "Don't forget the needle." Estefanita motioned to the syringe on the bed next to her arm.

Christina took the syringe off the blanket, raised it to her eyes, and studied the clear liquid as Estefanita watched nervously. Christina wished she could somehow save the potent sedative when she realized Estefanita was watching her and stuck the needle into the mattress before she turned to leave.

"You were chosen for your strength and courage. Do not give into your fears," Estefanita said.

Christina didn't answer as she walked out of the room. Handing the syringe to Jenny, Christina stepped around the large woman and walked in Roman's room. She was on edge and hoped Roman would be sleeping. Christina sighed when Roman sat up at the sound of the door opening.

"I'm just here to change the bedpan." Christina walked quickly across the room.

"What, no comment about Sarah?" Roman ignored Christina's foul mood.

"Nope." Christina hoped her short answer would end any further conversation.

"I'm surprised. Seems like everybody has an opinion about what I should do. My family, you the other night."

"And like I said, it's none of my business." Christina stepped into the bathroom.

"What brought about the change?" he asked, waiting for Christina to come back into the room.

"The change?" Christina asked. Her irritation was obvious.

"Your mood. You seem a little touchy." Roman remarked on Christina's casual indifference toward him.

"You're right, I am touchy," Christina answered as she slammed the bedpan back under the bed. "You're here because you want to be. The other people on this floor want to live but instead are slowly dying. You have someone who loves you and is willing to spend the rest of her life with you." Christina's voice shook with anger. "But I'm beginning to think maybe Sarah shouldn't waste her time with you. Not because of your legs, but because you expect everyone to feel sorry for you. Sarah loves you now but eventually she'll get tired of your pathetic game and move on, and when she does, you'll have a reason to pull the trigger." Christina leaned over and stared into Roman's eyes. "Either way, end the misery, Sarah's or yours. I don't give a damn whose—just stop wasting my time."

Roman swallowed the lump in his throat as he watched Christina walk out of the room.

# Twenty-Five

Christina worked the rest of her shift in a drug-induced daze. She completed each of her menial tasks until her shift was over. As she walked home the sun blinded her sensitive eyes and when she stepped into the kitchen the aroma of bacon and coffee upset her nervous stomach. Lucy sat alone at the kitchen table reading the *Santa Fe New Mexican* as she drank a cup of coffee. A plate with a half-eaten piece of toast sat on the table across from her, a sign John had spent the night. Lucy looked up worriedly as Christina walked into the kitchen.

"What's the matter?" Christina was on edge.

"They found a boy in the river just downstream from us." Lucy handed the paper to Christina. "I've let the kids play in the river without even thinking they could get hurt."

Christina looked at the photo and let out a gasp as she sat in the chair. Her heart pounded and the fear she'd felt was back as she remembered the image of the terrified young boy.

"Are you okay?" Lucy asked. Christina didn't answer as she stared at Johnny's smiling eyes in the photograph. "Jesus, Christy, why won't you answer me?"

Christina looked away from the newspaper. How could she tell Lucy about the dream without sounding like a lunatic?

"Christy?" Lucy nearly shouted.

"I'm sorry. It's just—I've seen this boy before." Christina moved John's plate and set the newspaper down on the table so she didn't have to see the young boy's smiling face.

"Where did you see him?"

"I need to go out for a few hours. Can you watch the kids for me?" Christina stood and walked to the door. Realizing she was still in her uniform, she turned and walked down the hall.

"Where are you going?" Lucy followed Christina into her room.

"You'll think I'm crazy if I tell you." Christina took off her uniform and changed into a cotton blouse and matching skirt.

"I already think you're crazy. Tell me what's going on."

Christina looked at Lucy. "I had a dream the other night. The boy was in my dream. He was scared and running."

"From you?"

"No, someone else was chasing him but I was there. I saw him. I saw her kill him. That boy's death wasn't an accident." Christina could see the concern and doubt on Lucy's face. "I knew I shouldn't have told you." She walked past Lucy into the hall.

"Hold on." Lucy grabbed Christina by the arm. "I didn't say I didn't believe you."

"You didn't have to." Christina pulled away from Lucy, mad at herself for thinking she'd understand.

"Wait." Lucy followed her to the front door. "Where are you going?"

"I'm going to the police."

"And what are you going to tell them? You had a dream about the boy? What do you think they are going to do when you tell them that?"

Christina hadn't thought about it. "I don't know and I don't care if they think I'm crazy. I've got to tell someone."

"You have told someone," Lucy reassured.

"Don't patronize me, Lucy," Christina said through clenched

teeth. "You didn't see the fear in that little boy's eyes. You didn't see him being carried into the river. I did and I couldn't live with myself if I didn't go to the police."

"Mommy?" Christina and Lucy both turned to Marie. "Are you okay?"

"I'm fine, sweetie." Christina wiped tears from her eyes. "Aunt Lucy is going to watch you for a few hours, okay?"

"What about our picnic? You promised to take us on a picnic today."

"I'm sorry, sweetie, but I can't today."

"But you promised," Marie whined.

"I said not today," Christina yelled. It was the first time she'd ever raised her voice in anger to one of her children.

Lucy walked over to Marie and put her arm around her shoulders. "Don't worry about the children. I'll take care of them."

Christina clenched her teeth as Lucy stepped in front of Marie protectively. "Go to the police and tell them what you saw and maybe if you get back before lunch, we can all go on a picnic."

Slamming the door behind her, Christina walked away.

Christina stared at the pudgy detective sitting across from her. She'd waited more than two hours for this interview and although the detective didn't look like someone she could confide in, she wanted the dreams to stop. She needed the police to catch the lunatic in her dreams and put an end to her nightmares.

Staring at Detective Winters's balding head, Christina clutched her purse against her chest. Detective Winters combed the thin gray hair over the top of his head, and when he spoke Christina noticed he was missing one of his front teeth. Christina glanced around the crowded room. Four men dressed the same as Detective Winters in short-sleeved dress shirts and ties worked in the cramped room. Six wood desks were crammed in the small office, each just as disorganized as the other. The untidy room looked as if it hadn't been cleaned in months. A coffeepot sat on one of the filing cabinets surrounded by used stirring sticks, spilled sugar, and unused coffee mugs. Although it was summer, winter jackets collected dust on the coat rack in the corner and cobwebs clung to the dead geranium on the windowsill.

Christina turned and impatiently watched Detective Winters search through the stack of papers for a notepad. "Here it is," the detective mumbled as he cleared a place on his desk to write. "Now, what is it you wanted to talk to me about?" He leaned back in his chair, put his hands behind his head, and studied the tired-looking woman.

"It's about the young boy in today's newspaper, the one who drowned." Christina's voice was soft as she sat at the edge of her seat.

"What about him?"

"I don't think his death was an accident. I mean I think he was killed."

"What makes you think that?" Detective Winters sat up to write on the notepad.

"I saw him the other night. I watched him die." Christina clutched her purse tighter against her chest as she looked around the room.

"Where did you see him?" Detective Winters leaned forward, suddenly interested.

Christina took a deep breath as she tried to find the words to explain. "I saw him in a dream," she whispered.

"A dream?" Annoyed, he dropped his pen on the notepad and leaned back in his chair.

"Yes." Christina looked down as she fidgeted with her leather purse strap.

"Look, I don't know what kind of game you're trying to pull here, Mrs. Dige—Dige—"

"Digerno, and it's not a joke."

"Then what do you call it?" he asked, irritated.

"I saw her kill him and last night I saw a young girl being chased by the same woman." Christina's voice broke, nearly in tears.

"What girl?"

"I don't know who she was. I just saw her running through the trees down by the river. She was being chased by a pack of coyotes and the same old woman."

"You saw all this and you didn't do anything to help her?"

Detective Winters leaned forward as he stared at Christina disapprovingly.

"I couldn't help her," Christina cried.

"Why not?" He questioned.

"She was in my dreams, but when I saw this morning's paper with the picture of the boy, I thought maybe she might be real, too." Christina wiped tears from her eyes.

Detective Winters looked over at the detective next to him. "Herb, is interview room two still empty?" The white-haired detective nodded. "Why don't you take Mrs. Digerno to the room where she can talk to us without any distractions." Detective Winters turned to Christina. "I need to get some paperwork and I'll be right with you."

Christina nodded as Herb walked over. "Follow me." The older man smiled kindly and escorted her out of the room.

Detective Winters waited until the door was closed when he stood and nearly shouted, "Is the Richards girl still here?"

"I think Mike is finishing the report now," one of the detectives answered as he poured a cup of coffee.

Detective Winters ran down the hall and opened the door as he knocked softly. "Mike?"

"Yeah?" Mike answered as he looked up from his notes. A scared young girl sat between her mother and father as she clung onto her mother's arm.

"Can I talk to you?" Detective Winters stuck his head into the room and smiled at the family watching him.

"Excuse me." Mike stood from the table and walked out into the hall. "What's going on?"

"You're not going to believe this, but I think your girl's attacker is in the next room." He was giddy from the excitement.

"What?" Mike asked in disbelief.

"This woman came in with some crazy story about the Jones boy being killed and then out of nowhere she started to ramble about your girl in there. She thinks she watched her being chased by a woman and a pack of coyotes."

"Where is she?"

"I've got her down the hall in interview room two. I'm on my way to get a statement from her now but it'd make my case easier if we could get a positive ID on her." It wasn't a case yet but it would be as soon as he was done.

"I'm on my way." Mike walked back into the room.

Detective Winters tugged on his belt and hiked up his pants. He whistled as he walked down the hall and smoothed his greasy hair over his head. Christina fidgeted. Across the room was a large mirror. She knew she'd been deliberately seated across from the mirror, and she tried hard not to stare at her ghostly reflection.

She watched Detective Winters shuffle through a stack of papers and knew he was stalling.

"So tell me, Miss—"

"Christina," she interrupted, tired of him butchering her name.

"Christina," he whispered as he wrote her name down at the top of the notepad. "Tell me, Christina, where exactly did you see this girl?"

"I already told you, I had a dream about her last night while I was at work."

"Where do you work?" He continued to write.

"I'm a nurse at St. Vincent's Hospital."

"How long have you been working there?"

"Less than a week."

"Could you describe the woman you saw chasing the girl?"

Christina leaned back in her chair and closed her eyes, wishing she could erase the image from her mind. "She had long white hair. She was wearing a white gown splashed with mud." She opened her eyes and looked up into the mirror.

"What did she look like?"

"She was thin, skinny. She didn't wear any shoes."

"Did you see her face?"

Christina stared into the mirror. She knew she was being watched and when she answered, she spoke directly to the mirror. "She was old. Her face was disfigured. You could see her black teeth and the muscles on her face." Christina looked away and shook her head.

"Excuse me for a moment." Detective Winters stood and

stepped out of the room. Mike was in the hall with the young girl and her parents. The girl's mother held her as the girl sobbed uncontrollably.

"Well, is it her?" Detective Winters asked eagerly.

Mike took Detective Winters by the arm and led him away from the family. "It's not her."

"Are you sure?"

"I'm positive. But she described the old woman the girl saw."

"Maybe she was there?" he asked hopefully.

"The only thing she saw was the old woman, the pack of coyotes, and a big black dog, like a wolf, but she didn't see anyone else."

"A wolf? We don't have wolves around here."

"I know that, you know that, and they know that," he said, motioning over his shoulder, "but that's what she saw."

"What about her?" Detective Winters pointed to the room.

"That's your baby. Do what you want." Mike shrugged.

"You said it yourself. She described the woman who chased your girl. She knows something," Detective Winters pressed.

"Even if she was there, my girl can't identify her or place her at the scene." Mike lowered his voice. "You heard what she said. She had a dream. I don't know about you but I'm not willing to stick my reputation on the line for a dream."

Detective Winters slumped and walked back into the room. Christina glared at him as he sat down. "Is there anything else you'd like to tell me?" he asked, only half interested.

"You don't believe me, do you?" Christina didn't wait for an answer. "I knew I shouldn't have come here!" She grabbed her purse and stood. "You're wasting my time. Am I free to leave or do I have to answer more of your ridiculous questions?"

Detective Winters shook his head as Christina stormed out of the room.

"What do you think?" Herb asked as he sat on the table.

"What do I think? I think she's crazy, that's what I think." He picked up the notepad and pen. "I wasted her time? Hell, no! She had a dream." He waved his hands mockingly around him. "She wasted my time on a fucking dream." He slammed the chair against the table and stormed out of the room.

Herb laughed, amused someone had gotten the best of the ego-driven Detective Winters.

# Twenty-Six

Tension filled the air as Christina and the children ate dinner in silence. Setting her fork down, Christina watched her children stare somberly into their plates.

"Will you stop moping? I said I was sorry." She tried not to sound angry but it was hard to hide the edge in her voice.

Marie looked up from her plate. "You promised you'd take us on a picnic."

"I know I did, and I promise I'll take you on one tomorrow, okay?" They all looked up at her.

"Promise?" Jessica asked.

"I promise. Now finish your dinner."

"Yeah, a picnic!" Mark Anthony yelled excitedly as he scooped a spoonful of peas into his mouth.

Christina replayed her meeting with Detective Winters and felt like a fool. The acid in her stomach burned and she dropped her fork onto her plate. She picked up her dirty plate and began to wash the dishes while the children finished eating.

"Get ready to take a bath," Christina ordered as she turned to wipe down the table and accidentally tripped over one of the kittens. "Damn it!" She kicked the kitten out from under her and sent it scooting across the floor.

"Mom!" Jessica yelled as the kitten meowed in pain. "You hurt him!" Jessica quickly picked up the kitten.

"Get those damn cats out of the kitchen and throw them outside!" Christina yelled as Marie and Mark Anthony chased their kittens around the kitchen.

"They can't go outside. They're too small," Marie pleaded as she and Mark Anthony stood next to Jessica. Tears streaked down Jessica's cheeks as she cried softly and stroked her kitten.

Christina glared down at the children. How dare they talk back to her? She took a step toward them.

"Please, Mom," Mark Anthony pleaded as he held his kitten in his arms. "They're just babies."

Her anger softened when she saw the fear in their eyes, the same fear she'd seen on the children's faces in her dreams. She wanted to reach out and hold them. She wanted to tell them she was sorry for getting angry but she stepped back to the sink and stuck her hand in the hot soapy water.

"Go take a bath and get ready for bed," she mumbled without looking up as the three children quickly ran down the hall with their kittens into their room.

La Llorona sat in the chair next to the table and slowly rocked back and forth. Her eyes fluttered as she mumbled with her arms outstretched. Wax from the burning candle dripped onto the table and the flame cast an orange glow against her pale skin.

A small mouse raced across the floor and stopped at her bare feet. Curiously, it circled around her before it scurried up onto the table. The mouse looked over at La Llorona. Standing on its hind legs, it sniffed the air cautiously before it darted over her arm.

La Llorona opened her eyes but continued her throaty chant, rocking as she watched the mouse. The mouse climbed freely over her arm down to her hand. After letting the mouse nibble on the rotted flesh, she grabbed the mouse and lifted the squirming animal.

She studied the mouse with her cold eyes and wrapped her fingers around its tail, dangling it out in front of her to watch it squirm.

Taking the mouse in her hand, she stroked its tiny head. She lifted the mouse to her cheek to feel the soft fur against her skin. Her black eyes rolled back as the chant resonated deep within her chest.

Trapped, the mouse fought and bit into the soft flesh of La Llorona's cheek. La Llorona tightened the grip around the mouse and held it out in front of her. She sneered as she watched the mouse fight for its life. Thrashing its head from side to side, it bared its tiny teeth and bit her thumb.

La Llorona screamed out in pain and squeezed harder. Feeling the animal snap, La Llorona watched the mouse loosen its teeth from her thumb before she dropped the twitching mouse onto the table next to the candle. She squeezed her thumb and let the blood drip into the burning flame. The blood sizzled on the hot wax and snuffed out the candle.

Without the candlelight, the shack was blanketed in darkness. La Llorona lifted the lifeless rodent off the table. She bit off its tiny head and warm blood oozed from the headless mouse onto her hand. Crushing the rodent's skull in her jaws, La Llorona relished every delicious bite. She sucked on the decapitated mouse, threw it on the floor, and laughed wickedly as she wiped the blood from the corners of her mouth.

Christina tossed and turned. Unable to sleep she looked over at the ticking clock on the nightstand. It was ten thirty-five. "My first night off and I can't sleep." Frustrated, Christina put the pillow over her head to muffle the ticking. After several seconds she threw the pillow onto the floor. Walking across the room, she stopped at the dresser. She stared down at her wedding picture and the intricately hand-carved jewelry box, the only mementoes she brought with her from Chicago.

Christina remembered the feel of Mark's arms as he held her close for the picture. Her mom gave her the jewelry box just before she died. The jewelry box had been a family heirloom handed down from mother to daughter for five generations. Gently lifting the lid,

Christina pulled back the red satin lining. Discreetly hidden in the lining was the pill she'd taken from the hospital. Holding the pill, she looked over at Mark's picture. His smiling eyes stared at her as if watching her every move. Looking away from the picture to her reflection in the mirror over the dresser, Christina felt shame rising in her cheeks.

"How dare you judge me?" She looked back at Mark's smiling face. "You left me alone to raise our children. I loved you and gave you three children but that wasn't good enough for you, was it?" Christina grabbed the picture and slammed it down on the dresser. Popping the pill into her mouth, she walked out of the room and into the bathroom. Turning on the water, she drank from her cupped hand. She felt a warm sense of ease wash over her. Walking back to the bedroom, she looked over at the picture. She ran her fingers over the metal frame and velvet backing.

Not bothering to pick up the picture, Christina walked back to bed. She turned off the light and slid under the soft quilted blanket. Staring up at the dark wood ceiling she relaxed and closed her eyes. Dulled images of the old woman and the black wolf played through her mind but she was numb to them now. Her eyes fluttered and she drifted into a troubled sleep.

A soft scratching and rustling on the wood ceiling pulled her from her sleep. She looked up at the wood planks over her bed and she got up. Turning on the lamp on the nightstand, Christina listened. Christina stood on the bed and peered cautiously into the corner of the ceiling. The muffled sound of scurrying footsteps sped over her. Christina stood on her tiptoes as the scratching grew louder. Sawdust and dirt fell from the hole. Putting one foot on the nightstand, Christina moved closer.

Christina muffled her scream with her hand when she saw the head of a mouse poke through the hole. The beady black eyes looked around as the mouse sniffed the air and fell from the crevice onto the floor with a soft thump. Panic swept over her as she watched the mouse scurry across the floor and disappear under her bed. She looked up at the hole as the scratching continued to grow louder and another mouse dropped to the floor. Christina watched in horror as mice fell from the ceiling around her. On the dresser the infestation of brown mice climbed over her wedding picture and jewelry box.

Her heart seemed to stop in her chest when she saw the blankets on the bed ripple. Kicking the blanket back with her foot, Christina screamed at the swarm of mice covering the bed. She climbed onto the iron headboard to get away from the rodents.

Christina looked up and to her dismay she saw mice running along the rounded vigas toward her, dropping down around her head. She screamed again as she shook her head to throw the entangled mice from her hair. Losing her balance, she slipped and fell off the headboard into the swarm of mice. Christina was paralyzed as she felt the tiny nails prick her skin when the rodents ran over her. She felt mice run along her flesh under her nightgown and over her face. Tiny teeth nipped at her skin and tore her clothes.

Slipping further into a state of shock, Christina screamed as the door swung open and the light turned on.

"Get away!" Christina yelled at Jessica and Marie as she thrashed around wildly on the bed.

"What's wrong, Mommy?" Marie asked.

Christina stopped. She flung the sheets off and stared at the empty bed in disbelief. Jumping to her feet, she stood on the bed and looked up at the ceiling. The hole was gone. Searching the room, Christina let out a small gasp.

"Come on, let's go." Christina jumped off the bed and pushed the two girls out of the room. With one last look behind her, Christina quickly closed the door.

"What's the matter?" Jessica asked as they walked sleepily back to their room.

"Nothing. I just had a nightmare, that's all. Now let's get you back to bed." Her hands shook uncontrollably as she pulled the covers over them.

"Do you want to sleep with us?" Jessica asked.

Christina looked over her shoulder and knew she couldn't go back to her own bed tonight. "I'd like that." Christina scooted Mark Anthony over as Jessica and Marie slid over to make room for her. Lying on her side and still shaking, Christina closed her eyes.

Perched at the edge of the mountain, La Llorona listened to the festivities on the plaza. "Fiestas," she whispered as she followed the sounds of merriment. La Llorona stood behind Zozobra, the tall white marionette with large sunken green eyes, red painted hair, and bulging red lips. His long arms moved up and down as his head turned from side to side with the aid of men manipulating the wires attached to the puppet. La Llorona watched the traditional dancers dressed in long white robes gather below her, and she slowly made her way down the hill. Unseen, La Llorona grabbed a robe lying on the ground and swiftly put on the ceremonial dress. Looking up at Zozobra, La Llorona listened to his deep throaty moan and felt the pain of her own life. The loss and loneliness she'd endured long ago haunted her soul and drove her to destroy all that was in her path. Following the procession of dancers, La Llorona walked toward the front of Zozobra and the crowd of spectators cheered. She turned and raised her hands in triumph. With her simple gesture the revelers screamed with joy and chanted.

"Burn him! Burn him! Burn him!"

Behind La Llorona, a tall man dressed in a red costume and headdress ran by and began to dance energetically in front of Zozobra. The marionette moved and his groans grew louder as the performer danced at his feet with a flaming torch. La Llorona watched with pleasure as smoke surrounded Zozobra, and in a fiery display of power, the dancer torched a fuse that ignited a thunder of fireworks. Burning sulfur filled the air as the crowd screamed with satisfaction as Zozobra's hair caught fire. Still moving, the puppet moaned as flames engulfed him and the spectators cheered.

Feeling the power of the symbolism, La Llorona threw her robe into the fire and, with her arms open, she welcomed the intense heat to burn her flesh. The dancer dressed in red threw his arms up once more before he disappeared into the thick smoke. Seeing La Llorona's naked, scarred body, he stepped back and gasped. He coughed on the thick smoke as he watched La Llorona step into the flames. The dancer watched as a ball of fire shot out of the flames and flew out across the night sky.

# *Twenty-Seven*

Christina woke up alone. The sun shone brightly into the room and she could hear the children and Lucy talking in the kitchen. She got out of bed and walked down the hall into the kitchen. Ignoring Lucy's gasp, she poured herself a cup of coffee.

"Good morning," Christina snapped as Lucy and the children stared at her. She knew they were just as appalled by her appearance as she was. "What, no Johnny for breakfast this morning?" She looked smugly around the kitchen. "Don't tell me you've already lost your charm."

"Good morning to you, too," Lucy answered sharply. "Not that it's any of your business, but John had to go in early today. I hear you had an interesting night."

Christina glared over her coffee cup at Jessica and Marie as they both looked down at their cereal. "I had a bad dream, that's all." She tried to swallow the knot in her throat.

"A dream. Was that all it was?" Lucy may have been upset with Christina but she still loved her and she was worried about her best friend.

"Of course. What else could it have been?" Christina gripped the cup of coffee to hide her trembling hands.

"I don't know. It seems these past few nights there's been something more to your dreams."

"It was just a dream." Christina lowered her voice to a whisper.

"The children tell me you're taking them on a picnic today." Lucy spoke lightly to change the subject and break the tension.

"Yeah, we're going to the river." Christina took a sip from her coffee trying to ignore the way Jessica and Marie looked at her.

"Sounds like fun. Mind if I come?"

Christina was about to tell her she wanted to spend some time alone with the children when Mark Anthony spoke up.

"Yeah, come with us!" He was excited by the idea of a big picnic with his mom and new aunt.

"Can she, Mom?" Marie quickly added.

"You don't have anything more important to do?" Christina asked hopefully.

"Nope."

"Suit yourself." Christina shrugged as she dumped her coffee into the sink. "You can come if you want."

"Great." Lucy stood from the table and walked over to the refrigerator. "By the way, this came in the mail for you." Lucy tossed the letter onto the kitchen counter. "What do you kids want for lunch?"

Christina watched the letter slide toward her and immediately recognized Simon's writing. Grabbing the letter, Christina watched Jessica and Marie standing next to Lucy. Anger and jealously seeped through her veins. Crumpling the letter in her fist, Christina turned and walked out of the room.

Christina sat on a wool blanket in the shade of a cottonwood. Mark Anthony poured water into a hole in the sand as Jessica and Marie walked along the edge of the river, occasionally stopping to pick up a colorful rock and Lucy sat with her feet in the water.

Christina had purposefully secluded herself from Lucy and the children. She was tired and although she'd never admit it to Lucy, she was glad she came. The children seemed to be overly demanding these past few days and she didn't have the patience or the energy to deal with them. She leaned her head back, closed her eyes, and listened to the sound of rustling leaves and trickling water. The sounds reminded her of her nightmares and she quickly opened her eyes. Christina watched Lucy and the children splash and run along the edge of the river. She was envious—a part of her wanted to go to her children but something made her stay away.

Filled with jealously and resentment, Christina watched her children play with Lucy. She tried to fight her growing anger until she couldn't take it any longer and walked over. She stood on the riverbank and watched them playfully splash each other.

With her eyes closed, Jessica splashed water at Lucy and Marie. Not seeing her mother beside her, in her excitement, she splashed Christina. Lucy and Marie stopped when they saw muddy water dripping off Christina's face and hair. Jessica opened her eyes when she realized the game had stopped and turned to her mother.

"I—I didn't see you," Jessica stammered fearfully as she stepped away.

"It's okay. You were just playing." Christina wiped the muddy water from her face and forced a smile.

"Come on, you two. We'd better dry off." Lucy smiled uncomfortably as she walked out of the water.

"I don't want to get out of the water," Marie whined.

"It's almost time for us to go," Lucy answered.

"It's okay, I'll stay with you," Christina smiled as Marie looked apprehensively at her before she turned to Lucy.

"Is it okay?" she asked Lucy.

"Don't ask her." Christina narrowed her eyes and pointed at Lucy. "I'm your mother, not her." She turned to Lucy. "I didn't mean that the way it sounded. It's just that she doesn't need to ask you for permission." Lucy nodded, accepting Christina's apology. "If you want to play for a little while longer I'll watch you." Christina turned to Marie and smiled.

"Okay," Marie whispered.

Lucy took Mark Anthony and Jessica by the hand and walked them over to the blanket. She wrapped towels around the wet children.

Christina sat on the sand and watched Marie play in the water.

Marie wandered out into the river until the water reached her knees and then turned back toward the bank. Christina watched her and knew she wanted to venture farther into the water but was afraid.

"Do you want to learn how to swim?" Christina stepped into the water as Marie looked at her and nodded. "Do you want me to teach you?" Again Marie nodded. Christina reached out and this time Marie didn't hesitate as she grabbed her mother's hand. Ignoring the water washing around her, Christina walked deeper into the river. She turned to face Marie. Taking her other hand, she led her farther into the water until the water ran around Marie's small chest up to her neck. "Don't worry, I won't let anything happen to you," Christina reassured Marie.

Marie bobbed up and down trying to keep her head above the water as Christina led her into deeper water. Marie panicked and began to cry as water splashed over her face and into her mouth.

"Don't be afraid," Christina urged, pulling her farther into the river.

"No, Mom, please," Marie pleaded as she tried to turn around. Loosening her grip on Marie's hand, Christina let go. "Mom, help!" Marie reached out as she tried to keep her head above the water and splashed frantically. Christina didn't move as she watched Marie disappear into the rushing river.

"Marie!" Lucy yelled as she dived into the river. Christina watched Lucy come up for air and disappear to search for Marie.

Christina slowly backed out of the water as she searched for Marie and Lucy. "Oh, my God, what have I done?" she whispered.

Lucy gasped for air as she held Marie. Christina ran into the water to take Marie's lifeless body but quickly stepped back when Lucy glared at her as she walked by and laid Marie down on the sand.

Putting her ear to Marie's chest, Lucy listened for a heartbeat and checked for breathing. "She's not breathing." Lucy straddled Marie's small body and pushed on her chest.

Tears rolled down Jessica's cheeks as she held onto Mark Anthony. "Don't let her die, Auntie," she pleaded.

"She's not going to die," Lucy reassured as she pushed on Marie's chest again. "Come on, sweetie, breathe." She pushed harder and faster until water poured out of Marie's mouth. Marie coughed and began to cry. "You're okay, you're okay." Lucy held Marie in her arms as she rocked her back and forth and stroked her face. "I've got you. Don't worry, you're okay," she reassured.

Christina knelt next to Marie with her arms out. "Come here, Marie, let me hold you." Marie looked at her mother fearfully as she clung to Lucy.

"Leave her alone," Lucy growled.

"What do you mean, 'leave her alone'? What's the matter with you?" She looked at Marie. "You don't think I did this on purpose, do you?" Marie didn't answer as she buried her face in Lucy's neck. "I was teaching her how to swim." Christina looked at Lucy. "This wasn't my fault."

"She nearly drowned and you just stood there."

"I didn't know what to do," Christina cried.

"I don't know what the hell has gotten into you but it had better stop or I'll take them away from you."

"They're mine!" Christina yelled. "You can't take them away from me!"

"I can and I will if you don't get your shit together."

"What's that supposed to mean?"

"You're making yourself crazy and I won't let you hurt them!"

"I'm not crazy!" Christina yelled and looked over at Jessica and Mark Anthony. She closed her eyes and whispered. "I can't explain what's happening to me but I know I'm not crazy."

"You need help, Christy." Lucy's voice softened. "I want to help you but you've got to let me know what's going on."

Christina looked up at Lucy and narrowed her eyes. "Quit trying to read into something that's not there. Nothing's wrong."

Lucy sighed as she helped Marie to her feet. "Come on, we'd better get going."

Christina closed her eyes as Lucy and the children walked by.

Christina sat on the back porch swing, still shaken from what happened, and watched the children playing with their kittens. They sat quietly together and occasionally looked over at her watching them. The screen door creaked open and Lucy, dressed for work, walked out onto the porch.

"I have to go to work." Lucy didn't look at Christina as she watched the children. "I want to think what happened today was an accident, but I would be lying if I didn't tell you I'm scared because I see my best friend turning into someone I hardly recognize. I'm scared for them. You're their mother and they love you and I wouldn't just take them from you." She turned to Christina staring at her hands folded in her lap. "But I won't sit idly by and watch you destroy yourself and those children. I'll be home at eleven—sooner if I can find someone to cover for me." Not waiting for an answer, Lucy stepped off the porch and walked over to the children.

Christina watched as the children huddled around Lucy. It was obvious they didn't want her to leave. Christina stood from the swing and walked inside, slamming the screen door behind her.

# Twenty-Eight

L a Llorona woke to the sound of rain and looked at the puddles on the floor around her. She got up from the tattered mattress and looked out the window into the forest. Dusk settled early in the forest as rain poured down on the dry ponderosas, causing the branches to droop and sway in the howling wind. La Llorona lit a candle and walked over to the shelf on the wall. Not finding what she was looking for, she strained to see in the dark room. Searching through a pile of torn blankets, her search became more frantic as mice scurried from the corner and dust filled the air. La Llorona searched blindly until she felt a searing pain rip through her hand. Quickly pulling her hand back, she watched blood drip down her hand from a deep wound. She saw a broken jar on the floor and carefully picked it up.

La Llorona set the jar on the table, carefully stuck her hand inside, and took out a coiled dead snake. La Llorona laid the snake on the table and sat in the chair. Her eyes rolled back and she swung her head from side to side. She moaned deeply as she caressed the snake with her long white hair. After a moment La Llorona started to chant.

"*Víbora, víbora saca la lengua. Víbora, víbora saca la lengua.*" She repeated the chant as she slammed her fist down on the dried snake, breaking it into small pieces. She took several pieces of the dried snake into her palm, lifted them to her mouth, and breathed on them. Slapping her hands together, she crumbled the snake and blew the dusty particles into the flickering candle.

"*Víbora, víbora saca la lengua. Víbora, víbora saca la lengua.*"

As she blew on the pieces again they began to move. Filled with life, black snakes grew until the table was covered in a nest of slithering snakes. Grabbing the fattest snake, La Llorona lifted it to her face. She mimicked the snake's flickering tongue and stuck out her own blackened tongue.

Christina opened the door and walked into the children's room. She sat on the edge of the bed and gently caressed Marie's cheek as she looked lovingly down at her children. Tears welled up in her eyes and rolled down her cheeks. "Oh God," she whispered. "What's happening to me?" She wiped her eyes as she leaned over and kissed the children before she left the room.

She leaned against the door and looked up at the light bulb in the hall. With Lucy gone, the house felt cold and empty. She rubbed her arms to take away the chill as she stepped into the bathroom.

Locking the door behind her, she opened the medicine cabinet and searched for Lucy's bottle of pills. The place where it had been was bare and her search became more frantic when she realized the pills were gone. Infuriated, Christina knocked the aspirin out of the cabinet, scattering white tablets across the floor.

"Son of a bitch!" she yelled. Her hands trembled as she picked up the aspirin. Losing her patience, Christina put the cap on the bottle and set it back on the shelf, not caring that most of the aspirin remained scattered on the floor. She checked the shelves in the medicine cabinet again and slumped down on the toilet lid. "The bitch threw them away." Christina rubbed the sides of her head, trying to control her anxiety. She turned on the water to fill the porcelain bathtub.

She tossed her blouse on the floor and accidentally knocked over the wastebasket. Christina watched the brown bottle roll noisily across the floor and stop under the sink. She picked up the bottle and held it to her chest as a reassuring calm washed over her. Opening the bottle, she poured two pills into her palm. Normally she'd only take one but tonight she needed two. Tonight she needed to sleep without dreaming. Popping both pills into her mouth and not bothering to swallow them with water, she stuck the bottle into the pocket of her bathrobe. Easing into the hot water, she closed her eyes and rested her head against the tub. Water continued to pour from the spout and slowly rose around her neck.

Opening her eyes and not wanting to move, Christina extended her leg and turned off the water with her foot. Holding her breath, she slipped under the water for several seconds before she came up and pushed her long red hair from her face. Leaning back, she closed her eyes and listened to the slow rhythmic drip of water in the quiet room. She felt foolish for crying over what happened with Marie. There was nothing wrong with her—she knew that now—and it wasn't her fault Marie swallowed a little water. Lucy just panicked. Marie had been doing fine on her own. How else was she going to learn how to swim? Lucy had just blown things out of proportion like she always did. She didn't have a problem. Lucy was the one with the problem. Lucy had always been jealous of Christina and this was just her way of drawing attention to herself. Christina relaxed as she leaned farther down into the water.

High from the pills, Christina didn't notice the faucet gurgle and the drip stop as a black snake slithered out of the spout. With half of its body out of the faucet the snake stopped, flicked its tongue, and looked around before it slipped quietly into the water. The snake skimmed around Christina's leg as another snake dropped from the faucet and another immediately took its place.

Christina moved her leg as the snakes swam around her shoulders and behind her neck. She groggily opened her eyes and saw the water ripple. Christina noticed something fall from the waterspout and quickly sat up. Rubbing her eyes, she saw the black snakes skimming across the water.

Screaming, Christina tried to stand but she lost her footing on the slippery tub and fell back into the water. Gasping for air, she tried to stand again as the snakes attacked.

Christina thrashed in the tub as she tried to fight off the attack. Blood dripped from the bites on her arms and legs. Christina pulled herself out of the water and stood but she was weakened from the poison. Using the wall for support, she steadied herself and put one leg on the floor. Feeling something under her foot, she looked down. The floor was covered with black snakes. Unable to move, Christina looked frantically around the room. Snakes slithered out from under the radiator and the sink was filled with an entwined black mass. Snakes continued to drop out of the waterspout and fill the room. Christina screamed as snakes struck and bit her legs, tearing her flesh. The attack was relentless. She looked at her bloody hands, down to her tortured body, and screamed.

The bathroom door slammed against the toilet. John stopped in the doorway as Lucy ran past him, grabbed the robe, and covered Christina.

"Help me!" Christina cried as Lucy draped the robe over her body and looked around the room. "No, not again," she whispered as she looked frantically from the sink to the floor heater to her wet hands. She gasped. The snakes were gone. Blood rushed from Christina's head and she collapsed. John quickly lifted her.

"Let's get her to bed." Lucy led John out of the bathroom into the hall as Marie and Jessica stood in the doorway watching their mother being carried into her room.

"Is Mommy okay?" Jessica asked as she watched John lay Christina on the bed.

"Your mom is going to be fine, sweetie. Now, why don't you go back to sleep?" Lucy led them back into the room and closed the door behind her.

"What's the matter with Mom?" Marie asked as she climbed into bed next to Mark Anthony.

"I don't know, but I'm sure she'll be fine in the morning," Lucy reassured.

"Why was she screaming?" Jessica asked as Lucy pulled the covers over her. "Was she having another nightmare?"

"I don't know, but I don't want you to worry. John and I are going to take care of her, okay?" The two girls nodded. "I'll see you in the morning." She leaned over and kissed them on the forehead before she turned off the light.

John waited for Lucy in the hall. "How is she?" Lucy whispered as she looked over at Christina asleep on the bed.

"These fell out of her robe." John put the bottle in Lucy's hand. "Where did she get them?"

"They're mine." Lucy turned the bottle and read the label.

"I know that, but what is she doing with them?" His eyes narrowed. "And why are you taking pills?"

"I'm not taking pills," Lucy defended. "In case you didn't notice, this prescription is over a year old. I didn't take them then and I don't take them now. As a matter of fact, I cleaned out the medicine cabinet today and threw them away."

"I don't know how many she took but she's pretty out of it. I don't think it would be a good idea for her to be alone."

"I'll stay with her," Lucy agreed.

"I didn't mean to imply anything." John reached out to her.

"Yes, you did." Lucy ignored his apology. "I would like to think you knew me better that."

"I do know you but I know how easy it is for us to get this stuff and I know how it can mess people up."

"I know."

"Then you'd better tell your friend in there, because if she keeps it up, it'll only be a matter of time before it takes hold of her." John took Lucy in his arms. "I'm sorry. Do you forgive me?" He smiled as Lucy nodded. "Good, now I'd better get going. Call me if you need me." He kissed her and walked away.

Lucy waited in the hall until she heard the front door close, and then she walked into Christina's bedroom. Christina lay on the bed still wet and in her bathrobe. Lucy took a nightgown out of the dresser. As she closed the drawer, Lucy looked down at the back of the picture frame and picked it up. She ran her fingers over the pictures, from the happy couple on their wedding day to the picture of Mark in his military uniform. "Help me, Mark," she whispered. "Help me help her." Lucy set the picture back on the dresser facing the room.

# Twenty-Nine

Christina opened her eyes and looked around the room. Lucy was asleep in a chair next to the bed. Christina looked down at her nightgown and rubbed her throbbing head. *How did I get here?*

"How do you feel?" Lucy asked as she walked over and sat at the edge of the bed.

"What happened? How did I get here?"

"John carried you to bed."

"What?" Christina pulled the blanket protectively around her.

"I dressed you. He just brought you here," Lucy reassured.

Christina looked over at the wedding picture on the dresser and quickly looked away from Mark's knowing stare.

"What happened last night?" Lucy looked over her shoulder at the picture.

"I don't know." Christina looked at her hands.

"Was it another dream?" Lucy moved the hair away from Christina's face.

"No," she mumbled.

"What was it then?" Lucy waited. "I found these in your robe." She held out the bottle of pills. "How long have you been taking them?"

"I knocked over the wastebasket. The bottle fell out and I put them in my robe. I was going to throw them away today." She fiddled with the satin lace on her nightgown to avoid Lucy's eyes.

"Christy, I wish you'd let me help you."

"I'm fine," she whispered.

"You're not fine." Lucy took a deep breath. "I don't want to sit here and lecture you about what's right and wrong."

"Then why are you?" Christina interrupted.

"Because I want to help you."

"You keep saying you want to help me. Well, you can start by leaving me alone. There is nothing wrong with me."

Lucy narrowed her eyes. "Take a good look in the mirror, Christina, and tell me nothing's wrong with you. You look like hell, you're losing your mind, and you refuse to let anyone help you."

Christina looked up at her wedding picture. Her face was vibrant and radiated with joy, her long red hair was shiny and full, and her green eyes sparkled. She looked from the picture to the reflection in the mirror over the dresser. Her hair was dull and limp with streaks of gray, her green eyes were lost in dark circles, and her complexion was gray. She hated the way she looked. "I'm just tired, that's all."

"You're not just tired. Something else is going on with you. Does it have anything to do with those dreams you've been having?"

"They're not dreams, they're—" She knew Lucy wouldn't understand.

"They're what?" Lucy urged.

"Nothing."

"Why won't you talk to me?" Lucy pleaded.

Christina wanted desperately to tell Lucy about her visions and the nightmares, but how could she explain to Lucy what she couldn't understand herself?

"You're shutting out everyone who cares about you. You can't blame what's happened in your life on Mark anymore." Christina stared up at Lucy with hate. "Don't look at me like that." Lucy narrowed her eyes. "I can understand you not wanting to get involved with Simon, but you should at least give him the courtesy of opening his letters."

"What are you talking about?" Christina hissed.

"I found his last letter to you unopened in the trash can in the bathroom. If you don't want anything to do with him, tell him, but don't string him along like some puppy."

"You had no right to read that letter!"

"I didn't read it," Lucy answered sharply. "I said I found it."

"You think you know everything," Christina growled. "But you don't know anything. You can't even tell when a man lies to you about being married. What gives you the right to tell me about leading men on?"

"Don't say things you can't take back, and don't make me regret bringing you here." Lucy heard the children in the next room and stood up. "I'll take care of the children. Why don't you get some rest?"

Christina lay back in bed and rolled over. "Thank you," she whispered with her back turned.

Lucy closed the door behind her and walked into the hall where the children waited anxiously.

"Is Mom still sleeping?" Marie asked worried about her mother.

"Yes." Lucy reached down, picked up Mark Anthony, and walked down the hall into the kitchen.

"Is she okay?" Jessica asked as she followed.

"She's fine. She just needs her rest, that's all." Lucy sat Mark Anthony on a chair and walked around the table.

"I wish Daddy was still alive," Jessica whispered. "He'd know how to take care of Mommy."

"I know, sweetie." Lucy reached down and wiped the tears from Jessica's cheek. "But I know a place where we can go to ask for his help."

"Where?" Jessica looked up at Lucy.

"Church."

"Church?"

"Today is Sunday and we can ask your dad for his help in church." Lucy put a pot of coffee on the stove.

"But you don't go to church, Aunt Lucy," Marie pointed out.

"My mom always told me going to church never hurt anyone but the devil and I think your mom needs our prayers right now.

So we'll go and ask for God's help." Jessica and Marie looked at each other with a puzzled look. "Cut it out, you two." Lucy laughed. "You're making me feel like a heathen."

"What's a heathen?" Marie asked.

"Someone who doesn't go to church."

"But you don't go to church. You said it makes you uncomfortable to be around all those saints," Jessica added.

"Well, I used to go to church." Lucy laughed as she put bacon into a hot pan. Jessica and Marie looked at each other, shrugged, and giggled.

Christina lay in bed most of the morning. Unable to sleep, she stared up at the water-stained plank ceiling listening to Lucy and the children in the kitchen. Lucy came in to check on her before they left but she pretended to be asleep. She didn't feel like talking anymore. She wanted to be alone. Christina nearly went mad with the incessant rhythmic tick of the clock and forced herself out of bed. Christina walked down the hall staring timidly at the bathroom door. Her breath caught in her chest at the memory of last night's attack. The razor-sharp teeth ripping into her skin and the poison burning through her veins sent a shiver down her spine. She swallowed back the bitter taste of bile and knew the pain she felt last night had been real. She stared helplessly at the door, expecting black snakes to slither out to attack her at any moment. She ran to the kitchen.

Leaning her head over the kitchen sink, Christina took a deep breath. The wave of nausea slowly passed as she closed her eyes. With trembling hands, Christina poured herself a cup of cold coffee. Sitting at the table, she looked out the window and watched Lucy and the children walk down the drive. Her eyes narrowed with envy. Lucy and the children walked hand in hand, laughing and talking as they stepped into the house.

"Hi." Christina forced a smile.

"Mommy!" Mark Anthony ran to her with his arms open while Jessica and Marie stood in the doorway behind Lucy. "We went to church." He jumped on his mother's lap not noticing his mother's indifference.

"Church?" Christina pushed Mark Anthony off her lap as she looked at Lucy. "What did you pray for?"

"Come on, kids, let's get you out of your good clothes." Lucy quickly ushered the children out of the kitchen.

Christina waited for the children to close the door to their room before she turned to Lucy. "You took them to church?"

"Yes," Lucy answered lightly as she walked to the refrigerator.

"I've never known you to put your faith in God," Christina mocked, knowing her simple act of faith was a waste of time.

"I've never had the occasion until now," Lucy retorted. "I made a casserole for dinner tonight and I asked Mrs. Sanchez to keep an eye on the children."

"Why would you do that?"

"Because you need to rest." Lucy closed the refrigerator and set the glass casserole dish into the oven. "I'll talk to Jenny after my shift tonight and let her know you won't be coming in."

"What? You can't do that!" Christina stood, nearly knocking over her chair.

"Do what?" Lucy asked calmly, knowing the best place for Christina to work things out in her head was at home.

"There's nothing wrong with me and I will be going to work tonight." Christina was infuriated. How dare Lucy treat her like a child?

"Look, if they're shorthanded I'll find someone to take your shift, but you should stay home tonight and rest."

"No!" Christina slammed her cup down and splashed coffee on the table.

"Why not?" Lucy lowered her voice and turned to face Christina.

"Because nothing is wrong with me, that's why!"

"The hell nothing's wrong with you! Take a good look at yourself!" Lucy softened her voice with concern. "I'm worried about you, Christy. Please, just stay home tonight and rest."

"No." Christina narrowed her eyes. "And quit lecturing me. I don't need you or anyone else telling me what to do."

"Fine, go to work, but Dolores will be in to check on the kids."

"I don't need her to—"

"She'll be here." Lucy didn't wait for Christina to answer as she walked out of the kitchen into her room, slamming the door behind her.

# Thirty

Christina walked down the long dark hallway and stopped at the door to the medication room. She glanced around the empty hall before she checked the knob. *Damn it,* she thought. But she knew Jenny wouldn't be as careless as to forget to lock the door. She would have to wait before she could sneak the key out of the drawer again. Christina turned to the sound of voices and footsteps coming down the hall and quickly slipped into the adjoining room. At the sound of the door closing, a frail old man turned to Christina.

"Good evening, señorita." The old man smiled a wide, toothless grin.

"Hello, Mr. Romero. How was your weekend?" Christina forced herself to be cordial as her mind raced with anticipation and she reached under the bed.

"When can I go home?" the old man pleaded.

Christina looked down into his sad eyes. He'd been a patient since she started working and every night he'd asked her the same question and every night she'd given him the same answer. "Soon."

"My crops need tending. I need to get back to work," he begged.

Michelle had told her Mr. Romero was a widower. He had been out working in his fields when he fell and broke his hip. Unable to move and hidden in the tall alfalfa, he had waited hours before anyone found him. The neighbor in the next field heard his cries for help and saved him from what would have surely been a painful night.

"I thought your children were taking care of your crops." Christina took out the heavy pan and walked into the bathroom.

"Ugh!" He threw his arms up in disgust. "If I know them, the alfalfa is wilting under the sun." Christina flushed the toilet, walked back into the room, and put the bedpan back under the bed. "My wife visited me last night," he whispered as he timidly looked around the room. Christina looked into his eyes as she slid the metal pan back under the bed. "Don't look at me like that. I'm not crazy. I know my wife is dead, but she came to me this weekend." He swallowed the lump in his throat, leaned closer to Christina, and whispered, "She didn't say anything. She just stood next to the bed as plain as you're standing next to me."

"What did she do?" Christina smiled, knowing some patients, while in a delusional state, would imagine dead relatives visiting them. She'd been taught to be sympathetic and understanding, no matter how bizarre the story.

"She didn't do nothing. She just stood there. It scared the hell out of me."

Christina smiled. "I'm sure she just wanted you to know her spirit was still with you."

"That's worse. The priest said 'til death do you part. He didn't say anything about after that."

Christina thought he was joking until she saw the fear in his eyes. "Well, I'm sure she didn't mean to scare you."

"You don't know my wife." He pulled the thin blanket up to his chin as if he were suddenly cold in the hot room. "She was a bruja and I'm not just saying that. She really was a witch."

"Is there anything else I can get for you?" Christina asked. The old man shook his head and wrapped the blanket tighter around him. "Call if you need anything," she said and walked out of the room. She didn't have time to listen to the old man's ramblings about his dead wife and wilting fields. She needed to get back to work. It was almost time for her break.

"The old lady needs her shot," Jenny snapped when Christina walked out of the room.

Christina cringed at the sound of Jenny's harsh voice. Without looking at Jenny, she took the syringe, turned, and walked down the hall. With Jenny one step behind her, she stepped into Estefanita's room without looking back, leaving Jenny in the hall. "Get her to eat," Jenny ordered impatiently as the door closed.

The smell of stale urine in the stuffy room hit Christina like a brick. She stepped into the room. Disgusted, Christina ran across the room and opened the window. Closing her eyes, Estefanita took a deep breath and welcomed the cool air rushing over her.

"When was the last time anyone was here to check on you?" Christina walked around the bed to take the spoiled bowl of oatmeal and flushed it down the toilet.

"No one knows I'm here except you," Estefanita whispered through her dry throat.

Christina filled a pitcher with water and walked back into the room. "No one's been here in two days?" Estefanita nodded anxiously as she watched Christina pour a glass of water. The thought of no one attending the old woman while she was gone infuriated Christina. She lifted Estefanita's frail head off the pillow and held the glass to her lips. Water spilled out of her mouth onto her chest. "Slow down," Christina urged, but Estefanita ignored her and forced the water down her parched throat.

Christina emptied the last of the water into the glass. "No more," Estefanita whispered as she leaned her head back against the pillow and closed her eyes.

"I brought you a sandwich." Estefanita lifted her head off the bed as Christina put the sandwich to her mouth and took a bite of the savory meatloaf sandwich. Christina took the bedpan and walked into the bathroom.

"I'm sorry," Estefanita said as she watched Christina walk out of the bathroom and slip the pan back under the bed.

"Don't be sorry." Christina smiled. "It's my job."

"That's not what I'm talking about." Estefanita shook her head. "You've seen the evil. You've felt her anger and I was wrong to pass my troubles to you. You're having difficulty dealing with the gift I've given you and she can sense your weakness. She's feeding off your fears and will do everything in her power to destroy you." Christina stared at Estefanita in disbelief. "I know you don't believe me but I'm telling you the truth." Estefanita lifted her wrists to Christina. "Let me go. I can stop her. I am the only one who can stop the evil."

"I can't," Christina whispered apologetically.

"You must," Estefanita begged.

Christina took the dinner tray from the end table. "I'm sorry, but I can't," she said and walked out of the room.

"What took you so long?" Jenny snapped.

Christina had forgotten Jenny had been waiting, "I was feeding her and changing the bedpan."

"You got her to eat?" Jenny studied the empty bowl.

"Yes, she was starving. It was as if she hadn't eaten in days," Christina answered sarcastically.

"Did you give her the shot?" Jenny searched the dinner tray from the syringe.

"Yes—I, uh, left it in the room."

"Go get it," Jenny growled as she grabbed the tray from Christina.

Christina walked back into the room as Estefanita stared out the open window. Estefanita closed her eyes in relief. An open window was like an invitation, beckoning the evil inside to claim her. Estefanita watched Christina pick up the syringe off the windowsill and squirt the liquid out the open window.

The room was hot and the odor of urine lingered in the air. Looking over her shoulder at Estefanita, she slowly cranked the window. She couldn't afford for Estefanita to have one of her outbursts but she left it open a crack for ventilation and walked out of the room.

Christina stepped out of the room holding the syringe out in her hand for Jenny but the hall was empty. Stepping around the corner to the nurses' station, Christina expected to find Jenny but no one was there. Walking around the desk, Christina looked down at the phone and found a note taped to the receiver. Down the hall she heard the door to the stairwell open. She looked up and saw a shadow slip into the stairwell. Setting the syringe down on the table, Christina picked up the note.

*On break. Be back in 15.*

Christina's heart raced with anticipation. She'd been waiting all night for this moment. She looked around anxiously. She slid open the drawer and took out the small key ring and held it firmly. Her body yearned for the comfort of one of the pills and she stepped around the desk. After taking several quick strides, Christina stopped. Something wasn't right. She sensed it and she set the key back in the drawer. Walking over to the stairwell, Christina opened the door and listened to the echo of footsteps.

Stepping inside, Christina looked down the center of the circular stairs. She could see Jenny descending the metal stairs and instinctively followed her.

At the basement Christina stood in the shadows as she watched Jenny walk down the long narrow hall until she disappeared behind a door hidden in the shadows. Christina waited several minutes before she retraced Jenny's steps. Walking against the wall, Christina looked over at the door marked *Morgue* and wondered if the young boy from her dreams was inside. The image of his cold, lifeless body lying on the metal slab under a sheet sent chills through her. Contemplating whether she should turn back, Christina stopped and listened. The only sound she could hear was her heart pounding and she forced herself to swallow the dry lump in her throat. Christina wanted to know where Jenny disappeared to every night and against her better judgment, she walked farther down the hall.

Reaching the door at the end of the hall, Christina turned the brass knob. It was locked. Kneeling down, she peered through the keyhole into the dark room.

A black candle burned in the center of the room. Smoke from burning incense drifted from the room and the pungent odor stung her nose but she leaned closer for a better look. The room was empty. Puzzled, Christina stood and looked around the hall but turned back to the door in front of her. She was certain this was the door Jenny had gone through. She stepped away and quickly retraced her footsteps. Reaching the stairwell, Christina ran up the stairs, taking the steps two at time.

The black wolf emerged from the darkness and growled as it watched Christina.

Reaching the top of the stairs, Christina ran into the hall and checked her watch. She still had five minutes before anyone would get back from break. Breathless, she ran to the desk and took the key from the drawer. Christina ran down the hall, stopped at the medication room, and unlocked the door.

Closing the door behind her, Christina strode quickly through the dark room and opened the glass case. Taking a bottle from the shelf, she poured the red pills into her hand. She felt a sense of relief wash over her.

Hurriedly twisting the lid back on the bottle, she fumbled and watched it slip through her fingers and roll across the floor. Her heart pounded in her chest and her hands shook uncontrollably. The pills rattled nosily inside the bottle and Christina knew it was happening again. Unable to control her rising fear, Christina shut her eyes as dark images flashed through her. Trying to keep her balance, she reached out and knocked several bottles off the shelf. The glass bottles shattered and pills scattered around her feet. The powerful vision flashed again and Christina fell to her knees. Shards of glass tore into her hands and knees as she crawled toward the door. Christina reached for the brass knob when the door swung open.

Jenny stood in the doorway. Her large shadow cast across the floor as she stared down at Christina. Christina reached her bloody hand out for help before she collapsed. Sneering, Jenny watched Christina wither in pain.

As quickly as the vision came, it was over. Gasping for air, Christina slowly stood and looked down at her bloody hands. "Oh, my God!" Christina cried out in shock, running past Jenny, out of the hospital and through the empty parking lot. The muscles in her legs burned and the stitch on her side felt like a dull knife but Christina forced herself to run faster.

From the fourth-floor window Jenny smiled as she watched Christina disappear into the night.

# Thirty-One

P eering through the window, La Llorona watched the three children asleep in bed. She smiled as she tapped on the glass with her long nails to awaken one of the kittens. La Llorona motioned with her bony finger and the kitten walked up to Mark Anthony and licked his cheek to wake him with her scratchy tongue.

La Llorona's concentration broke the moment she heard Lucy walk down the dark driveway and she quickly stepped away from the window. Slipping into the shadows, she watched Lucy walk into the house.

La Llorona watched Lucy through the kitchen window. Setting her cap down on the table, Lucy ran her hands through her long black hair and let it fall loosely around her shoulders. She reached into the pocket of her sweater and took out a pack of cigarettes. Lighting the cigarette, Lucy blew a cloud of smoke into the air as she rubbed the tension from her neck.

La Llorona watched Lucy finish the cigarette and walk down the hall to check on the children. Quietly opening the door, Lucy peeked into the dark room and smiled. The moonlight cast a soft glow on their faces.

Turning off the light in the kitchen, Lucy walked into her room and closed the door. La Llorona watched and waited until the house grew silent before she left the safety of the shadows. Walking back to the children's room, she peered through the window.

Gently tapping on the glass again, she woke the sleeping kitten. The kitten gently nuzzled Mark Anthony's cheek to wake him, purring as it jumped off the bed and meowed at the door. Rubbing his tired eyes, Mark Anthony climbed over Marie, jumped off the bed, and opened the door. Groggily following the kitten into the kitchen, he watched the kitten meow and paw at the door to be let out.

"No, kitty. Potty inside," Mark Anthony whispered and pointed to the litter box. The kitten looked at the litter box but turned back to the door. "Meow," it cried again as it continued to scratch the door. "Shh, kitty, don't wake Auntie." Standing on his toes, Mark Anthony opened the door and the kitten ran out onto the porch.

"Bring him to me," La Llorona whispered as she watched Mark Anthony follow the kitten onto the porch, and with her hand she lured the kitten away from the house.

"No, kitty," Mark Anthony whispered as the kitten ran away. Straining to listen through the darkness, he heard its soft meow and stepped off the porch to follow its cries.

Lucy woke when she heard the door open. Grabbing her robe, she ran into the kitchen and closed the door. Sensing something was wrong, she ran down the hall into the children's room and turned on the light. "Oh, my God, Mark!" Seeing the empty space between the two sleeping girls, Lucy ran back into the kitchen and out the door. "Mark!" Lucy shouted as she stood on the front porch. With their kittens at their feet, Jessica and Marie stepped out onto the porch.

"What's the matter, Aunt Lucy?" Jessica rubbed her eyes. "Where's Mark?"

"Mark Anthony!" Lucy ignored her as she strained to listen and heard the faint meow of a kitten in the distance.

"Go back inside and lock the door. Don't open it until I get back." Lucy jumped off the porch and ran out into the darkness, following the distant meow.

Too tired to question her, the girls walked back into the house.

Lucy ran through the darkness. Branches scratched her face, pulled her long hair, and tore her robe. "Mark Anthony!" she yelled again as the meows got farther away.

Mark Anthony stopped when he heard Lucy. He turned to go back but the kitten rubbed against his leg and beckoned him deeper into the forest. La Llorona watched Mark Anthony from the shadows and lured the kitten into the thick woods. Hearing Lucy call for the boy, La Llorona motioned to the black wolf and in an instant it bolted through the forest toward the sound of Lucy's voice.

Lucy stopped when she heard branches break in front of her. "Mark Anthony?" she called out as she strained to see through the dark forest. She screamed when she saw the black wolf leap out from the shadows. Lucy raised her arm to protect herself but it was too late. The black wolf was a powerful and skilled killer. Unleashing its vicious instinct, the black wolf's jaws locked on her neck.

Stopping its attack, the black wolf stepped off its victim and watched her struggle to breathe through her broken windpipe.

Blood gurgled in Lucy's chest. Holding her hand over her throat, Lucy desperately tried to crawl away. Lucy could go no farther and collapsed. With her eyes fixed on the black wolf, Lucy lay motionless as she listened to the distant meow of the kitten drifting through the quiet night.

Christina stumbled onto the porch as Jessica and Marie peeked out the kitchen window. "Where's Lucy?" Christina asked between breaths as she pulled on the locked door.

"She went into the woods to look for Mark Anthony," Jessica answered, unlocking the door.

Exhausted, Christina staggered to the phone on the kitchen counter. Her hands trembled as she dialed. "Come on, answer!" She wiped the perspiration from her brow.

"Sheriff's office," a male voice answered.

"This is Christina Digerno. I'm at 604 Canyon Road. Send an ambulance and the police!"

"What's the problem, ma'am?" The man's voice was slow and patient.

"She's hurt and my son is missing!"

"Who's hurt?"

"Please," Christina pleaded. "Just send someone right away to 604 Canyon Road!" Christina hung up the phone as the voice on the other end continued to ask questions and she ran to the door. "Lock the door and wait for the police."

"Mommy, I'm scared," Marie began to cry.

"Do as I say! Now, get inside," Christina ordered before she stepped off the porch and ran into the darkness. "Mark Anthony! Lucy!" Christina yelled, holding her side. Running though the thick grove of cottonwoods, Christina held her arm out in front of her as branches whipped at her face. Christina saw something move and walked closer. "Lucy?" she asked as she timidly walked toward the torn and bloodied robe and gently rolled Lucy onto her back. "Oh, my God, no!" Christina cried. She wasn't prepared for what she saw and gasped at the gaping wound. Blood gushed from Lucy's neck and soaked into Christina's white uniform. Crying, Christina moved Lucy's bloody hair from her face and pressed her hand onto the open wound.

"Oh God, Lucy, no!" Christina cried, tears running down her cheeks. *Why is this happening?* She rocked Lucy gently in her arms.

Lucy opened her eyes. Her breathing was labored and shallow but she was still alive.

"Where's Mark Anthony?" Christina asked as Lucy's glassy eyes looked up at the yellow moon. Lucy moved her lips but couldn't talk. Lucy lifted her arm and pointed toward the river.

Christina closed her eyes. She didn't have the courage to go farther. She knew what awaited her and she wanted desperately to stay with Lucy until help came.

Lucy pointed again toward the river. "I can't leave you," Christina cried, torn with the decision of leaving Lucy, knowing she would die, and the uncertainty of what might lay ahead with Mark Anthony.

"Go!" Lucy forced herself to speak.

"Oh God, Lucy, I'm so sorry," she sobbed as she gently laid Lucy down on the ground. "I love you." She leaned over and kissed her gently on the cheek. "I'll be right back. Just hang on."

Lucy watched Christina disappear into the darkness and closed her eyes.

Christina ran toward the river. The sound of rushing water grew louder with every step. "Mark Anthony!" she yelled as she reached the edge of the river. The moon reflected off the rippling water and illuminated the area. Across the river Christina saw a woman's silhouette. Beside her, poised to attack, was the black wolf. Its yellow eyes glared at her as it growled threateningly, baring its bloody teeth.

Christina stood in horror as she recognized the woman from her dreams. Feeling her legs grow weak, Christina took a step back and knew this wasn't a dream. This was real, and so was her fear.

"Leave!" La Llorona shouted across the rushing river. "Leave or I'll take all of your children one by one."

Christina cringed at the threat. Her whole body trembled and she wanted to turn and run away from the sinister woman but she had to find Mark Anthony. "Where's my son?" Christina yelled.

La Llorona didn't answer as she pointed to the river and turned to walk away.

"Mark Anthony!" Christina panicked. She ran along the river-bank, searching the rushing waters. "Mark Anthony!" she screamed again as she stumbled and fell into the water. She saw the small kitten floating in the shallow water. "Oh, no," she whispered as she gently lifted the dead kitten out of the water and held it in her arms. "Mark Anthony! Mark Anthony!" Christina cried out as she frantically searched the rushing river. "Oh, God, no! Mark Anthony!"

Estefanita cried out and opened her eyes. Tears burned her cheeks as she sobbed. The image of La Llorona dragging Mark Anthony into the river and watching him drown in the fast current haunted her. She gave Christina the gift without realizing the danger she'd placed her and her family in and now another innocent child was dead because of her.

She stopped struggling against her restraints and stared at the ceiling. It would only be a matter of time before they came for her and this time she would not fight. She didn't have the strength or the desire to live. Her guilt was overwhelming and she knew it was time to die. She was ready.

# Thirty-Two

Christina sat alone in the same interview room at the police station she'd been in just a few days before. She looked around the empty room, from the dark gray walls to the mirror across from her, and stared at her sullen reflection. Her hair and face were muddy, and Lucy's blood stained her white uniform. Leaning back in the hard chair, Christina looked down at her hands in her lap and tried to stop thinking about the emptiness she felt in the depths of her soul. Mark Anthony was missing and the witch's omen echoed in her head. The image of Lucy dying in her arms and her grisly wounds were more than Christina could endure and she began to weep. With trembling hands she rubbed the mud from her arms.

The police found her at the river still clutching the dead kitten and brought her back to the house. Lucy's body was being loaded into the ambulance and although the paramedics were working diligently to save her, Christina knew it was useless. Lucy was going to die. There was no doubt in her mind about that. Just like there was no doubt where they'd find her son. She sobbed quietly at the thought of Mark Anthony. The dull ache of losing another loved one ripped into her. Christina's whole body shook as she cried uncontrollably.

Christina looked up as the door opened. Detective Winters nervously cleared his throat as he walked into the room and set his notepad on the table. Folding his arms, he looked down at Christina in disgust. He had a murder and a missing child, and this woman was his prime suspect.

Christina shut her eyes. Her disappointment was obvious. Of all the officers in the police department, it had to be him. He was the last person she wanted to talk to. She tried to warn him and he didn't believe her. It was his fault Mark Anthony and Lucy were dead. If he'd done his job they might still be alive. Now they wanted him to take her statement?

Detective Winters tugged at his belt, purposefully drawing attention to the .38 Special holstered on his hip.

"Good evening, Mrs. Digerno. I'm Detective Winters." He sat down, took a pen from his shirt pocket, and began to write on the notepad.

"I know who you are," Christina answered sharply.

"Right." Detective Winters clenched his jaw, his face expressionless and if Christina knew him any better, she would know he was having difficulty controlling his anger. "You know why you're here, so why don't you tell me what happened tonight so we can sort this mess out?"

What was there to sort out? She wanted to yell. She lost two people she loved and he wanted to sort things out? Christina leaned back and brushed the hair from her face. Christina let out a long, exasperated breath. "Where are my children?" she questioned, refusing to be intimidated.

"They're safe," Detective Winters answered as he looked up and shifted in his seat, feeling a little uncomfortable from the way she was staring at him.

"What do you mean, 'they're safe'? Where are they?" Christina narrowed her eyes, matching the anger in her voice.

"Right now they're here at the police station, and whether they can go home with you tonight will depend on what happens with our investigation."

"What the hell is that supposed to mean?" She raised her voice.

"As long as you cooperate with our investigation, you can take you children home."

"And if I don't?" Christina folded her arms and leaned back in her chair.

"Then we'll have to keep you here and they'll be placed in state custody." Detective Winters paused. "Unless you have family who will take care of them while we sort out the pieces of our investigation."

Christina knew Jessica and Marie were being questioned right now but she didn't care as long as they were safe, and right now they were safe.

"Where were you tonight?" Detective Winters asked.

"I was working at the hospital. I'm a nurse, remember?" Christina sarcastically pointed to her stained uniform.

"Was your shift over and that's why you came home?"

"No," Christina answered softly.

"Why did you leave work and go home?"

"I had a—" Christina stammered. She knew he wouldn't believe her, just like he didn't believe her when she told him about her nightmares but it was the only answer she could give. "I had a vision," she whispered.

"A vision? Is that like one of those dreams you told me about?"

"Yes, something like that," Christina answered, rubbing the dried blood off her hands.

"So what happened in this vision of yours?"

"I saw Lucy being attacked, so I ran home but by the time I got there she was already gone."

"What made you think this vision was real?"

"I've had them before, remember? And what I saw happen to the little boy, the young girl, and Lucy was real, even if you don't believe me."

"Lucy wasn't there when you got home. Where was she?" He ignored her comment and kept to his line of questioning.

"She went to look for my son." Christina sighed.

"And where was he?" Detective Winters showed no emotion.

Christina shut her eyes, remembering the old woman. "I don't know," she whispered.

"When the police found you, you were down at the river, is that correct?" Detective Winters asked as he methodically wrote down her answers.

"Yes," Christina whispered.

"Why were you at the river?" He looked up to make sure she was still responsive to his questions.

"When I found Lucy she showed me where Mark Anthony had gone." Christina shifted nervously in her chair. The image of Lucy's neck and the dark pool of blood sent a chill through her.

"She was still alive when you found her?" Detective Winters stopped writing and noticed her uneasiness.

"Yes." Christina rubbed the chill from her arms.

"So you went to the river. Was your son where she said he'd be?" Detective Winters searched her eyes for the slightest hint of remorse.

"No." Christina knew what Detective Winters was implying and she wasn't going to be a part of it.

"Was anyone else at the river?"

"Yes," Christina whispered.

"Who?" Detective Winters looked up with interest.

"A woman."

"Did you recognize this woman?" Detective Winters leaned closer to Christina.

"Yes," she answered impatiently.

"Who was she?" Detective Winters tried to mask his eagerness.

"The same woman I told you about the other day." Christina glared at Detective Winters.

"Did she say anything to you?" The disappointment on his face was obvious.

Christina looked away from him as she shook her head and tears rolled down her cheeks. "She told me to leave before she took the rest of my family."

"This was the same woman from your dreams?" Detective Winters wrote without looking up from the notepad.

"Yes." She nodded.

"How could you be so sure? It was dark."

"Yes, it was dark, and she was standing across the river but I know it was her and she knew it was me." Christina wiped tears from her eyes and stared at her ghostly reflection in the mirror.

Detective Winters set his pen down on the notepad and stared at her for what seemed like an eternity. "I'm not buying it. I'm just not buying it. I've had a chance to do a little checking around and do you know what I think?" Christina didn't answer as she looked across the table at him. "I think you killed Lucy." He stood from the chair, walked over, and sat on the table next to her. "And I think you killed your own son because he saw you do it."

"Why would I kill Lucy?" Christina glared at him.

"She knew about you stealing drugs from the hospital." He paused for effect and studied her reaction. "What were you doing in the medication room?" Christina didn't answer as he stood and leaned against the wall behind her with his arms crossed.

"Like I said, I was working."

"Now, you know and I know you don't have the authorization to access that room where the medications are stored. All the problems we've been having around here started right after you came to our quiet little town and do you know what I think? I think you're behind it all." He smiled smugly at the mirror knowing the adjacent room was filled with officers watching the master at work. He had this woman figured out the first day she came in to see him. It would only be a matter of time until he was inside her head and after that she'd be begging to sign a confession. He'd never had the opportunity to interrogate a murderer; crime wasn't a problem in Santa Fe like it was in the bigger cities. Around here, solving the occasional robbery was the highlight of a detective's career, but solving the town's most gruesome homicides would definitely be his greatest achievement as an officer.

"Are you finished, Detective?" Christina's harsh tone startled him and he looked down at her. Christina had had enough. This man was repulsive, and she wanted to go home. "Don't tell me after all the years you've been a detective this is the only thing your feeble little mind could conjure up? I killed Lucy and my son because I'd taken a few pills. Did you come up with this brilliant deduction on your own or did this bright idea come to you after you read one of your detective magazines?"

Detective Winters looked nervously over at the mirror, it was no secret he was a subscriber and avid reader of *Detective Magazine*. He even submitted several stories on cases he'd solved and although he embellished to make them more interesting, none had made it to print.

"You're out of your league," Christina continued. "You don't have a clue what's going on in this town and you're too damn lazy to go out and find the real killer. It would be easier for you to blame everything on me, wouldn't it? Tell me, Detective, before you came up with your brilliant deduction that I killed Lucy and my son, did you examine Lucy's body?" Christina waited. "Did you see the hole ripped in her neck? She was attacked by a wolf. Find the wolf and you'll find the killer."

"It's convenient for you to blame someone no one has ever seen, isn't it?" Detective Winters walked around the table and deliberately put his back to the mirror. He was losing control of the interview and the thought of the men in the next room watching suddenly made him nervous. He fumbled with the notepad in front of him. He was the detective, damn it. He was in control, not her. "I may not have the proof I need right now but it'll only be a matter of time before I find out the truth." Detective Winters leaned over the table and looked in Christina's eyes.

"Can I leave?" Christina stared back, undaunted by his threatening demeanor. She had no respect for the detective. He was lazy and she was wasting her time talking to him. She needed to see Jessica and Marie to make sure they were all right and she knew Detective Winters couldn't keep her any longer, not yet anyway.

"You can leave." Detective Winters looked over at the mirror.

"Where are my children?"

"They're in the hall. I'll arrange a car to take you home."

"Don't bother." Christina stood and walked to the door. She didn't want to go home. It was the only place she had to go but the thought of being there alone, without Mark Anthony or Lucy, was unbearable.

"It's three o'clock in the morning—" he started.

"I don't live far." Christina walked past him into the hall.

"Mrs. Digerno, I would feel more comfortable if you let someone give you and your children a ride home."

"I don't give a damn what would make you feel more comfortable, Detective." Christina found Jessica and Marie sitting alone on the bench outside the interview room. "Come on, let's go home." Both girls stood solemnly and took Christina's hands.

"Mrs. Digerno, until my investigation is finished, I'm going to ask that you don't leave town."

Christina stopped and turned to face Detective Winters. "I won't be going anywhere until my son has been found."

Detective Winters watched Christina walk out the front door.

"She figured you out, Winters." Mike laughed as he slapped the detective on the back.

"What did the kids say?" Detective Winters asked as he walked into the squad room.

"Their mom came after Lucy left the house to look for their little brother. One thing they mentioned that was strange was that they heard a wild howl, like a wolf."

"You said it yourself. We don't have wolves around here, but just to be sure let's check the area for wild dogs. Have they found her son yet?"

"Not yet, but we've got several men searching the river."

"Good. Let me know as soon as they find him. I'd like to wait a few days before we tell her. I'd hate for her to leave town before I finish my investigation."

"I think you're barking up the wrong tree."

"No, she knows something. I can feel it in my gut."

"It's a pretty big gut." Mike poked Detective Winters's stomach and walked away.

Detective Winters sat behind his desk, opened the top drawer, pushed aside his latest edition of *Detective Magazine,* and searched for his notes from his last meeting with Mrs. Digerno.

# Thirty-Three

Looking out the window into the darkness, Mana Mercedes studied the dark sky. The night was eerily calm. Not even a breeze broke the stillness. She reached into the pocket of her nightgown and took out a rosary. She made the sign of the cross and began to pray quietly.

Mana Mercedes jumped when she saw the ball of fire dance across the sky toward the forest. Her breath stopped as she watched and waited as three more fireballs raced across the sky. She made the sign of the cross to end her prayers and stepped away from the window. She walked over to the bed and grabbed her clothes off the chair. She changed out of her nightgown into her dress as she watched her husband sleep. His snores rattled deep within his chest and she tiptoed across the squeaky wood floor to the door.

"Where are you going?" her husband grumbled when she opened the door.

"I can't sleep," she answered without turning around.

"What time is it?" He rolled over to look at the windup clock on the nightstand.

"It's three. Go back to sleep," she whispered as she nervously looked out the window and saw the balls of fire race from the forest toward town. She looked over at her husband to see if he noticed the witch's display but he had already fallen back to sleep. "Crazy old man," Mana Mercedes whispered as she closed the door. She took a leather pouch from the cupboard and a canning jar filled with water and shoved the items into her black purse. Mana Mercedes took the wool shawl hung by the door and stepped out onto the front porch. Searching the dark sky until she saw the orange glow, she stepped off the porch and walked down the dirt road, slowly making her way toward the dancing fireballs.

Christina walked past the bright lights of the hospital as she held Jessica and Marie's tiny hands. Her body was numb, her heart ached, and the emptiness she felt resonated like a steel drum deep in her soul. Christina's head throbbed and the rhythmic sound of her feet on the dirt echoed in her mind. Dreading each step, Christina pushed herself farther down the road. She was alone and left to cope with the death of two more people she loved. The agony of losing Mark Anthony and Lucy was overwhelming but she needed to stay strong for Jessica and Marie. She needed to grieve but now was not the time. She couldn't show the children how vulnerable she really was.

A cold chill ran down Christina's spine. She let out a gasp. Unable to breathe, Christina waited in horror as another vision flashed before her eyes.

"What's the matter, Mommy?" Jessica looked up at her mom. Terrified, Christina had let go of Jessica's hand.

The blood pounded in Christina's ears as she tried to clear the image from her mind but it was no use. She felt herself flying through the night sky surrounded by fire. Looking to her left, she saw a woman dressed in black dancing inside a ball of fire. To her right was another fireball but the woman inside seemed vaguely familiar. Straining to see through the flames, Christina stared at the woman inside dancing provocatively. Letting go of Marie's hand, Christina stepped away from the two girls when she recognized the woman.

Christina saw Jenny's face clearly. The same overbearing and demanding woman from the hospital was now dancing inside the fire. Her long gray hair hung loose from its usual tight bun and swayed in the wind with every turn of her head.

"Oh, my God," Christina gasped as she slowly backed away.

"Mommy!" Jessica began to cry, afraid to be left alone.

Christina shook the image from her mind. Grabbing Jessica and Marie by the hand, she led them quickly down the dirt road.

"What's the matter, Mommy?" Jessica asked, running to keep up with her mother.

Christina didn't answer as she scanned the night sky. She saw a ball of fire drop out of the sky and she began to run. Unable to keep up, Marie tripped and fell. Christina stopped and watched the fire dance closer with each bounce. Letting go of Jessica's hand, Christina ran over to Marie and picked her up.

"Mom!" Jessica screamed when she saw a ball of fire fall on the road in front of them. Christina picked up Jessica in her other arm and ran with what little strength she had.

Jessica and Marie held onto their mother as they watched the balls of fire in horror. In a flash they saw five more fireballs race across the sky and drift around them on the tops of the trees.

"Mom!" Jessica shouted as Christina ran down the driveway.

The balls of fire dropped from the sky, surrounding Christina and the girls. The front door was only a few steps away. Holding Jessica and Marie tighter, Christina frantically searched for a way out but the blazing balls of fire blocked her every step.

Christina was surrounded but she refused to give up. Clenching her jaw, Christina closed her eyes and ran. She flinched when she passed through the fire but was surprised when the flames didn't burn. With the balls of fire one step behind, Christina ran up the front porch and bolted through the door.

She hadn't bothered to lock the door when the police took her away. She hoped Mark Anthony might somehow be alive and find his way home and she didn't want him to come home to a locked house. Christina locked the door behind her and looked out the window as the balls of fire danced around the house.

Holding Jessica and Marie in the middle of the dark kitchen, Christina got to her knees as the whole house began to rumble. The tin roof shook violently as the balls of fire slammed onto it. The windows rattled in the frames and the locks slowly loosened. A bright white light poured into the house from the windows. The door bowed and shook with such an incredible force that Christina covered Jessica and Marie's heads to protect them from the imminent blast of shattered wood. The door hinges bent and loosened as the assault grew more violent. Jessica and Marie cried fearfully as they clung to Christina until suddenly everything fell silent.

The house went dark and the night fell still. Just as suddenly as the attack had begun, it was over. The windows and doors stopped rattling and the house settled into an eerie calm. Streams of dust fell from the ceiling planks. Slowly Christina stood and searched the darkness.

The hollow sound of footsteps echoed on the worn planks of the front porch and Christina held her breath when they stopped at the door. A loud knock thundered throughout the quiet house followed by a second that was harder and quicker. Jessica and Marie cried softly as they held onto Christina, afraid of whoever was out there. Easing their arms from around her legs, Christina motioned them to be quiet as she walked toward the door. Christina cautiously stepped closer to the door. She jumped away as Mana Mercedes stepped in front of the window.

"Please open the door," Mana Mercedes asked as she peered into the window. "They're gone."

Christina put her hand on the lock and hesitated. She trusted Mana Mercedes but didn't want her here. Christina wanted to forget about the woman in her dreams and she was going to do just what the woman ordered her to do. She was going to leave, take the girls, and get the hell out of town. Christina knew Mana Mercedes would try to talk her out of leaving but it was too late; she'd already lost too much.

"Please open the door," Mana Mercedes pleaded and reluctantly Christina opened the door. Mana Mercedes stood alone on the front porch. Dried leaves and twigs hung from her hair and her white wool shawl was covered with dirt.

"Come in." Christina turned on the lights. Taking a quick glimpse outside, Christina immediately closed the door behind Mana Mercedes.

"Hi there," Mana Mercedes smiled warmly at Jessica and Marie as they timidly stepped away from her. The two kittens ran into the kitchen and affectionately rubbed their purring bodies around Mana Mercedes's legs. "Look how big they've gotten." She smiled as she bent over and stroked their soft fur. She looked for the other kitten and the little boy, and her smile quickly faded. The kittens shared a special bond with the children and when she gave the children the kittens she knew their souls were bound together in life and death. They were both gone, she felt the sadness around her, and she quietly whispered a prayer.

"Why don't you take the kittens to your room and try to get some sleep?" Christina walked Jessica and Marie to the bedroom. Slowly she opened the door and prayed by some miracle Mark Anthony would be asleep in the bed, but the room was empty. Christina knelt and took Jessica and Marie in her arms. "I love you," she whispered as Jessica and Marie held her tight. "Now go to bed." They looked at her fearfully. "Don't worry, I'm not going anywhere."

"What about Mark Anthony and Aunt Lucy?" Jessica asked.

"Aunt Lucy had an accident and she's gone to heaven." It was the same answer she gave them about their father and grandmother.

"What about Mark Anthony?"

"I don't know where Mark Anthony is."

"Is he dead, too?" Marie whispered.

Tears fell from Christina's eyes as she looked into their sad faces. "I don't know, but if he is, he's with Daddy and Daddy is taking care of him now." The thought of their little brother being with their dad comforted them. "Now go to bed." Christina tucked them in and kissed them gently on the forehead. "I'll be in the kitchen if you need anything, okay?"

Christina left the door open and the light on in the hall. She walked into the kitchen where Mana Mercedes stood over the stove watching the kettle steam. The old woman smiled at Christina. Reaching into her purse, she took out the small leather pouch filled with dried leaves and crumbled the handful into the steaming water.

"Sit down." Mana Mercedes motioned to the chair. "I've made you some tea to help you sleep."

Christina sat down. She looked at the opened pack of cigarettes on the table and picked it up. Running her fingers over the smooth white package, Christina closed her eyes as she tried to draw from Lucy's courage and strength. Mana Mercedes put the cup of steaming tea in front of her, breaking her concentration.

"Thank you." Christina set the cigarettes down on the table.

Mana Mercedes looked at the almost full pack of cigarettes and reached into her purse and took out a cloth pouch filled with tobacco and rolling papers. Mana Mercedes sat across from Christina and rolled a cigarette effortlessly. It wasn't perfect like the ones from the factory but it would do. She took out a wooden match from the pocket in her dress and blew a puff of smoke into the air.

"Drink your tea." She motioned to the cup with the cigarette in her fingers.

Christina blew on the hot liquid and took a sip. The tea was bitter but sweetened with just enough honey. "It's good, thank you."

"You're welcome." Mana Mercedes smiled as she took another puff of her cigarette. "It'll help you sleep."

"I don't think there's a drink out there that could help me sleep tonight," Christina said bitterly as she took another drink. "What are you doing here?" she asked, suddenly realizing it was four o'clock in the morning.

"The balls of fire led me here." Christina slowly put down the cup of tea. It never occurred to her that Mana Mercedes came with the balls of fire. "No, that's not what I meant." Mana Mercedes sensed her apprehension. "I saw them gather in the sky for one of their meetings and I knew they were planning an attack so I followed them." She took another puff from her cigarette. "Do you know what the balls of fire are?" Christina slowly shook her head no, although she had a pretty good idea what they might be. "It is one of the ways the witches travel, but you knew that, didn't you?" Mana Mercedes smiled knowingly. "You've been given the gift. You can see through the eyes of the darkest soul."

Christina stared at the green tea in her cup, afraid to look at Mana Mercedes, afraid to accept the reality of what she'd witnessed in her dreams. It was easier for her to believe her visions were a figment of her imagination and not the result of some gift she'd been given by an old woman strapped to a hospital bed.

"You have been helping Estefanita. Why?" Mana Mercedes snubbed out her cigarette in the ashtray, pushing aside Lucy's half-smoked cigarette. She quickly rolled another.

"I don't know what you're talking about."

"You've been feeding her with your own food, bringing her fresh water to drink, and you've stopped giving her those dreadful shots." Christina didn't answer. When she first started helping Estefanita it was to spite Jenny but lately it had become something more. Protecting the old woman had become an obligation. Christina wasn't sure why but she knew she had to take care of Estefanita.

"Estefanita is the only one who can put an end to your nightmares and without you to protect her at the hospital, it'll only be a matter of time before they kill her."

"Who's going to kill her?"

"La Llorona has regained her position of power in the circle of witches. She will stop at nothing to kill Estefanita and destroy you now that she knows you have the gift."

"What are you talking about?" Christina struggled to control her frustration. She'd lost her only son and her best friend and if it was because of this so-called gift she'd been given, she wanted to know why.

Mana Mercedes blew out the match with a puff of smoke. Taking several small pieces of tobacco from the tip of her tongue with her fingers, Mana Mercedes studied the small tear on the cigarette. Mending the rip with her wet finger, Mana Mercedes carefully chose her words. "Estefanita is the key. Help her, and she'll help you."

"Help her what?"

"You need to get her out of the hospital before it's too late."

"Look, as soon as they find my son I'm getting the hell out of this town." Christina shook her head.

"You can't run from the gift you've been given."

"Well, take it back because I don't want it!" Christina yelled, forgetting Jessica and Marie were asleep in the next room. She quickly lowered her voice. "I didn't ask for any of this. I lost my son and my best friend tonight and if what you are saying is true, then they were killed because of this gift. The only family I have left are those two little girls in the next room and I can't let anything happen to them."

"That is why you must help Estefanita."

"Why me? Why don't you help her?"

"I can't."

"Why not?"

"My fate has already been decided. I can only help guide you."

"That's just great. You can only guide me," Christina mocked. "Well, my fate has already been decided too and I'm getting as far away from this town as I possibly can. I'm sorry if it's not what you or Estefanita want but that bitch told me she'd take my family one by one, so you see I don't really have a choice now, do I?"

"Very well." Mana Mercedes stood from the table, pulled the dusty shawl over her shoulders, picked up her handbag from the table, and walked to the door. "I won't be back to bother you." Mana Mercedes looked around the kitchen as if she sensed something. "Follow your heart and the truth will be revealed to you."

Christina didn't want to hear anymore of Mana Mercedes's coded riddles. Opening the door for the old woman, Christina looked up and noticed the writing over the door, the same words written in Spanish over Estefanita's door at the hospital.

"*Pasen con el amor de Dios.*"

"What is that?" Christina pointed to the writing.

"It is a blessing." Mana Mercedes smiled. "Only those with the love of God can enter your house. It'll keep you safe until you leave." Mana Mercedes stepped onto the front porch as the sun slowly rose over the mountains. Christina watched the old woman walk up the driveway as the sounds of morning broke the silence of the night.

Christina closed the door and stood alone in the cold empty kitchen. She looked down at her dirty uniform and walked down the hall to the children's room. Jessica and Marie held onto each other as they slept, their heads resting on the same pillow with the two kittens curled up on the pillow next to them. Christina left the door open and walked down the hall into the bathroom. She closed the door behind her, pulled the shower curtain around the tub and turned on the water.

Staring at her reflection in the mirror, Christina saw a dried streak of Lucy's blood on her cheek. Turning on the water in the sink, she splashed water on her face gently at first, until her anxiety took control and she scrubbed harder desperately trying to wash away the memory of Lucy's lifeless body. Water splashed on the mirror and distorted Christina's reflection. She pulled frantically at her uniform as she tore it off her body and threw it on the floor.

Standing naked in front of the mirror Christina reached out and opened the medicine cabinet. She searched for anything to take away her pain. Throwing the medicines onto the floor, Christina became more frantic.

Christina realized what Lucy had been worried about as she stared at the empty cabinet. She stepped into the bathtub and began to cry until she could no longer bear the pain in her heart. Leaning against the wall, she slowly slipped down into the tub. Curling her knees to her chest, Christina sobbed uncontrollably as she rocked back and forth. She cried for her baby, she cried for Lucy, and she cried for her lack of desire to continue to live.

# Thirty-Four

There was a hard knock on the front door. Christina lifted her head off her arms, which were folded on the table, and looked around the kitchen. She squinted to see through the sun shining through the kitchen window. She looked down at her watch. It was one thirty and before she could gather her senses, another knock rattled the door. Christina slowly stood. Her neck and back were stiff from sleeping on the table. She hadn't been tired after her bath so she came to the kitchen to drink another cup of Mana Mercedes's tea. She had been determined to stay awake and watch the door, afraid Jessica or Marie might leave while she slept, but after the second cup of tea she hadn't been able to keep her eyes open.

Christina ran her fingers through her dry hair as she walked to the door and looked out the window. She moaned softly when she saw Detective Winters.

"Afternoon, Mrs. Digerno." Detective Winters smiled as he awkwardly held out a plate of cookies. "Someone left these on the swing."

"The neighbor across the street must have brought them." Christina took the plate.

"Those sure do smell good." He nodded as he hiked his pants around his waist and jingled the key ring hooked onto his belt. "Mind if I—?" He pointed to the cookies. "I've been working all night and I haven't had a chance to eat," Detective Winters explained as his stomach grumbled noisily.

*He's pathetic,* Christina thought. *At a time like this all he can think about is eating?* "Go ahead."

He reached over and eagerly took two cookies off the plate and took a bite.

"What can I do for you, Detective?" Christina quickly realized he didn't have any news about Mark Anthony.

"I need to talk to you about Mr. Romero." He spoke with his mouth full.

"Who?" Christina was surprised by the question.

"Mr. Romero, room 405."

"What about him?" She remembered the frail old man.

"He passed away last night. I've done some checking. You were the last one in Mr. Romero's room and the last one to see him alive."

"And?" Christina couldn't believe where he was going with this.

"And Mrs. Digerno, I want to know what you were doing in his room."

"You want to know what I was doing in his room?" She glared at him.

"Yes, ma'am," Detective Winters answered as he took another bite of cookie.

"I was changing his bedpan."

"His bedpan?" He looked disappointed.

"Yes, Detective," Christina sneered. "That's my job."

"Was he alive when you saw him last?" He closed his notepad and stuck it into his shirt pocket.

"Of course he was alive." Christina was annoyed that Detective Winters was bothering her with Mr. Romero's death.

"Did he say anything to you?"

"No." Her conversation with Mr. Romero was personal, something Detective Winters would not only not understand but would distort and use against her. He was grasping at straws and she wasn't going to let him pin every death in this town on her. "What about my son, Detective?"

"I'm sorry, but we haven't been able to find him yet and we don't have any new leads."

Christina was amazed by this man's audacity to be asking her questions about Mr. Romero when her son was still missing. She wanted to yank off his dingy brown tie and shove it down his throat. Christina was tired and she was about to close the door when the phone rang. She walked into the kitchen, set the plate of cookies on the table, and answered the phone.

"Hello?" she answered.

"Christina Digerno?" The woman's voice on the other end was soft and gentle.

"Yes."

"This is Sister Martha from the hospital."

"Yes, can I help you?" Christina asked but already knew the reason for her phone call.

"I would first like to extend my condolences. Lucy was a wonderful woman and she will be greatly missed. The sisters are praying for her and the safe return of your son."

"Thank you." Christina marveled at how quickly bad news traveled through this small town.

"I'm also calling regarding your position here at the hospital." Sister Martha paused. "It seems there has been some controversy regarding your duties here last night and I hate to do this in your time of sorrow, but we're going to have to let you go until the police finish their investigation."

"I understand," Christina mumbled as she slowly lowered the phone onto the cradle, cutting off Sister Martha as she continued to explain why she was being fired, as if it really mattered.

"Bad news?" Detective Winters asked as he stood in the doorway.

Christina looked up and glared at him. What kind of asshole was he? Her son was missing, her best friend had been killed brutally, and he was asking a stupid question like "bad news"? "I lost my job, Detective, or didn't you already know that?"

"Look, Mrs. Digerno, I'm only doing my job."

"Well then, why don't you do your job and find my son?"

"We're doing everything we can."

"That's not good enough!" She sat in the chair and put her head in her hands as tears streamed down her face.

"I'll be leaving now, but I would like to remind you not to leave town."

Christina looked up, her eyes burning with hatred. "Just find my son."

Detective Winters tugged on his belt as he nodded and stepped out of the doorway.

Christina locked the kitchen door and glanced up at Mana Mercedes's blessing. *Maybe the blessing did work,* Christina thought as she walked down the hall to look in on Jessica and Marie. They hadn't moved since the last time she checked on them. She desperately wanted to lie down with them and hold them. She wanted to fill the void in her aching heart with their love but she didn't want to disturb them. She would draw from their strength later. She quietly closed the door and walked into her bedroom. Leaving her door open, she lay on the bed and slowly drifted off into a troubled sleep.

# *Thirty-Five*

Soaked from the pouring rain, Christina chased Jessica and Marie through the thick forest. Christina squinted through the rain to keep them in sight. Branches scratched her face as she climbed over tree stumps and boulders. Losing the girls, Christina stopped.

"Don't run away from me!" Christina narrowed her eyes. The anger in her raged. Her only thought was to find her children and unleash her fury on them. Her reasoning was clouded by her hate. Clenching her fists, she turned and saw the sleeve of Marie's white sweater behind a thick ponderosa. This was the moment she'd waited for. Breathing through clenched teeth, she strode toward the cowering girls. Grabbing Marie's long black hair, she lifted her off the ground. The thundering rain drowned out the young girl's screams. With her other hand Christina knocked Jessica to the ground. Crying, Jessica looked helplessly up at her mother.

Christina sat up in bed. Her breaths were short and fast. Her heart pounded so hard it felt like it would explode. Disoriented, Christina looked around the room and relaxed. She was home. She looked across the hall and jumped out of bed. Jessica and Marie weren't in their room. Stumbling down the hall, Christina was relieved when she saw Jessica and Marie at the kitchen eating cookies.

"How long have you been awake?" Christina looked up at the clock on the wall. It was seven thirty-five and the sun had begun to set over the mountains.

"Not long." Jessica shrugged as she took a bite of a milk-soaked cookie.

"How many cookies have you eaten?"

"Just a couple," Jessica answered between chews.

"Why don't you put them away and I'll make us some dinner."

Jessica and Marie drank their milk as Christina searched the bare refrigerator and took out a half-dozen eggs. She'd make egg salad sandwiches, not the best dinner she could think of making but she didn't feel like cooking and she doubted any of them would really eat. Right now they were just going through the motions.

She wanted to cry out and damn God for taking Mark Anthony and Lucy. Hadn't he taken enough from her? How could he let an innocent child die at the hands of someone so evil? Her blood raced every time she let herself think about all she'd lost. Here, she was again faced with another death, and the dull, aching pain.

She needed to put the torn pieces of her life back together for Jessica and Marie. They needed her, and she needed to stay strong for them. Nothing else mattered. Christina spread the boiled eggs onto slices of bread. When she didn't keep herself occupied she'd find herself slowly slipping into the dark recesses of her mind, and she didn't know if she could pull herself from her depression. The sound of a passing truck prompted her to stare out the window. She'd waited all day for Detective Winters to bring news about Mark Anthony and with each passing car she'd look out the window awaiting the impending anguish. Waiting for the truck to disappear down the dirt road, she shook her head and set the plate of sandwiches on the table. The waiting was the hardest. Each passing hour brought more torment and uncertainty. She didn't have any hope they would find Mark Anthony alive. She just wanted closure.

The three of them sat quietly around the kitchen table as they ate their sandwiches, each lost in their own thoughts.

"I miss Mark Anthony," Marie whispered as she nibbled on the corner of her sandwich.

"We all do." Christina's voice broke. "Why don't you finish eating?"

"I'm not hungry." She put the sandwich down on the plate.

"Me neither," Jessica whispered.

"I guess I'm not that hungry either." Christina picked up her plate and set in the sink.

"What are we going to do, Mommy?" Jessica asked as she set her plate on the counter.

"About what?" Christina answered.

"What are we going to do after they find Mark Anthony?"

"It depends."

"On what?"

Christina hadn't given it much thought. She knew she wanted to get as far away from Santa Fe as she could but she didn't know where she would go. In addition, Detective Winters wasn't going to let her leave town until his investigation was over, which could take months, if not years. "I don't know," she finally answered.

"I don't feel so good." Marie leaned against her mother's leg.

"What's the matter?" Christina dried her hands on a dishtowel and felt Marie's head.

"My stomach hurts."

"Mine, too," Jessica added.

Christina knelt down. Both of their faces were pale, and their eyes were hidden in dark circles. She felt their foreheads to check for a fever and then pushed gently on their stomachs. "Does that hurt?" she asked and they both shook their heads. "Do you feel like you're going to throw up?" They looked at each other, not sure exactly what that felt like. "Why don't you go to your room and lie down? I'll fix you some tea to help settle your stomach."

The two girls walked slowly down the hall with the kittens following close behind. Christina put a pot of water on the stove to boil and searched the cabinet for her bag of dried peppermint. It was the only remedy her mother used when she was sick as a child.

To her mother it was a cure-all for everything from fevers to stomachaches. It even cured her mother's occasional headaches.

Christina threw the dried leaves into the boiling water and made three cups of tea with honey. Her stomach wasn't upset but she could use the soothing taste of the peppermint. Peppermint tea reminded her of her mother and now more than ever she needed to draw from her mother's strength.

Both kittens meowed around Christina's feet as she walked down the hall into the bedroom. Jessica and Marie were curled up on the bed and groaned as they held their stomachs. Christina quickly set down the cups to feel their foreheads. Their skin was cold and clammy and they trembled under her touch. Brushing the wet hair from their faces, she saw the clouded gaze in their eyes. "Oh my God." Christina tried to sit Jessica up. "Sit up, honey," she urged, but Jessica's small body went rigid.

Christina ran down the hall through the kitchen and out the front door. She stepped out onto the front porch and looked around. She saw Mr. Sanchez walking across the street toward his house and ran out to him.

"Help me!" Christina cried, meeting him on his front porch. The old man looked fearfully down at Christina. Without saying a word he walked past her and quickly stepped into the house. "My children are sick. I need a ride to the hospital!" Christina pleaded as he shut the door behind him.

"Mrs. Sanchez, please!" Christina saw Dolores watching her from the living room window. "I need to take my children to the hospital." Dolores let the white lace curtain fall. "What's the matter with you people?" Christina cried as she looked at the houses around the neighborhood and watched people step into the safety of their homes. Santa Fe was a small town. It didn't take long for people to find out what happened and to condemn her.

She ran back to the house. Taking the blanket off the bed, Christina wrapped the two sick girls and carried them out of the house. As fast as her legs would carry her, Christina ran down the dirt road.

# Thirty-Six

Christina sat in the long hall of the emergency room. She watched the nurses and doctors walk by hoping one of them would have information on Jessica and Marie's condition.

When she ran into the hospital Jessica and Marie were quickly whisked away and wheeled through two large metal doors. A young nun stopped Christina from going with them. She led Christina away by the arm and handed her a clipboard with several forms.

"You can fill out the forms in the hall." She pointed to the long row of chairs against the wall.

"What about my children?" Christina looked over her shoulder as the doors swung open and she tried to catch a glimpse of Jessica and Marie.

"Your children are being taken care of. As soon as the doctors know something, someone will be out to talk to you." The nun tried to sound reassuring but Christina recognized the rehearsed speech.

Christina reluctantly sat down. After she finished filling out the forms, she set the clipboard on the chair next to her and continued to stare at the two large metal doors, wishing she could be with her children.

"Christina?" John cleared his throat beside her.

"John?" She'd been so caught up with her own grief she'd forgotten about him. *Oh my God, was he here when they brought in Lucy?*

"I just came from seeing Jessica and Marie."

"How are they? When can I see them?" Christina stood up.

"They're resting and you can see them after we talk."

"About what?" Christina took a step back. She dreaded what he might tell her.

"Let's go into the lounge where it's a little more private." Christina glanced around the empty hall and reluctantly followed John into the makeshift doctors' lounge, which was a converted patient's room. A round table and chairs stood in the middle of the room, a refrigerator whined noisily in the corner, and a coffeepot sat on the counter.

"Would you like a cup of coffee?"

Christina nodded as John poured two cups of coffee and sat next to her.

"How are Jessica and Marie?"

John sighed as he carefully chose his words. "We sedated them but we still don't know what's making them sick. We're running a series of tests but so far we haven't been able to make a prognosis. They don't have a fever but they're sweating like they have one and they've slipped into shock and aren't responding to any external stimuli."

"What does that mean?"

"They're in a coma and because we have no idea what's wrong with them we don't know how to treat them." John rubbed his eyes as he leaned back in the chair.

"Oh God." Christina rubbed her temples. "I can't lose them."

"You're not going to lose them," John reassured. "But I need to know if you have any idea what could have gotten them sick."

"I don't know." Christina shook her head.

"Did they eat anything out of the ordinary?"

"They ate some cookies the neighbor brought over, and I made egg salad sandwiches for dinner."

"Not things they'd get food poisoning from." John rubbed his tired eyes. "If you think of anything, no matter how trivial it may seem, I need to know, okay?"

"Can I see them?"

"They're being moved to a room. I'll take you there."

"Thank you." Christina paused, wishing she could say the right words to John. "I'm sorry about Lucy." Her voice broke as she stared down at her coffee. She was afraid to look him in the eyes. Afraid he thought she was to blame for Lucy's death.

"I am too," he whispered.

"I didn't have anything to do with her death." Christina looked up. "I don't know what Lucy told you about me and I know things were kind of strained between us but I never would have hurt her."

"I know." John nervously cleared his throat and stood from the table. "Jessica and Marie should be in their room now."

Christina followed John out of the lounge down the hall into a small room. Jessica and Marie's beds had been moved so that they were no more than a few feet apart. Christina walked quietly through the room. They looked small and helpless in the big hospital beds. Standing between them, Christina reached down, took their small hands in hers, and began to cry.

Christina sat with Jessica and Marie for two hours waiting for them to wake up. Emotionally and physically exhausted, she stepped out of the room and leaned against the wall. Rubbing the tension from her stiff neck, she closed her eyes as hot tears burned her cheeks. Her whole body ached. She missed her son and she couldn't lose her daughters. Feeling a wave of nausea rising in her throat, she stumbled across the hall and collapsed into a chair. Blood rushed from her head and the hall began to spin.

"No," Christina whispered. The pounding in her chest and her quick breaths meant only one thing. Waiting for the sensation to pass, Christina shut her eyes as the vision flashed through her mind. At first the image was distant and gray but slowly her vision cleared and Christina was certain who was reaching out to her.

Estefanita struggled to free herself from the restraints binding her wrists and ankles. She tried to bite the cloth with her teeth but it was no use. Looking fearfully at the curtain blowing in the wind, she could hear the flutter of wings outside the window. A black owl swooped down and perched on the windowsill. The bird watched Estefanita struggle and relished her fear. Estefanita watched in horror as the owl flew into the room and transformed and the evil she'd fought so hard to destroy stood before her.

La Llorona's thin frame was cloaked in a black hooded robe. Standing in the middle of the room, she lowered her hood and walked over to Estefanita as four other owls transformed around her. Estefanita tried to make out the faces of the other witches but she couldn't see through the black hoods. Estefanita thrashed on the bed, desperately trying to get away. Grabbing Estefanita by the hair, La Llorona forced the old woman to look into her evil eyes.

"Estefanita," La Llorona whispered. "It's been a long time."

"Not long enough." Estefanita spit into La Llorona's face.

"Don't worry. Your suffering will soon be over." La Llorona laughed as she wiped her face with the back of her hand and motioned the other witches to gather around.

Looking into the cold dark eyes looming over her, Estefanita began to pray.


Christina ran down the empty hall, around the corner to the emergency room, and bumped into Detective Winters. Sweat ran down his pale face as he held his stomach. Weak and unable to stand, Detective Winters fell back against the wall.

"Detective?" Christina reached out and grabbed him by his shirt to keep him from falling. "What are you doing here?"

"Sick," Detective Winters mumbled, using every ounce of his strength to hold himself up.

Christina looked around at the nurses walking down the hall oblivious to the sick man. "Can someone please help me?" she shouted to the two nurses.

"What's the problem?" one asked as they walked over and Detective Winters collapsed onto the floor. "Doctor!" the nurse yelled over her shoulder as an elderly doctor walked out of the lounge.

The doctor knelt beside Detective Winters. "What happened?" he asked, pressing his fingers into the side of the detective's neck.

"I don't know," Christina stammered. "I walked around the

corner and he just collapsed." Christina watched nervously as the doctor flashed a small light into Detective Winters's eyes. The large metal doors slammed against the wall as a male intern pushed a gurney through the doors and ran toward them. As the intern unlocked a latch, the bed dropped to the floor next to the detective and four medics lifted Detective Winters off the floor. Once Detective Winters was on the bed, the intern pushed the gurney through the metal doors as the doctor shouted orders to the nurses.

Christina stood and watched them disappear through the same metal doors through which they'd taken Jessica and Marie. Christina looked around for Detective Winters's family and realized he was alone. She backed away slowly, hoping the admissions nurse hadn't seen her with the detective. She didn't want to answer any questions and she didn't want anyone to know she knew him.

As she turned the corner to go back to Jessica and Marie's room, she saw John inside.

"Is everything okay?" John asked as she walked into the room.

"Yes," Christina stammered. "John, I need to ask you for a favor." Her voice trembled.

"What is it?" He draped his stethoscope around his neck and looked up.

"There's something I need to do and I want to know Jessica and Marie will be taken care of."

"I don't understand."

"I think I know who killed Lucy," she blurted. "Or at least I think I know where to find her, but I need to know they're safe." Tears welled up in her eyes at the thought of the possibility of losing Jessica and Marie.

"Who killed Lucy?" John's face reddened with anger and he clenched his hands by his side.

"I can't tell you." Christina shook her head.

"Why not?"

"It's too difficult to explain right now but you've got to help me," Christina pleaded.

"Help you what?"

She took a sheet of paper and pen from the nightstand between Jessica and Marie's bed. "I want you to call this man. He's my father and the only family I have. If something should happen to me, I want him to take care of Jessica and Marie." Christina handed John the paper.

"What do you mean, if something happens to you?" John looked down at the paper.

"If I don't stop her, she'll kill them." Christina pointed to the two unconscious girls. "Just like she killed Mark Anthony and Lucy. I can't lose them. They're all I have." She cried. "Just promise me you'll call him."

"This is crazy." John waved the paper in her face. "Why don't you tell the police and let them take care of things?"

"I can't." She shook her head. "At least not yet. They think *I* killed Mark Anthony and Lucy. I have to prove to them I didn't." She bent down, kissed Jessica on the forehead, and gently nuzzled her soft cheek. "I love you." Christina wiped the tears from her eyes before she walked over and kissed Marie. Summoning the courage to leave her children, Christina walked out the door.

"Where are you going?" John followed her into the hall. "You can't just leave them. They need you. You're their mother, for God's sake." He grabbed Christina by the arm and turned her to face him. "Don't you care about them?"

Christina pulled her arm from his tight grip. Hadn't he been listening? She was doing this for them. "How dare you." She glared. "Of course I care about them. I wouldn't be doing this if I didn't. Look at them in there. You don't know what's wrong with them and for all I know they're in there because of me. The police won't let me leave this Godforsaken town because they think *I* killed Lucy and Mark Anthony and if I don't stop this woman, she'll come after Jessica and Marie. I'm doing everything I can to protect them, so don't ask me whether or not I care about them!" Christina turned and walked away, leaving John holding the sheet of paper with her father's name.

# Thirty-Seven

Christina ran up the four flights of stairs hoping she wasn't too late. Bursting through the door on the top floor, she wasn't surprised to find it deserted. Christina ran past the nurses' station toward Estefanita's room.

Christina nearly screamed. Sarah stepped out of Roman's room and grabbed her shoulder.

"I'm sorry, did I frighten you?" Sarah quickly pulled her hand away from Christina.

"No, I was just—" Christina stammered as she turned her back to Estefanita's door to face Sarah.

"I was hoping you'd be here tonight," Sarah began excitedly. "Roman is giving us another chance." She smiled.

"I'm glad," Christina answered halfheartedly as she glanced over her shoulder.

"I don't know what happened but he called me out of the blue and told me he loved me." Tears streamed down Sarah's face.

"That's nice." Christina backed away from Sarah. "I'm sorry but I really can't talk right now."

"Of course," Sarah apologized. "I just thought you'd want to know."

"I'm happy for you. Now, I've got to get back to work." Christina turned and put her hand on the metal door handle.

"Where's your uniform?" Sarah asked as she studied Christina's clothes. Christina stopped and shot Sarah a hard look. "Yes, well . . ." Sarah stammered as she slipped back into Roman's room. Christina entered Estefanita's dark room and quietly closed the door behind her.

Christina's eyes struggled to adjust to the darkness. A black candle cast a soft glow in the otherwise dark room. Five cloaked figures stood around Estefanita's bed as they chanted quietly, working their evil magic. Still bound to the bed, Estefanita prayed as she stared at the ceiling. She was unable to scream through the gag tied around her mouth.

Undaunted by Christina's entrance, the witches continued to chant as La Llorona looked up at Christina and laughed. Her face was hidden in the shadows but Christina recognized her as she stared into the cold dark eyes of the woman who killed her son. The courage she'd felt a few minutes ago vanished as the woman who plagued her dreams laughed at her. With a wave of her hand La Llorona motioned and one of the witches turned. The hooded figure glided across the floor and stood in front of Christina.

"I'm going to enjoy this," Jenny hissed as she slowly lowered the hood. Christina stumbled back as Jenny grabbed her by the throat and squeezed. "How are the children?" She snickered. "Did they enjoy the cookies?"

"You!" Christina's eyes widened in dismay.

"Yes, me," Jenny snickered. "But don't worry. They won't suffer for long."

Christina grabbed Jenny's hand and tried to loosen the pressure around her throat. Struggling to breathe as Jenny backed her against the wall, Christina fought as she felt her feet leave the floor. With incredible strength Jenny lifted her as she dug her fingers deeper into Christina's throat. Frantically searching around her, Christina felt the cool metal of a lamp. Gripping the lamp, Christina struck Jenny on the side of the head. Stunned, Jenny dropped Christina to the floor. Christina gasped for air as she stumbled toward the door. Jenny kicked

Christina, slamming her against the wall. A sharp pain ripped through Christina's side and she felt her ribs crack from the force of Jenny's kick. Jenny grabbed Christina by the hair and pulled her away from the door, dragging her back into the room. Christina grabbed Jenny's hand, which was entwined in her hair, and turned and scratched Jenny's face. With her eyes watering, Jenny fell back into the wall.

Christina's eyes darted around the room. She knew she wasn't strong enough to defeat Jenny. Christina crawled on her knees across the floor toward the intercom on the wall and reached for the button as Jenny shoved her under Estefanita's bed. Jenny wrapped the cord from the broken lamp around Christina's throat and squeezed.

"Not exactly the way I wanted to kill you, but it'll do," Jenny growled as she pulled the cord tighter.

Christina pried her fingers between her neck and the taunt cord but Jenny wrung the cord tighter. Christina's eyes rolled back. The pressure around her neck was excruciating. Christina began to lose consciousness. She reached out for the metal bedpan as Jenny jerked her out from under the bed. Christina was unable to hang on, and the metal pan clanked nosily to the floor, splashing urine around the witches' feet. The echo of the pan hitting the floor broke the witches' concentration. They stopped chanting as La Llorona looked up and glared at Jenny. Jenny looped the cord tighter around her hands and pulled.

Christina looked up at Estefanita. The old woman's eyes pleaded and Christina realized what the witches feared. They worked quickly and silently, using the cover of darkness to torment Estefanita. Managing to ease the pressure off her throat, Christina screamed. Her cry resonated loudly in the small room.

La Llorona and the other witches turned to Christina. Startled, Jenny let the cord slacken as Christina took a deep breath through her sore throat and screamed again.

The tranquility of the fourth floor had been broken. Patients were awakened by the shocking screams and the sound of running echoed down the hall. Estefanita stopped her struggle and rested her head on the pillow. The witches quickly stepped away from the bed and gathered around La Llorona.

"This is only the beginning," La Llorona whispered through clenched jaws before stepping onto the windowsill and jumping out into the darkness.

Jenny was the last to leave. She turned to Christina as the footsteps in the hall drew nearer. "First your children, then you." She lifted the hood over her head, slipped out of the window, and disappeared.

Unwrapping the cord from her neck, Christina had the salty taste of blood in the back of her throat. In an instant Michelle and Monica ran into the room and turned on the lights.

"Christina?" Michelle stammered, surprised to see Christina and helped her to her feet. "What are you doing here?"

Christina wondered the same thing as she braced herself against the wall. John had been right—she should be with Jessica and Marie. Instead, she'd gotten herself involved in something she couldn't possibly understand and had nearly gotten killed. Christina turned to Estefanita as Monica loosened the gag tied around her mouth.

"What the hell happened?" Monica asked as she looked around the room. The lamp lay broken on the floor. The black candle still burned on the nightstand and the smell of urine filled the room. "We were told you were fired after what happened last night."

"I was," Christina whispered. "My children are downstairs in the emergency room. While the doctors are running tests I came up here to check on Estefanita." Christina didn't dare tell them what had just happened. She didn't know if she could trust either of them with the truth.

"What's the matter with the children?" Monica's demeanor softened.

"They don't know yet."

"I'm sorry, but you still can't be here," Michelle whispered nervously. "If Jenny finds you here, she'll go through the roof."

"I know." Christina whispered as she looked over at Estefanita and knew what she had to do. "Can I have a few minutes?"

Monica looked over at Michelle who just shrugged. "Okay, but clean this place up." They were shorthanded now that Christina was gone, and although she didn't work there anymore they could use the help, especially with spilled bedpans. If she wanted to visit, she would have to work.

"Thank you." Christina didn't move until the two nurses stepped out of the room. Christina doubted they would be back anytime soon but she needed to hurry. She walked over to the bed and loosened Estefanita's restraints. Weak from being confined for the last two weeks, Estefanita leaned on Christina for support. Christina took the blanket from the bed and draped it over Estefanita's frail shoulders. With Estefanita's arm around her shoulder, Christina held her firmly around the waist and they walked toward the door. Looking up at Mana Mercedes's blessing, Christina began to understand why Jenny wouldn't come into Estefanita's room, at least not through the door. Opening the door, Christina peeked into the hall before leading Estefanita out of the room. Christina tried to decide which would be the quickest way out of the hospital. She knew the stairs would be the safest way to get out without being noticed but Estefanita was too weak. They would have to take their chances and use the elevator.

Walking past the nurses' station, Christina looked down the adjoining hall toward the elevator. At the opposite end of the hall she heard Monica and Michelle talking as they delivered medications to the patients. She would have to hurry.

With trembling fingers Christina pushed the call button for the elevator, expecting Jenny to emerge from the shadows at any moment. The two women anxiously watched the numbers light up over both elevators. Both elevators were coming up at the same time.

The elevator's loud ring caused Monica and Michelle to turn, a habit they had when the silence was disturbed on the otherwise quiet floor. They looked down the hall in disbelief as Christina and Estefanita stepped toward the unopened elevator door.

"Christina!" Monica yelled as she ran toward her with Michelle close behind. "Wait!"

The metal doors slid open and Christina quickly stepped inside as the second elevator rang, signaling it had stopped. Christina rammed her finger into the first-floor button several times as if each push would make the door close faster. She could hear Monica and Michelle's footsteps get closer as the door to the other elevator opened.

Jenny stepped out into the hall and stopped. Startled to see Monica and Michelle running toward her, she straightened her shoulders, oblivious to Christina and Estefanita inside the adjacent elevator. As Christina pushed the button again, the door slowly began to slide shut and Jenny turned and saw them.

Christina breathed a sigh of relief as the elevator slowly descended toward the first floor. Realizing Jenny would call down to the front desk to have her detained, Christina pushed the button for the basement. If they couldn't get off on the first floor, she'd have to find a way to get out before they got caught. Time seemed to stand still as both women stared at the numbers over the elevator door and they descended toward the first floor.

Christina closed her eyes. The first floor was where Jessica and Marie were, and she wished she could see them one more time. Her thoughts were broken by the gradual stop of the elevator. Christina held onto Estefanita as the door slid open and she steadied herself for a barrage of interns to rush into the elevator but nothing happened. Peeking into the empty hall, Christina walked Estefanita out of the elevator into the hall as the door closed behind them. Step by step they gradually made their way to the front door and out into the warm summer night.

Christina looked around. The night was still but she knew that was about to change. La Llorona was out there, watching and waiting, and she had no doubt Jenny was one step behind her. Holding Estefanita close, Christina walked as fast as she could through the dark parking lot. She looked back and saw Jenny run out of the front entrance with two male interns by her side, and Christina ran faster as the two men easily closed the distance.

"Hold it!" one of the men yelled as he ran awkwardly, holding the keys jingling on his belt.

Christina knew she wasn't going to get away. Maybe if she was alone she would have a chance of outrunning the overweight men but Estefanita could barely walk, much less run, and the men were gaining on them. Not knowing where else to go Christina took the familiar route home and turned onto Canyon Road.

Estefanita didn't have the strength to keep up. Her feet dragged on the ground as Christina pulled her. Christina looked up and saw two balls of fire bouncing toward her and stopped. Christina held back a startled scream. Her breath wheezed out of her tight throat and she turned around. Being locked in jail was more appealing than an encounter with a vengeful clan of witches.

"No!" Estefanita stopped her.

Taking another look over her shoulder, Christina saw an old truck rattling down the dusty road. Christina took a step toward the truck. Estefanita motioned to Mana Mercedes as she recklessly steered the Ford Model T toward them. Christina opened the door and helped Estefanita into the still-moving truck. Running to keep up, Christina stumbled and was barely able to grab the door as Mana Mercedes stepped on the gas.

"Stop!" Estefanita yelled as she reached out and grabbed Christina's arm.

"I can't!" Mana Mercedes yelled as she struggled to steer the truck. She didn't know how to drive, and if she stopped now, she wouldn't be able to get it started again.

"Hang on." Estefanita weakly held onto Christina.

"Leave me here," Christina answered as her foot slipped and her feet dragged on the dirt road.

"No!" Estefanita's tightened her grip.

Seeing the determination in the old woman's eyes, Christina struggled to regain her footing and pulled herself into the truck. Christina closed the door as they drove past one of the interns and screamed as he reached out to the slow-moving truck. He yanked open the door and Christina nearly fell out of the cab.

"Hurry!" Christina yelled as she held onto the swaying door.

Changing gears, Mana Mercedes popped the clutch and the truck lurched forward. The door yanked out of the intern's hand, and he tripped and rolled away onto the dusty road. Mana Mercedes stomped on the gas and revved the engine, steering the truck toward the other intern blocking the road. He jumped out of the way as the truck sped by without slowing down.

Mana Mercedes had never had the occasion to learn how to drive. José drove her to town once a week in the ratty '26 Ford and she liked to walk the short distance to church for daily Mass. But she had watched her husband and driving didn't look that hard. Push a pedal with one foot, move the stick, and step on the other pedal with the other foot. She thought it would be easy, but as she grinded the gears and the truck jerked down the road, she knew if her driving didn't kill her, her husband would.

Driving past the hospital, Christina saw Jenny standing in the middle of the parking lot, glaring at her. Looking past Jenny to the hospital, Christina prayed Jessica and Marie would be safe.

# Thirty-Eight

The three women drove in silence. The truck engine whined as Mana Mercedes no longer felt compelled to change gears. As long as the truck was moving, she was fine, even if they were only going five miles an hour. Christina held onto Estefanita. The old woman was still weak and bouncing around in the front seat of the truck wasn't going to help her recover any faster.

"What did they do to her?" Mana Mercedes asked without taking her eyes off the road.

"I'm not sure," Christina looked over at Estefanita, who was barely conscious. "She was tied up and gagged when I got there."

"*Gracias a Dios.*" Mana Mercedes let out a sigh of relief. "They weren't able to finish the spell."

"How can you be so sure?"

"In order to complete the spell, she would have had to drink their tainted brew."

"How do you know she didn't?"

"For one thing, she's still alive."

"Watch out!" Christina yelled. Mana Mercedes clutched the wheel and steered the truck straight toward the balls of fire dancing in front of them. Undaunted by the menacing witches, Mana

Mercedes stomped on the gas and drove faster until they flew away into the night sky and disappeared.

"Are they gone?" Christina asked as she searched the dark sky through her closed window.

"No, they're still out there. They will not leave us alone until they have her," Mana Mercedes answered.

"What do they want with Estefanita?" Christina asked but before Mana Mercedes could answer, a ball of fire swooped down and slammed into the front end of the truck, jerking the wheel out of Mana Mercedes's hands.

"Don't let off the gas!" Christina yelled as she reached over Estefanita and steered the truck away from the ditch on the side of the road. Grabbing the wheel, Mana Mercedes stomped on the gas. The truck sputtered and accelerated, revving the strained engine.

Another ball of fire dropped out of the sky and slammed the driver's-side door, pushing the truck farther toward the ditch. Mana Mercedes jerked the wheel away from the embankment when they were hit again from behind and the back window shattered.

Christina screamed as shards of broken glass flew around her. Clearing the glass shards from her face, Christina saw Estefanita's frail body being pulled out the back window. Christina grabbed Estefanita's waist and held on as the old woman slowly slipped from her arms.

"Do something!" Christina pleaded to Mana Mercedes as she struggled to hold onto Estefanita.

The window next to Christina shattered as a cold bony hand reached into the truck and grabbed her throat. Christina struggled to breathe.

Mana Mercedes jerked the truck into her driveway, slamming the corner fence post with the front bumper. The engine sputtered and died and everything became silent. The hand around Christina's throat was gone and Estefanita's body slumped halfway out of the truck. Christina eased Estefanita back onto the seat.

"Get inside!" Mana Mercedes yelled as she jumped out of the truck and scanned the dark sky. Christina carried the weak woman onto the front porch. Mana Mercedes followed them into the house as the balls of fire dropped out of the sky.

Mana Mercedes locked the door and thanked God for getting them home safely. Mana Mercedes helped Christina carry Estefanita into the living room, and together they laid her down on the couch. Christina saw a flash outside the window. Slowly she stepped over to the window and watched the balls of fire dance on the fence.

"They can't harm us in here," Mana Mercedes reassured. "Would you like a cup of tea?" she asked and walked out of the room.

Christina followed her into the kitchen, sitting in the same chair she'd sat in the first time she'd visited the old woman. "Is she going to be all right?" Christina motioned to Estefanita in the other room.

Mana Mercedes nodded as she poured two cups of tea. "She's a strong woman, much like yourself."

"I'm not strong." Christina shook her head.

"Ah, but you are. It took great courage for you to risk your life to save Estefanita."

Christina sipped her tea. "I need to get back to my children."

"I will take care of your children. The doctors may know a lot about some things but they do not know anything about the *brujería*."

"The what?"

"They've eaten food that's been cursed by a witch."

"Jenny," Christina whispered, remembering Jenny's devious admission at the hospital. "And Detective Winters." He had also eaten some of the cookies.

"He'll be taken care of as well, although a little suffering might do his heart some good." Mana Mercedes smiled coyly.

"What are you going to do?" The thought of Jenny deliberately trying to kill Jessica and Marie turned her stomach.

"I will make a *remedio* that will rid their bodies of the *brujería*. Now, finish your tea." She nodded to the half-empty cup. "You need to rest. You'll need your strength."

After Christina finished her tea she left Mana Mercedes alone in the kitchen grinding herbs in the stone metate. She walked into the living room and sat in the rocking chair next to Estefanita and closed her eyes.

The instant Christina closed her eyes she fell asleep. Her dreams were plagued with images of Jessica and Marie lying helplessly in the hospital as Jenny stood in the shadows and watched them die.

# Thirty-Nine

Christina opened her eyes and looked around the small living room. She was alone. The couch was empty and the blanket that had covered Estefanita had been draped over Christina. Getting up out of the rocking chair, Christina rubbed her stiff neck and walked into the kitchen. The house was quiet and she thought she was alone until she heard the wood creak on the front porch.

Estefanita sat alone on the porch slowly rocking back and forth in Mana Mercedes's rocking chair. She stopped when she heard the screen door open and turned to Christina with a smile. "Sit." She motioned to the wood bench as she resumed rocking. Her face was kind and gentle. Her hair was combed neatly into a bun and she was rested, looking like a different person from the one Christina had gotten to know at the hospital.

Too stiff to sit, Christina walked to the edge of the porch and looked out at the lush green valley.

"I thought I'd never see the light of another day." Estefanita took a deep breath and filled her lungs with the sweet smells of summer.

Christina knew how she felt but unlike Estefanita, she didn't share the same joy for life anymore. It had been hard to move on after Mark had been killed in the war but now with Mark Anthony and Lucy gone, she wanted to die and leave the pain of this life behind. Now only Jessica and Marie kept her going. She dreaded the idea of her children being raised by her father but she now wondered if anything would be better than the fate that awaited them here, with her.

"Thank you for taking care of me at the hospital. I wouldn't have survived if it hadn't been for you."

"You're welcome." Christina smiled and sat down on the wood bench across from Estefanita. "Where's Mana Mercedes?" She looked over at the broken fence post and noticed the truck had been moved next to the house.

"She's at the hospital."

Christina's heart sank. She should be there with Jessica and Marie but she couldn't bring herself to leave, not just yet. She had too many questions and Estefanita had all the answers.

"Your children will be fine," Estefanita reassured. "Mana Mercedes is the best curandera in Santa Fe." It comforted Christina to know they were not alone. "It'll be dark soon." Estefanita looked up at the sun slowly inching its way toward the western horizon. "Tonight I must finish what I started." Her gaze lingered on the high range of the Sangre de Cristo Mountains before she turned to Christina. "You have many questions for me." Christina didn't answer as she leaned back on the hard bench. "And I am ready to answer them." Estefanita once again looked toward the mountains.

"Many years ago my husband and I moved to Santa Fe. I met Santiago when I was sixteen. He was a coal miner working in Madrid and I still lived with my mother and father in Tesuque. We met at my cousin's wedding and from the first day I saw him I knew I was in love."

Christina smiled at her own memories of Mark. She knew the instant she saw him she would love him for the rest of her life.

"Santiago and I had two beautiful children, Lourdes and Antonio, and for the first few years of our marriage life was wonderful. We built a home and farmed our land. A simple life but a happy one." Estefanita's smile faded. "But things soon changed when

Constance Salazar came into our lives. She was a widow but many in town believed she killed her husband. It was told she had come home late one night after one of her witches' gatherings. Her husband Pablo had waited up for her until the early morning hours and demanded to know where she'd been. He confronted her with the rumors that she was a witch, and she became infuriated and cast a spell on him. He was never the same after that night. His black hair turned white from the terror he witnessed and he lost his mind. He wandered the plaza speaking to no one. Over and over he would mumble the curse Constance cast on him. He lived like a madman for two years, eating garbage out of his neighbors' trash cans and sleeping on the sidewalks until someone found him late one fall. His body had washed up along the bank of the river."

"Constance was a beautiful woman. She used her beauty to lure men into her bed and although men feared her, they could not resist her." Estefanita looked out at the tall grass swaying in the meadow. "Santiago was a good husband and a loving father until one day he just disappeared. When he didn't come home that first night I feared he was hurt but I soon learned the truth. He had been with Constance. When he came home two days later I threw him out of the house, angry for what he'd done, and he went back to her. They lived down the road from our house and passed our farm each time they went to town. She would hold onto his arm as he drove their wagon past our home and each time she always looked our way to make sure we'd seen them. It was especially hard for the children. Her smile was a constant reminder to us of everything we'd lost. A father, a husband, in essence our family, and each time he passed us he didn't have the courage to look at us. They too had children, a son and two daughters, and I hated those children. I was angry because Santiago was now showing them the love he'd once given our children." She stopped and looked thoughtfully at Christina. "It wasn't their fault, you know? They were just children who loved their father—just as Lourdes and Antonio had, but I couldn't see that back then. No, those children were the innocents and they were the first to suffer their mother's wrath."

Christina's mind raced with questions but she stayed quiet. She didn't want to distract Estefanita from her story. There would be time later to ask questions.

"I grew more jealous each day until finally I couldn't stand it any longer and I came here to Mana Mercedes. She had a cure for every ailment and she could cure any brujería. If she could cure a curse, then she could give one, and that's what I wanted. I was desperate. She was waiting for me when I got here and she told me what I so desperately wanted to hear. Santiago had been bewitched by Constance. Mana Mercedes gave me a remedio and I followed her instructions to break the curse. I can still remember the excitement I felt when I thought I could bring Santiago home again, and my hands trembled as I mixed the herbs. The next day when the children and I came home from church we found him sitting on the front porch, *perdido*, lost. He pleaded for forgiveness, wanting to come home, and for the first time in years I saw the man I fell in love with. I was not one to forgive easily but I did want him home and the children were happy once again, so I let him move into the barn. Several days passed and Constance came to our home demanding Santiago go home with her. But she no longer controlled his soul and he chose to stay with us, a decision that will forever haunt me."

Estefanita slowly stood and walked to the edge of the porch. Telling her story was painful. It brought back all the terrible memories she fought so hard to forget. But it was a part of her life and now that she'd given Christina the gift, it was now a part of her life, too.

"They found his children the next day on the bank of the river, the same place they found Pablo, and although Santiago did not love Constance, he did love those children. Santiago questioned her after the funerals and she admitted that she drowned them. Wanting him to feel the pain of losing someone he loved, Constance callously recounted their deaths in detail. The night after Santiago refused to go home with her, Constance realized she'd lost his love forever. She went into a jealous rage and her anger didn't stop with her own children. At night she wandered the river searching for her dead children and took any child she could lure away from his or her parents to replace the children she'd killed. The people in town called her La Llorona."

Christina watched Estefanita intently.

"It means 'the weeping woman.' At night her cries could be heard along the river as she searched for her dead children. Late one night I followed Constance into the forest to her wood shack and I watched from the shadows as she practiced her magic. I went to Mana Mercedes again and this time she showed me how to stop her. Late that next night I waited to hear Constance's cries along the river. I left my children alone in the house. Santiago was asleep in the barn and I went back into the forest. Before I could finish the sacred ritual that would put an end to her reign of terror, she came back and found me. We fought like two wild animals. She was stronger than me and she nearly killed me. She told me she'd been to my house and taken my children. Out of desperation to get back home I found the strength to defeat her but when I got home it was exactly as she had said: Lourdes and Antonio were gone. After the funerals, Santiago walked into the barn, tied a rope around one of the beams, and hanged himself."

"I'm sorry," were the only words Christina could muster.

"I have fought my entire life to keep her wicked soul buried but I have failed in my old age. She has been released from her grave and is among us again roaming the river, killing the innocents."

"I don't understand." Christina shook her head.

"She's a witch, the devil's whore, and when I defeated her, the spell only confined her body to a grave. Each year I made the journey into the forest before the rise of the summer's first full moon to bless her grave. It was the power of God that kept her in hell where she belonged. She's waited over forty years to be released and during that time she grew stronger while I grew weaker. I knew it was only a matter of time before I could no longer make the treacherous journey and this year the devil himself stopped me. My life was spared so I could be tortured by the bruja in the hospital while La Llorona regained her strength."

"Jenny," Christina whispered.

"Yes, Jenny. I gave you the power to see into La Llorona's evil soul. I placed you and your family in danger. For that I am sorry."

Christina was angry for what Estefanita had done but at the same time her heart went out to the old woman. Estefanita had suffered an incredible loss, one Christina could relate to.

"I want you to take it back," Christina whispered.

"It's not that easy. I'm sorry." Estefanita looked down at her hands folded in her lap.

"What do you mean, 'it's not that easy'?" She raised her voice. "Take it back!" Both women turned when they heard the gate open and watched Mana Mercedes walk up the path.

"Buenos días. I hope you slept well." Mana Mercedes stepped up onto the porch. "I've come from the hospital. Your children are fine."

"Gracias a Dios," Estefanita whispered as Christina let out a sigh of relief.

"Here are the things you asked for." Mana Mercedes handed Estefanita a leather pouch.

"Gracias." Estefanita smiled appreciatively.

"I know it's not my place to tell you what to do, Estefanita, but you are too weak. This is a battle you cannot win. You need your rest."

"I've had two weeks to rest."

"That's not what I'm talking about," Mana Mercedes protested.

"I know what you are talking about." Estefanita stood, grabbed the wood cane against the wall, and walked inside as Christina and Mana Mercedes followed her into the kitchen. "She has to be stopped and I'm the only one who knows how."

"For what? You stop her this year but who is going to stop her next year or the year after? You're only prolonging the inevitable." Mana Mercedes watched Estefanita move around the kitchen.

"I can't concern myself with something that hasn't happened yet. She is alive now and must be stopped."

"How can you stop her?" Christina asked. She'd seen La Llorona's evil and knew how powerful she was.

"I need to restore the spell to condemn her spirit back to hell."

"But you can't do it, not now." Mana Mercedes followed Estefanita around the kitchen.

"I can't wait another day." Estefanita filled the kettle with water.

"Why not? What good is it for you to go to her and she kills you?"

"Who cares if I die?" Estefanita slammed the kettle on the woodstove. "I deserve to die. It's my fault she's out there! How many more innocent children must suffer?"

Christina watched the two old women argue. Mana Mercedes knew she couldn't change Estefanita's mind. She sat at the table across from Christina and rolled a cigarette.

Christina watched Estefanita's every move as she mixed the dried leaves, dirt, and water. The leaves, Estefanita explained, were from the Crown of Thorns cactus plant, the same thorns believed to have been placed on Jesus's head before he was crucified. She collected the leaves and the holy water from the cathedral on the plaza and the dirt was from her children's graves. She mixed and poured the watery mixture into a jar and filled a leather pouch with the remaining dirt.

Estefanita walked into the living room to the hand-carved statue of the Blessed Mother and leaned her cane against the small altar. A single candle burned in front of the statue and illuminated the otherwise dark room. Taking the rosary from around the statue, she knelt and made the sign of the cross. Estefanita closed her eyes and began to pray quietly.

Christina watched in awe. The woman had incredible faith. After everything she'd been through, she still had the courage to turn to God for guidance.

# Forty

Estefanita knew the time had come. She dreaded facing La Llorona alone and knew deep within her soul she did not have the strength to prevail in tonight's encounter with the witch.

Not once in nearly fifty years had Estefanita faltered but tonight was different. Estefanita saw Mana Mercedes's trepidation, but she was ready. She didn't fear death; she embraced it. Death meant she would be reunited with her family but it also meant La Llorona's thirst for vengeance would be insatiable. Estefanita shut her eyes and prayed for the souls of the innocent.

Estefanita finished her prayers. Kissing the small crucifix in her hand, she slowly stood and walked into the kitchen where Christina and Mana Mercedes waited. Without saying a word Estefanita took the jar and the leather pouch from the table. Draping a wool shawl over her shoulders, she walked to the front door.

"Where are you going?" Christina asked.

"I'm going to find her and put an end to her madness."

"Now?"

"Yes, now." Estefanita tried to walk around Christina.

"But you can't go alone." Christina grabbed Estefanita's arm. She put her children at risk to save Estefanita. She wasn't about to let the old woman be a martyr and sacrifice herself because she was stubborn enough to believe she could stop La Llorona.

"It is the only time when the spell can be placed," Estefanita answered impatiently.

"I'm coming with you." Christina didn't want to go with Estefanita but she knew she had to. It was the only way to put an end to her nightmares and protect Jessica and Marie from the witch who was sure to prey on them.

"No." Estefanita shook her head. "You've been through enough. Stay here and take care of your family."

"I won't have a family to take care of if that witch isn't stopped. You gave me this so-called gift and you can't take it back." Christina shook her head. "No, I won't live the rest of my life watching her kill innocent children."

Estefanita turned to Mana Mercedes, who nodded encouragingly. "Very well," Estefanita reluctantly agreed. "You may come, but I warn you La Llorona has the ability to read your soul. She will prey on your weaknesses and force you to confront your deepest fears."

"She's taken my son and stalked my daughters. If I don't do this, my deepest fears will come true," Christina answered through clenched teeth.

Estefanita nodded knowingly.

"May God's blessing guide you." Mana Mercedes handed Christina a wool flannel shirt.

"If something should happen, will you tell my children I love them?" Christina's voice broke as she took the shirt.

"I've looked into your soul and your destiny is not to die tonight." Mana Mercedes smiled knowingly. "But have comfort in knowing your children will be taken care of." Mana Mercedes turned to Estefanita. "Good-bye, my friend," she said and gave her an affectionate hug. "Thank you for the journey. It was good to come home."

"Tell my children I'm coming home." A tear rolled down Estefanita's cheek. "Save a place for me at the banquet table." Estefanita quickly wiped away the tear and adjusted the wool shawl over her shoulders.

"They await your triumphant return." Mana Mercedes smiled, her eyes welled with tears.

Christina watched the two old women. Estefanita turned and walked out into the night. Putting on the wool shirt, Christina followed Estefanita out into the darkness. With the moon and stars as their guide, the two women made their way toward the towering mountains.

Christina struggled to keep up with Estefanita. Walking along a narrow path, Christina breathlessly followed Estefanita through the dense thicket of trees and brush. She was at least forty years younger than the old woman. Christina didn't need a cane to help her walk, and she still couldn't keep up. Christina looked up at the darkening sky. Thunderclouds loomed overhead and blocked the moonlight.

"We're almost there," Estefanita whispered over her shoulder as she sensed Christina's uneasiness.

"What are we going to do when we get there?" Christina answered as she ran to catch up to Estefanita.

"We wait."

"For what?"

"For her to return," Estefanita answered matter-of-factly.

"What?" Christina stopped. She'd asked to come but she never thought she was going to have to face the woman who killed Mark Anthony and Lucy. "What do you mean, we wait for her? Can't you just do your thing and leave?"

Estefanita looked up at the lightning flash from the dark clouds. She didn't have time for this. "If you want to go back you can," Estefanita said impatiently as she turned and walked away.

"Go back?" Christina shouted over a loud clap of thunder. She wouldn't be able to find her way out of the forest if her life depended on it. "I can't go back and you know it." She jumped as another bolt of lightning flashed across the sky. "Just what are we supposed to do when she comes back?"

"We fight her." Estefanita didn't know how else to explain what they were about to do.

"Fight her? Are you kidding?" Christina paced nervously. "We can't fight her. She'll kill us. Look what she did to Lucy."

"I don't blame you for being scared, but it is the only way to stop her."

"Scared?" Christina *was* scared. She wasn't afraid to admit it and she knew Estefanita was scared too. "You're damn right I'm scared!"

"She'll keep killing if we don't stop her. She gets stronger with each day that passes. You can leave Santa Fe. Your children might be safe and maybe you can shut yourself off from her evil, but what if you can't? And what about the innocents in this town, like your son?"

"Okay," Christina reluctantly whispered. Estefanita was right: Christina had to bury her fears no matter the consequence.

Estefanita and Christina continued to follow the path up the mountain. Bolts of lightning struck around them. The wind howled, moving trees with incredible force. Branches succumbed to the powerful winds and fell to the ground. The intensity of the storm grew. Christina pulled the flannel shirt tighter around her. Fingers of lightning ripped through the dark clouds. The electricity in the air made the hair on the back of Christina's neck stand. Lightning struck an aspen. Christina heard the deafening sound of splintered roots ripping from the ground as the tree fell on the path in front of them.

"We should go back!" Christina shouted over the howling wind and thunder.

"We must keep going." Estefanita climbed over the tree. "The storm is the work of the devil trying to keep us away. La Llorona's home is close."

Christina followed Estefanita over the fallen tree and deeper into the forest. The storm thundered over them. Branches from the pine trees pulled at Christina's hair and clothes as the hidden force tried to stop her from going farther. Christina's apprehension grew. Thunder shook the ground and lightning lit up the sky. In the blinding flash Christina saw the weathered shack. Its presence in the middle of the forest was frightening. Christina rubbed her arms through the thick shirt but the chill running down her spine wasn't from the weather.

"She's not here." Estefanita sat on the trunk of a fallen tree at the edge of the clearing.

"What do we do now?" Christina glanced around fearfully.

"Now we wait."

Unable to take her eyes off the shack, Christina sat on the ground and leaned against the fallen tree.

"Do you believe in God?" Estefanita asked as she reached into her pocket and took out two rosaries.

"Yes," Christina whispered. Her mother never missed Sunday Mass and worked hard to instill her faith in her but over the years Christina slowly lost her belief in what her mother called God. She hadn't always had contempt for God but after Mark was killed and she watched her mother suffer a miserable death, she questioned everything her mother taught her about God being kind and forgiving. Especially now after Mark Anthony had been taken from her, Christina wondered if God existed at all. She'd suffered enough, and if God was kind and loving, why had he abandoned her? She had lost her faith.

"Take this." Estefanita handed her a rosary. "Only with the love of God will we defeat her." Christina took the beaded rosary. Carefully studying the small crucifix, she tried to feel the love and strength Estefanita drew from God but there was only a cold emptiness within her.

"We need to place the rosary around La Llorona's neck. With it, she is powerless. Once her powers are gone, you take the pouch filled with dirt and pour it over her. The dirt will strip her of her human abilities and what's in the jar confines her to the grave. Do you understand?" Christina nodded. "Good." Estefanita made the sign of the cross and began to pray.

Christina put the rosary in her shirt pocket. She stared at the wood shack as she listened to the rhythmic whisper of Estefanita's prayer and closed her eyes.

# *Forty-One*

Awakened by an odor so foul and disgusting it was almost unbearable to breathe, Christina felt the warm breath on her cheek. Holding the air in her burning lungs, Christina felt the blood race through her veins. Unable to move and unwilling to face the creature before her, Christina forced herself to stay calm. *Estefanita is with me,* she reassured herself. Slowly letting the air out of her lungs, Christina turned to the witch.

Inches from Christina's face, shrouded in darkness, she recognized La Llorona's sinister shadow looming over her. A gust of wind swirled around the two women. Dead leaves rustled across the ground and La Llorona's long white hair lightly brushed against Christina's face.

In a bright flash of lightning and deafening thunder, Christina saw the horror of La Llorona's face. The rotted, scarred skin highlighted every detail of her grisly skull. The disfigured flesh peeled back from her blackened teeth and eased into a haunting grin. But it was La Llorona's dark ominous eyes that held Christina.

"Boo." La Llorona snickered and watched Christina scoot away from her fearfully until she was pinned against the fallen log. La Llorona reached out and ran her bony fingers through Christina's red hair, leaned in, and sniffed Christina like a rabid dog. "Ah, the smell of fear," La Llorona mused.

Christina jumped to her feet and clumsily climbed over the dead tree. Christina fell to her knees and then staggered to her feet. La Llorona's evil eyes pierced Christina's soul. Tripping on a fallen branch, Christina stumbled to the ground. Over a wave of thunder Christina heard a throaty growl and looked up at the black wolf looming over her. The wolf's fiery yellow eyes stared at her as it curled its snout to expose its yellow fangs. In an instant La Llorona jumped over the log and grabbed Christina by the hair. A sharp pain shot through Christina's neck as La Llorona jerked her off the ground.

"Where do you think you're going?" La Llorona snarled. "You came here to find me. Now you can't leave until I say you can leave." Christina frantically searched the forest for Estefanita. "Looking for the old bitch?" La Llorona snickered. "I hate to disappoint you, but she's gone." La Llorona wrapped her bony hand around Christina's throat and lifted her off the ground. "The old hag left you here to die. Don't you know it's easier to sacrifice someone else when your own fears become too great? She led you here like a lamb to the slaughter." La Llorona tightened her grip. "But don't worry; she'll suffer the same agonizing death you're about to."

Christina held onto La Llorona's bony hand as she felt the muscles on her neck pop from the force of the grip. Kicking her feet, barely able to breathe, Christina reached into the front pocket of her shirt. Losing consciousness, Christina felt the beaded rosary and with numb fingers and placed it around La Llorona's neck.

Seeing the rosary around her neck, La Llorona let go of Christina. "You bitch," La Llorona growled as she stared at the cross. Christina lay on the ground as she coughed and gasped for air. La Llorona stumbled backward before she looked up at Christina and laughed. "Estefanita was a fool to believe in you," La Llorona snickered as she took the rosary from around her neck. "This means nothing to you." She dangled the rosary from her bony fingers. "You have no faith, and because of it, this has no meaning for me." She crushed the beads in her hand and dropped the broken rosary to the ground.

"You have no faith, and who could blame you after everything you've been through?" La Llorona mocked. "How could one have faith in a God who has abandoned you?" La Llorona walked over to Christina. "You've lost the man you loved and your only son. How could he have forsaken you? What did you ever do to deserve his wrath?" La Llorona knelt next to Christina and lifted her chin to look into her eyes.

"Yes, I know your pain. You can see into my soul and I, my dear, can see into yours. By killing you I'm sparing you a lifetime of hell. Life isn't what it's made out to be. It's filled with pain, but in death there is no pain." La Llorona motioned over her shoulder. Mark Anthony, surrounded by a halo of hazy light, stood at the edge of the forest holding his kitten. He smiled and waved at his mother excitedly. "In death you can be with your son."

"Mark Anthony, baby," Christina whispered as tears rolled down her cheeks. The emptiness in her was overwhelming. Christina looked over at La Llorona. La Llorona was right: she did want to die. She wanted the pain to end. She couldn't take it anymore and the witch knew it. Christina stood slowly. She lifted her chin, offering her red and bruised neck. Unable to take her eyes off Mark Anthony, Christina surrendered herself to La Llorona.

"Yes, life is pain." La Llorona wrapped her fingers around Christina's throat. "Soon you'll be with your husband and son. Then I'll send your daughters to be with you. You'll be one happy family in hell."

Christina felt the blood pulsate painfully through her neck as she watched Mark Anthony disappear. La Llorona continued to squeeze and drain Christina's soul. Tears streamed down Christina's cheeks as joyful memories of Jessica and Marie raced through her mind. *She* wanted to die. Not Jessica and Marie. They deserved a life without misery, a life without her, and she couldn't bear the thought of La Llorona taking their delicate lives. Christina tried to pry the bony hand away from her throat but La Llorona laughed sadistically and squeezed harder. Struggling to breathe, Christina kicked her legs at the witch but La Llorona continued to drain the life from her.

The sharp blow knocked La Llorona to her knees. Estefanita stood over La Llorona and struck her again with the wood cane.

Falling to the ground, Christina gasped for air and crawled away from the two women. Christina watched in dismay as the black wolf emerged from the darkness. Blocking her escape, the wolf growled as it crept toward her. Behind her, Christina could hear the two women fighting.

"You can't defeat me!" La Llorona screamed in anger as Estefanita swung and struck her again with the cane.

Looking over her shoulder, Christina saw La Llorona tackle Estefanita to the ground. Christina tried to run to help Estefanita but stumbled back as the wolf leapt through the air and landed in front of her. The wolf growled as the fur on its neck raised on end. Backing away, Christina tripped and fell. Christina watched in horror as the wolf transformed before her eyes. The wolf's fur changed into a long black cloak rippling in the wind. The cloaked figure slowly stood up.

Jenny snarled as she lowered the black hood over her head and walked over to Christina. "It's going to give me incredible pleasure to drain the life from your body. I will savor your slow and painful death unlike your friend Lucy's."

Christina turned to run. In a flash of lightning Christina saw La Llorona unleash an assault on Estefanita. Sitting on Estefanita's chest, La Llorona struck the old woman repeatedly. Christina couldn't leave Estefanita to fight this battle alone and she turned back to Jenny. There was no other way for Jessica and Marie to be safe. Their lives depended on her and she would die to protect them. Jenny lunged at Christina and knocked her to the ground, overpowering her in a matter of seconds. Jenny wrapped her hands around Christina's throat and pinned her to the ground. With one hand Christina tried to loosen the pressure and with the other she searched the ground. Gripping a large stone, Christina swung with all her might and slammed the rock into the side of Jenny's head.

Dazed, Jenny let go as Christina struck her again. Succumbing to pain, Jenny collapsed as Christina rolled out from under her. Jenny held onto her head as blood gushed from a gaping wound over her eye. Blinded by the blood, Jenny crawled away as Christina stood over her and struck her again.

"That's for Lucy, you bitch!" Christina kicked Jenny's unconscious body and looked over her shoulder. Christina could see Estefanita lying helplessly on the ground. Unable to protect herself and nearly unconscious, Estefanita lacked the strength to fight. Blood trickled from Estefanita's broken nose and her eyes were nearly swollen shut. Christina ran the short distance to Estefanita. Still gripping the bloody rock in her hand, Christina hit La Llorona on the back of the head.

La Llorona stumbled off Estefanita and struggled to her feet as Christina swung again. Seeing Christina rear back, gripping the rock, La Llorona instinctively ducked. Christina lost her balance and fell to the ground.

Christina crawled on her knees and cried out in pain as La Llorona kicked her in the back. La Llorona straddled Christina and grabbed her head with both hands. Killing was one of her greatest pleasures. She liked to see her victims' fear before she took their lives but she was running out of patience and this one would have to die quickly.

Holding Christina's head between her hands, La Llorona would break Christina's neck with one quick motion. Her death would be quick and relatively painless.

Christina felt the pressure in her spine as La Llorona began to twist her neck.

A scream echoed through the forest. Startled, Christina opened her eyes as La Llorona's hands slipped from her head.

A paralyzing pain burned through La Llorona's soul. Letting go of Christina, she turned around to see the battered old woman beside her.

"I have faith," Estefanita said as she struggled to her feet.

La Llorona fell to her knees and let out a piercing scream as the rosary burned into her flesh. Taking the leather pouch from her pocket, Estefanita slowly unfastened the leather strings.

"No!" La Llorona screamed out in pain, fumbling with the rosary around her neck.

Standing over the dying witch, Estefanita poured the dirt on La Llorona's long white hair. La Llorona screamed in agony and watched as her body began to disintegrate. Maggots bore through her rotted flesh and fell to the ground. Taking out the small bottle of the green tea mixture, Estefanita slowly removed the cork, savoring the fear in the witch's eyes. She poured the liquid over La Llorona's body and prayed as the witch screamed.

La Llorona's flesh burned and sizzled as the spell sucked the life from her body. Leathery, dried flesh clung to her bony skeleton as clumps of long white hair fell to the ground. Losing all her strength, La Llorona took one last breath.

"No!" Jenny ran from behind Estefanita and tackled her. Christina heard Estefanita's fragile bones break from the force as Jenny slammed the old woman to the ground. Jenny turned to Christina, her eyes filled with rage. Christina slowly backed away as Jenny glared at her. "You bitch!" Jenny yelled as she transformed back into the black wolf and lunged.

Christina turned to run and tripped over the skeleton. The frail bones scattered around her as she fell. Rolling onto her back, Christina grabbed one of the shattered bones and held it out in front of her. Christina watched as the wolf leapt through the air.

The wolf's sleek fur blew in the wind as she flew toward Christina. Jenny saw the sharp bone in Christina's hand but it was too late, and she felt a sharp pain rip through her chest.

Christina watched the bone sink into the wolf's chest and felt the weight of the heavy animal pin her to the ground. The black wolf transformed back into Jenny and Christina rolled out from under her. Christina watched Jenny struggle to pull out the bone buried in her chest. Blood trickled out of the corner of Jenny's mouth as her lungs slowly filled with liquid.

Jenny glared at Christina until she lost herself in the darkness of death.

Lightning flashed. Thunder shook the ground. The black clouds ripped open as rain poured down. Christina ran to Estefanita and carefully rolled her onto her back.

"Estefanita," Christina whispered as she wiped the dirt from Estefanita's battered face.

Estefanita struggled to breathe. "You know the truth," Estefanita coughed as blood trickled out of her mouth. "Every year the journey must be made on the eve of the summer's first full moon," Estefanita wheezed. "You are the only one who has the power to stop her." Rain fell on Estefanita's face as she looked up toward heaven. "I am ready to be with my family."

Christina held Estefanita as she closed her eyes and breathed her last breath. Christina looked over at Jenny's lifeless body and La Llorona's scattered bones as she held onto Estefanita and cried. She cried for the old woman and for a life she knew would never be the same.

# Epilogue

As Christina sits in the bare white room of the nursing home she's lived in for the past fifteen years, in the same building where her life was forever changed, she watches the summer's first full moon rising over the Sangre de Cristo Mountains. The owls have gathered outside her window to taunt her with their cold gazes and haunting cries. Feeling the anxiety tightening in her chest, Christina knows the end is near and *she* knows it's coming, too.

*She*—after all these years Christina still cannot bear to speak her name. The very mention of her evokes fear in all who have heard of her and know the pain and suffering she inflicts on the innocent.

Late at night from her open window Christina can hear the laughter of naïve teenagers mocking the tormented spirit, hoping to hear the sorrowful cry as she searches the river for her lost children. Christina shudders at her own memories, knowing La Llorona is more than a tale told to scare little children.

Her muscles ache as she kneels in front of the old wooden statue of the Virgin Mary and begins to pray. She shuts her eyes as the pain and tragedy she's had to endure replays in her mind. Clutching the rosary, she struggles to control the vivid memories, wishing they could be forgotten. Her prayers have been the same since that fateful night in the forest with Estefanita. She asks for the hand of death to come down and end her miserable existence, to rid her mind of the horrible memories she's had to carry. Christina learned to pray and have faith in the years that followed Estefanita's death. Her lack of faith had nearly gotten her killed, and witnessing the power of God working through Estefanita was a wonder she'd never questioned.

Christina walks across the tidy white room to the small desk and looks down at the worn notebook. She'd written her life in these pages, sharing her story with anyone willing to listen. What she'd written in the pages was a warning that needed to be sounded like a siren in the dead of night.

Christina looks down at her weathered skin. She has lived a long life, longer than she could have ever imagined. She is eighty-nine years old, and life as she knew it ended over forty years ago.

After finding her way out of the forest she realized her nightmare had only just begun. She stopped at Mana Mercedes's house and found nothing more than a crumbled, abandoned adobe shell. The woman who had saved Jessica and Marie from Jenny's curse had been dead for more than fifteen years.

Mana Mercedes had thanked Estefanita for her journey back home and Christina had no doubt she came down from heaven to help them defeat La Llorona. Mana Mercedes was Estefanita's mentor and spiritual guide, much like Estefanita was hers.

Mark Anthony's body was found near the river just like Christina knew it would be, and Detective Winters, true to his word, worked diligently to charge Christina with the murders of Mark Anthony and Lucy but without any evidence the district attorney couldn't persuade the grand jury to indict her.

Christina buried Mark Anthony and Lucy together at Rosario Cemetery. She couldn't bear the thought of either one being alone. Lucy had risked her own life to protect Mark Anthony and Christina knew Lucy would always care for him.

Christina reluctantly sent Jessica and Marie to live with her father while she dealt with Detective Winters. She missed them dearly, and she regretted her decision every day. When she asked them to come back to Santa Fe to live with her, they wouldn't leave the safety of Chicago and she couldn't blame them. Santa Fe was no longer home for them. They lost their innocence when they lost their little brother and Christina hadn't been there to help them heal.

Jessica became a lawyer. By the age of thirty-five she was a partner in a successful law firm in Los Angeles and married a doctor who was very much like John. They have a daughter and a son they named Mark Anthony. Jessica still hasn't been able to come back to Santa Fe and Christina's short trips outside the city have not been enough to keep their relationship alive. Christina hasn't seen her in twenty years. Her grandchildren are grown and except for the occasional phone call and annual Christmas gift she is merely an acquaintance to her own daughter.

Marie chose to express herself through art. One of the greatest joys of Christina's life has been to sneak away from the nursing home on beautiful Sunday afternoons and walk to the galleries on Canyon Road to see her work. Marie's visited Christina several times over the years but the bond they'd once shared has been broken.

Christina's story did, however, secure her a room in the state mental hospital where she'd spent nine months trying to convince the doctors of her innocence and warn them of the evil horror that plagued Santa Fe. Realizing no one believed her and knowing it was the only way for her to be released from her institutional hell, Christina convinced everyone she no longer believed her own madness. She was released two weeks before the rise of the summer's first full moon the year after Estefanita's death.

After she was released from the state hospital, Christina vowed to leave Santa Fe but found she could not stay away. After a few days, visions of her past haunted her dreams and the only place she found refuge from the nightmares was in Santa Fe.

Christina made a promise to Estefanita and the thought of the witch who waits to be released from the grave each year is unbearable. She still has the gift and as the summer's first full moon draws closer each year, she visits Mark Anthony and Lucy. Taking dirt from their graves, she makes the treacherous journey into the mountains.

Christina stares out the window. The once small farming

community has transformed into a small city and a popular tourist destination. The house she'd once shared with Lucy is now an exclusive art gallery, and the river no longer winds its way through town.

Santa Fe may have changed over the years but Christina is certain about one thing and that is La Llorona. The witch has waited patiently for Christina's demise, just like she'd waited for Estefanita's. She is out there ready to be reborn and to inflict her fury on the innocents.

Setting the notebook on the desk, Christina knows this will be the last time she'll make the journey into the mountains.

The owls gather outside her window and the coyotes taunt her with their distant howls. They too know this is her last journey. Remaining strong throughout the years, waiting for Christina to fail, they know the time for the rebirth of their queen has come.

Taking the small leather pouch and jar, Christina looks around the room for the last time and closes the door.